Death
on a
Deadline

Death

on a

Deadline

A HOMEFRONT NEWS MYSTERY

Joyce St. Anthony

CROOKED
LANE

NEW YORK

Published in the United States by Crooked Lane Books, an imprint of The Quick Brown Fox & Company LLC.

Crooked Lane Books and its logo are trademarks of The Quick Brown Fox & Company LLC.

Library of Congress Catalog-in-Publication data available upon request.

ISBN (hardcover): 978-1-63910-115-3
ISBN (ebook): 978-1-63910-116-0

Cover illustration by Trish Cramblet

Printed in the United States.

www.crookedlanebooks.com

Crooked Lane Books
34 West 27th St., 10th Floor
New York, NY 10001

First Edition: November 2022

10 9 8 7 6 5 4 3 2 1

Note to the Reader

Thanks in advance for reading *Death on a Deadline*. It means a lot to me.

As you read, please remember that this is fiction. I've done my best to be factual about things that matter most, like dates and actual incidents (even the weather!). However, I've taken a few liberties to fit the story.

War bond drives and rallies featuring Hollywood stars did occur. In real life, the rallies were one-time events moving from city to city, and they usually featured big name stars. Clark Gable's wife, Carole Lombard, died in a plane crash returning to California after a rally. You'll see a mention of this early in the book. In *Death on a Deadline*, I have second-rate stars in town for a week, with the rallies occurring at the yearly fair to give Irene enough time to investigate and solve the murder.

I've also included a demolition derby at the fair on Friday evening. All car races, including the Indianapolis 500, had been banned for the duration of the war. It's possible that something like this could have occurred early in the war, but with gasoline

Note to the Reader

and rubber rationing, it's doubtful. In the book I explain that the cars (the metal and rubber) would be scrapped for the war effort and that the drivers used their own gas rations. I like to think anything is possible in fiction, as long as it fits the story.

Thanks again for reading. I hope you enjoy it!

Joyce

Chapter One

"Clark Gable is coming to Progress and will be appearing at our war bond drive," Ava Dempsey said. "I have it on good authority."

"Whose authority?" I asked. I was the only one questioning Ava's insistence that the star was coming to town. There were a half dozen of us gathered in Mayor Ralph Young's office. I was here representing my newspaper, the *Progress Herald*. Actually, Pop's newspaper—he'd put me in charge when he'd finagled an appointment to be a correspondent thanks to a friend of his in the War Department. At the moment, he was somewhere in the Pacific.

The others present in the mayor's office were members of the planning committee for the upcoming war bond drive that would be held during the county fair.

"You don't need to know that, Irene," Ava said.

"Yes, I do. I won't publish a rumor."

Ava patted her perfectly curled black hair. She'd recently traded her artificially colored flaming red hair for artificially colored black. "It's not a rumor. I don't repeat anything that isn't true."

If I'd been taking a sip from the glass in front of me, I'd have sprayed water all over the table. Ava Dempsey was a busybody and the owner of Ava's Beauty Shop, where just about everyone in town went. Gossip was her specialty.

Martha Feeney, the head of the committee and the wife of Sergeant Jimmy Feeney, spoke up. "Ava, dear, wouldn't it be better to tell us how you know Mr. Gable is coming?"

The other members of the committee—Dan Petrie, Roger Eckel, Mayor Young, and my future father-in-law, Chief Walter Turner—nodded, almost in unison.

Ava sighed loudly. "Oh, all right. If you must know, my sister Angela told me."

"You have a sister?" I said. "Since when?"

She gave me a look. "Since she was born thirty-one years ago."

"Why have we never seen her?" Dan Petrie asked.

"Or heard of her," I added.

"She doesn't live nearby," Ava said. "As a matter of fact, she lives in Los Angeles."

Mayor Young perked up. "California? I always wanted to go there. I only made it as far west as Texas. That's where the Rough Riders trained before we headed to Cuba. That was a time, let me tell you."

Roger Eckel, the manager of the A&P, interrupted before the conversation veered into the eight-term mayor's time serving with Teddy Roosevelt. "Let's stick to the subject at hand. How would your sister know anything about this?"

"Angela telephoned me two days ago to ask if she could come and stay with me for the next couple of weeks," Ava said. "She told me that Clark Gable is the chairman of the Hollywood Victory Committee that's doing these war bond drives."

"Just because he's the head of the committee doesn't mean he's coming here," I said.

"I'm sure it does," Ava said. "Angela said he participates all the time, even after the death of his wife, poor man." She looked around the table at each of us. "We'll have to be extra nice to him. Angela said he's still devastated at losing Carole."

Gable's wife, actress Carole Lombard, had died in an airplane crash in January after one of the bond drives. It was tragic, but I had a feeling Ava was thinking more of herself than the actor. She was probably imagining being such a great comfort that he'd whisk her off to Hollywood with him.

"How does your sister know so much about the goings on of Hollywood stars?" I asked.

Ava rolled her eyes. "Because she's one of them."

"She's one of them," I repeated. "A movie star I've never heard of."

"Angela is not a movie star," Ava said. "Not yet, anyway. She's married to Freddie Harrison. She's had a few bit parts and travels in their circles. Why, just last week she was at a party at—"

"Who in the world is Freddie Harrison?" Roger interrupted.

Ava gave him a look like he was the dumbest person on the planet. "He's an actor. He's been in plenty of movies."

"We're getting off track here," Martha said. "As of now, we don't know who will be participating."

"Of course we do," Ava said. "Angela will be one of the performers. She told me so herself."

Martha looked skeptical. "I'll contact the Victory Committee to find out for sure. In the meantime, does anyone have anything else to add?"

The chief raised his hand. "I do. What kind of security do these things have? With just three of us on the police force, I can't

3

guarantee anything. We might have to get the state police to assist if they don't have their own security."

"I'll check on it when I contact them," Martha said. "Anyone else?"

We all shook our heads.

Martha stood. "If that's it, the meeting is adjourned."

I walked out of the mayor's office with my future father-in-law. "Well, that was interesting," I said.

Dad smiled. "To say the least. What do you think? Is Gable coming?"

"I guess we'll find out soon enough," I said. "Did you know Ava had a sister?"

"Sort of," he said. "Years ago, Ava's mother left Ned and took the girls with her. When the mother died about ten years ago, Ava moved back to Progress to be closer to her father. I'd forgotten all about the sister. I guess it's none of our business anyway." He held the door to the stairway open and followed me through.

"I guess." My heels made a clacking noise on the marble stairs as we went down. When we reached the first floor and entered the police department, Jimmy Feeney was on the telephone at the front desk. I waved to him.

"Thank you for the Father's Day gift," Dad said. "It was very thoughtful of you."

"You're welcome." Father's Day was the day before and I'd bought him a paperweight for his desk and signed the card from Bill and me. I hadn't consulted with my fiancé because he was down south training with the Third Armored Division, but I knew he'd like the idea. Since I'd recently begun calling the chief "Dad," I thought it was only fitting to get him something, especially since my own father was overseas. I bought Pop a similar paperweight and put it away until he got home from the war. He'd have quite a few gifts to open when the war was over.

"Heading back to the paper?" he asked.

I nodded.

"Can I buy you lunch first?"

Before I had a chance to answer, Jimmy called out, "Hey, Chief."

Dad turned around.

"Mrs. Pinkley said someone stole two of her chickens from the coop in her backyard."

"Tell her I'll be right there." He turned back to me. "It's probably the neighborhood fox again, but I have to check on it."

"We'll go to lunch another day," I said. We parted outside and I watched him drive off in his squad car. My stomach took that moment to inform me that even though the chief wasn't buying, I still needed lunch. I crossed the town square to Woolworth's, wondering two things—was Clark Gable really coming to town, and was Ava's sister actually taking part in the bond rallies, or was it wishful thinking on Ava's part?

* * *

The lunch counter at Woolworth's was where I usually ate lunch if I didn't bring something from home. It was close to the newspaper, and the service was quick. The food was good most days, with the exception of the meatloaf special. I avoided that one. There was one empty stool next to Dan Petrie, who was perusing the menu even though it never changed.

I slid onto the stool. "Hi, Dan."

"Hi. I would have walked over with you if I'd have known you were coming here," he said.

5

"I didn't know until a few minutes ago."

Dan held the menu in front of me. "Here you go."

"I know what I'm ordering," I said. "I have the menu memorized."

"I do too." He returned the menu to the stand on the counter. "I look at it every time anyway, hoping there will be something new."

A waitress stopped to take our orders. I usually ordered an egg salad sandwich, but today I opted for a BLT and black coffee. Dan ordered a ham sandwich and a Coke.

"How is the Victory Garden doing?" I asked. "I haven't had time to give it a good look." It had been a month since Progress residents had gathered to plant a garden in the park in the town square. Dan owned the local garden and feed store and had done most of the legwork and organization.

"It's doing very well. I haven't had to ask anyone for help watering and weeding. I hope that keeps up over the summer."

"If interest wanes, let me know," I said. "I'll write up a reminder that it's everyone's patriotic duty to help out."

"So, do you think Ava's right?" Dan asked.

"About Gable?"

He nodded. "It would certainly make my wife happy. She's a big fan."

"As far as Ava's concerned, I'll believe it when I see it." The waitress poured my coffee and I took a sip. "I'm surprised the rumor isn't all over town yet."

Dan grinned. "I give it to the end of the day."

We chatted until our lunch arrived. Dan practically swallowed his sandwich whole. I wasn't even halfway through mine by the time he dropped fifty cents on the counter and said goodbye.

As it turned out, it didn't even take until the end of the day for Ava's unconfirmed news to get around. Peggy Reardon, my secretary and best friend, greeted me as soon as I returned to the *Herald*. Peggy was what the fellows called *a looker*, with her natural, almost-platinum blonde hair and blue eyes. Ava had been after me to dye my auburn hair a similar color, but I liked mine the way it was.

"Is it true?" Peggy said. "Please tell me it's true." She followed me into my office and sat in the chair opposite the desk.

I opened the bottom drawer of my desk and dropped my pocketbook in. "Is what true?" I took a seat. I had a pretty good idea what she was referring to.

"That Clark Gable is coming here for the bond drive," Peggy said. "It's the talk of the town." She reached down and straightened her skirt. "I want all the details."

"Where in the world did you get an idea like that?"

"I went in Thrift Drug at lunch and Mildred told me."

"Interesting," I said. "Who told Mildred?"

"Ava." Peggy's expression changed. "Dang it."

She looked so disappointed I took pity on her. "The truth is, we don't know if he's coming or not. Ava's sister told her—"

"Hold it right there," Peggy said. "Since when does Ava have a sister?"

I filled her in on what had transpired at the meeting. "Ava figures since Gable's the head of the Hollywood Victory Committee, it means he's coming to Progress."

"So it's still possible," Peggy said.

"Maybe. Martha Feeney is going to contact them. I told Ava I'm not mentioning any names until we have some kind of confirmation."

"That's not going to stop her, you know."

"I know." I rolled a sheet of paper into my typewriter. "But rumors don't matter in the long run, and people should know by now to take what Ava says with a grain of salt."

Peggy nodded, making her platinum waves bounce on her shoulders. "Well, I hope it turns out she's right. It would be so exciting to have an honest-to-goodness movie star in Progress." The telephone on her desk outside my office rang and she stood. "Keep me posted."

"Will do." After she left, I typed up a short piece on the war bond drive. I ended it with *The celebrities participating in the drive have yet to be determined.* When I'd finished, I wrote a draft on keeping house for Wednesday's edition. Before Pop left for the war and made me editor-in-chief, I was the home, garden, and fashion reporter. Unfortunately, I still had that duty in addition to the others. Each week featured a different topic. This was the fourth week in June, which meant clothing and fashion. I wrote about how fashions were beginning to change in order to use less fabric. I hadn't thought of it before, but some of the cotton, nylon, and other materials were needed for various supplies for our troops. Hems were becoming smaller and skirts were inching up. No more wide pleats or big collars. There would be no excess fabric on anything.

I pulled the sheet of paper out of the typewriter and placed the draft in my top drawer. I'd go over it tomorrow and make any changes before I passed it on to my cousin Donny, who took care of layout. Donny and I had never gotten along, but we'd come to a partial truce lately when I'd given him a little more responsibility. He still tended to whine and complain like his mother—my aunt Rita. She was Mom's younger sister, and Pop had given Donny a job here to keep peace in the family.

I pushed out of my chair and walked into the newsroom. Rex Griffin and Frank Mitchell were both at their desks. I'd known Rex since I was a baby. He used to bounce me on his knee, and he'd had a rough time getting used to the fact I was now his boss. I was slowly gaining his respect due to how I'd handled myself during the events of last month when I'd discovered who was responsible for the sabotage at Tabor Ironworks and helped solve the murder of a fellow reporter.

Ken Stafford's desk was empty at the moment. He was our sports reporter and was out covering a local baseball game. Ken was also Peggy's fiancé. He was twenty-two—the same age as Peggy and me. Unlike Donny, who was happy to be 4-F, Ken would like nothing more than to be among the boys fighting the war. But he'd been injured in a serious car crash right around the time we graduated from high school. The crash had destroyed his dream of playing professional baseball, but surprisingly, he wasn't bitter about it.

Rex waved me over to his desk and yanked a sheet of paper from his typewriter. "I just about finished this if you want to take a look," he said. "It'll save me a trip to your office."

My office was only thirty feet away. Rex could use the exercise. He smoked like a chimney, and his chair groaned every time he sat down. I took the paper from him. The headline read *Jap Sub Fires on Oregon Coast*. "That's not entirely accurate," I said. I had already read an AP report that came over the wire, so I knew what had happened.

"But it's catchy."

"It'll make readers panic. Change it to *Japanese Sub Fires on Fort Stevens, Oregon*. Then add a subtitle something like, *Shots Miss* or *Shots Harmless*."

"You're no fun," Rex said. "You're just like your pop."

I took that as a compliment. For the last few months all I had heard was how something wasn't how Pop would do it. I scanned the rest of the article, which gave the whole story. A Japanese submarine had reached the mouth of the Columbia River by following fishing boats and avoiding mines that had been set. The commander of Fort Stevens had wisely ordered a blackout and no return fire. Most of the shots from the sub had landed harmlessly in a neighboring baseball field and in a swamp. The worst damage was to a few telephone poles. I passed the paper back to Rex. "The article's good. Just fix the headline and send it down to Donny."

"Yes, boss." He gave me a half-hearted salute and went back to work.

I was about to go back to my office and do the same when Ava walked in, followed by a woman a few inches shorter than her five foot eight. Ava glanced around the room, and Frank and Rex suddenly looked extremely busy, both of them typing furiously.

Ava's gaze fell on me and she headed my way. "Irene! You're just the person I wanted to see." She stopped in front of me. "I'd like you to meet my younger sister, Angela Harrison."

Chapter Two

Japanese Sub Fires on Fort Stevens, Oregon

The Progress Herald, June 22, 1942

A ngela stepped forward and held out her hand. "Call me Angel. Everyone does."

"It's nice to meet you," I said.

Her hand was limp and soft as I shook it. Angel seemed an appropriate nickname for her. She had an ethereal air about her, almost as if she floated beside her older sister. Ava wasn't exactly coarse and clunky, but next to Angela she was. Ava had curves in all the right places and so did her sister, but Angela's were softer. While there was a facial resemblance between the two, Angela's features were more delicate, her nose tinier, her lips fuller. Even Angela's hair was a contrast—a shade of blonde somewhere between platinum and honey.

The newsroom was suddenly quiet as the typing stopped. Frank jumped out of his chair and hurried over. Rex was a little slower. Both reporters looked like puppy dogs waiting for a treat. I introduced them to Angela before they started drooling.

Ava tapped her foot and placed her hands on her hips. "If you don't mind, gentlemen, my sister and I have business to discuss with Irene." Before they could respond, she grabbed Angela by the elbow and marched to my office door.

I had no choice but to follow. Once inside I closed the door and made my way around my desk. "Take a seat, ladies."

"Thank you," Angela said.

"What can I do for you?" I asked.

Ava looked at her sister. "Tell her."

Angela straightened her skirt, then reached up and readjusted a hairpin holding a curl in place. She seemed to be stalling to annoy Ava.

"Tell her," Ava said again.

Angela leaned back in her chair and smiled. "My sister tells me no one believes that Clark Gable might be coming in for your war bond drive."

"Not exactly," I said. "Ava told everyone that Gable is definitely coming here. *Might be coming* isn't the same."

Ava sniffed. "It is to me. He's not going to pass up a chance to visit the part of Pennsylvania that's producing almost all the steel and hardware to build the planes and tanks. He might even combine it with a trip to his hometown."

"His hometown?" I asked.

Ava rolled her eyes. "Cadiz. Cadiz, Ohio. It's near Steubenville."

Angela broke in. "I told Ava that it's very possible that Clark will participate. When I saw him last week, I mentioned that my sister lived here, and he seemed very interested."

I was getting a headache. "You talked to Clark Gable last week."

Now Angela was the one who looked at me like I was an idiot. "He's my next door neighbor. I worked on his last film."

If this were true, Ava surely would have bragged about her sister working with Gable.

There was a quick rap on the door, and Peggy peeked in. "Can I get you ladies some coffee?"

"Nothing for me," Ava said.

Angela turned in her chair. "I would love a gin and tonic with some lemon, please."

Peggy looked at me.

"I'm sorry," I said. "All we have is coffee and water."

Angela turned back to face me. "What kind of water? I only drink mineral water."

The Allegheny River certainly contained plenty of minerals, but I didn't think that was what she had in mind. "It's tap water."

"Oh my," she said. "That won't do." She looked at Ava. "Why didn't you tell me this? I can't drink ordinary water."

Ava reached over and patted Angela's arm. "Don't you fret. We'll find some mineral water. I'll bet Roger at the A&P will have some."

That seemed to soothe Angela. I hoped she wasn't counting on a snooty brand. I was pretty sure the A&P only carried White Rock. I had a feeling Roger stuck with that brand because of the half-naked fairy in the advertisements.

Peggy left, and I attempted to get the conversation back to the subject at hand. "In other words, we still don't have any idea who is coming for the bond drive."

"Besides me, I know everyone who will be here, including one I wish wasn't," Angela said.

"Who?" I asked.

"My no good, cheating creep of a husband, Freddie Harrison."

The name had sounded familiar when Ava had first mentioned it, and it suddenly dawned on me why. Peggy and I had gone to the movies a week ago to see a detective film. It was so bad I couldn't remember the name of it—something like *Killer in the Night*. The actor who had played the killer was Freddie Harrison. It had not been an Academy Award–winning performance. Not even close.

"Are you an actress?" I asked.

"Yes," Angela said. "I did a few radio shows—one with Bing Crosby. I've had some small parts as well. I was supposed to be in Freddie's next movie, but I've been replaced by *her*."

I was about to ask who she meant when I caught Ava shaking her head. I was sure she'd fill me in later.

Ava patted Angela's arm again. "Don't think about that woman right now. Freddie Harrison doesn't deserve you."

"He doesn't, does he?" Angela said. "He'll regret the day he took up with that . . . that . . . floozy."

That explained why all of a sudden Angela had decided to come a few days early to visit her sister. Her husband must have been doing the horizontal tango with someone else. While this conversation was interesting, I had work to do. They really hadn't told me anything, and I wondered what the point of the visit was, other than for Ava to show off her younger sister. She could have done that anywhere. And she probably would. "Is there anything else? I hate to be rude, but I need to get back to work."

Ava and Angela stood. "I just wanted to set the record straight about Clark Gable," Ava said. "I didn't want you thinking I made the whole thing up."

"It was a pleasure meeting you," Angela said. "I hope to see you again."

I opened the door, and before I could ask Peggy to show them out, Rex and Frank rushed over. I'd let them handle it. I closed the door and went back to work.

Death on a Deadline

The big news that came over the wire that afternoon was about a speech given on French radio by Pierre Laval, the head of the Vichy government. Although everyone knew the Vichy had been collaborating with the Germans, it was a shock to read what Laval had said. *"In the event of a victory over Germany by Soviet Russia and England, Bolshevism in Europe would inevitably follow. Under these circumstances, I would prefer to see Germany win the war."* It was almost press time, and I could have used the AP article, but I assigned Rex to write one up for tomorrow's paper, then went down to the basement to tell Donny to leave room for it.

As expected, my cousin complained. "I can't do my job right when you keep sending articles down at the last minute."

"Would you rather work somewhere else?" I asked. "I'd be more than happy to give you a reference."

Donny's eyes widened. "No! That's not what I meant. I only want the *Herald* to look perfect."

"As do I. I know you'll do your best. You always do." It was painful to say, but it was true. I only wished he didn't whine so much.

He nodded. "I'll do what I can. Tell Rex I'll be waiting for his article."

*　*　*

My fourteen-year-old sister, Lily, accosted me the minute I walked in the door after work. "Clark Gable is coming to town," she said. "Can I meet him?"

I kicked off my shoes before answering. I'd made the mistake of wearing brand new peep-toe shoes all day without breaking them in first. They'd felt all right until the last hour. The walk home had just about done me in. My dogs weren't just barking, they were howling. I sat on the chair beside the hallway telephone table, crossed a leg over my knee, and began massaging my toes. "Where did you hear that?" I knew the answer but figured I'd ask anyway.

"Mom said she heard it from Mrs. Anderson, who heard it from Miss Dempsey," Lily said. "Do you know when he'll be here?"

I switched legs and rubbed the toes on my other foot. "We don't know if he's coming or not."

"But Miss Dempsey said—"

"What did I tell you, Lily?" Mom came through the doorway from the kitchen. She looked as fresh as she had when I'd left for work that morning. Her pink and cream floral dress didn't have a wrinkle in it. I could never figure out how she managed it. Much to my dismay, I hadn't inherited that ability.

"But Clark Gable—" Lily said.

Mom put up a hand. "There are enough rumors going around without you contributing to them."

"They're spreading like wildfire." I stood and gave my mother a kiss on the cheek. "Martha Feeney is going to call and verify who is coming."

Lily sighed. "I'm going to put some records on."

She disappeared into the living room and in seconds had Frank Sinatra crooning "Night and Day." My sister was nuts about the singer. I hadn't thought it possible, but she was even more infatuated with him since she had received a personally autographed picture of him from my friend, Katherine Morningside, just days ago. Katherine had roomed with us for a few weeks while she was working at Tabor Ironworks, and now she was in New York singing with Sinatra.

I followed Mom into the kitchen. She opened the oven door and took out a pan of pork chops. "How was your day?"

I opened a drawer and took out the potato masher. "I met Ava's sister Angela today. I never knew she had a sister." I reached for the pot of potatoes that Mom had already drained, and set it on the counter.

"It's a sad story," Mom said.

"Dad said Ava's mother left Ned and took the girls with her, and Ava only moved back to town after her mother died." I added butter to the potatoes and began mashing.

"Did Walt tell you the rest?"

I shook my head. "There's more?"

"Angela ran away from home when she was fifteen—this was about five years before Ava came back here."

I did the math in my head. It took me longer than it would have taken Lily. She was a whiz. "So that was about fifteen or sixteen years ago?"

"Approximately. No one knew where she'd gone for about a year. Ned received a Christmas card saying she'd married an actor."

"Freddie Harrison?" I splashed some milk into the potatoes.

"I don't remember the name."

"Did Ned keep in touch with Angela?" I asked. "Or did Ava?"

"I really can't say." Mom handed me a bowl for the potatoes.

"Well, I'm sure Ava will tell me and everyone else the whole story sooner or later."

Mom smiled. "That's one thing you can depend on."

Over dinner, Lily mentioned that she was drawing some posters for the bond drive. She had designed the ones advertising the

Victory Garden and the scrap drive that the mayor had put up all over town. I had already asked Martha Feeney about it. She'd take a look at them whenever they were ready, and Lily could distribute them.

That evening, Lily was up in her room, and I'd just turned on the radio so Mom and I could listen to *Cavalcade of America* when the telephone rang. "I'll get it," I said since I was already on my feet. Every time it rang, I hoped it was Bill or Pop, though the chance of that was unlikely, especially since Bill had called less than a week ago. Pop was somewhere in the Pacific—safe at the moment and nowhere near a telephone. The article he'd written on Midway had been picked up by the AP and wired all over. I had proudly featured it on the front page.

It was Sylvia Fontaine. Sylvia had been dating the reporter who had been killed about six weeks ago. We'd become friends since then. "I hope I'm not interrupting anything," she said.

"Not at all."

"Would it be all right if I moved in on Saturday?"

Shortly after Pop had left on assignment, Mom had decided to rent one of our three bedrooms to a boarder. We'd been without anyone since Katherine had left, and I'd temporarily moved back into my former room. Part of me didn't want to give it up and return to sharing a room with my sister, but I knew it was for the best. Besides, Sylvia needed a break. Ever since her former apartment had been broken into and the contents destroyed, she'd been staying in Butler with her sister, which was a thirty-minute drive from her job at Tabor Ironworks. She had been grateful when I'd asked her if she'd be interested in staying with us.

"That would be fine," I said. "Do you need any help with anything?"

"I doubt it. I just have a couple of suitcases and whatever I was able to salvage from my apartment. I'm glad I don't have to go back there."

"Me too."

"I really appreciate you doing this for me," she said. "Places to stay are hard to come by these days. And expensive. My former landlord doubled the rent for the poor sap who moved in. Are you sure your mom doesn't want more to rent the room? She could triple it and I'd still be ahead."

"You can take that up with her, but I'm sure she'll say no."

We chatted a few more minutes. As I hung up the phone, I glanced through the front door sidelight and saw a car pull up in front of the Finnertys' house across the street. Richie Finnerty was an ensign on a flight crew in the navy. I had an awful feeling the family was about to get bad news. There had been over three hundred casualties during the battle for Midway two weeks ago. Mrs. Finnerty had been on pins and needles waiting to hear from him. When the man in the Western Union uniform got out of the car, I knew she never would.

Chapter Three

Vichy French Laval Wishes for German Victory
The Progress Herald, June 23, 1942

"Mom, come here. Quick," I said.

"Why? Is something wrong?"

As soon as she entered the hallway, I pointed outside. "Western Union is at the Finnertys'."

"Oh, no," she said. "It can't be."

I didn't want to believe it either. Richie Finnerty had been a year ahead of me in school. I'd had a massive crush on him when I was in ninth grade. He couldn't possibly be dead.

"Maybe it's not what we think," Mom said. "Maybe he's only missing or injured, or captured."

From the stories I'd heard about how brutal the Japanese were to prisoners, being captured wasn't a better option. "Should we go over?"

She nodded. "Let me tell Lily where we'll be."

Mom and I crossed the street just as the Western Union car pulled away from the curb. They sure didn't waste any time getting away from the bereaved. Some places had teenage boys on bicycles delivering the awful telegrams. It made me glad the Western Union offices were too far away to do that here. It would be bad enough getting that kind of news from an adult.

The Finnertys' front door was wide open, but Mom knocked anyway. "Rose," she said. "Can we come in?"

There was a muffled response from the living room. We took the sound as a yes and went inside.

Rose Finnerty sat on her sofa, staring at the telegram in her lap. Her face was so pale it was almost white. She didn't look up when we entered the room.

Mom took a seat beside her and touched her arm, while I stood in the middle of the room feeling helpless. There had to be a better way to let a soldier's loved ones know he'd been killed. Telegrams were so impersonal. The military should have someone do the notification in person.

"It's not true," Mrs. Finnerty said after what seemed like an eternity. "I would know it if my boy was dead. It has to be a mistake. The government makes mistakes sometimes, doesn't it?"

"Sometimes," Mom said.

Mrs. Finnerty looked up at me. "You know people in the War Department, don't you?"

"A few," I said.

She pushed up off the sofa. "Then you can tell them this is a mistake. They need to correct this. They need to send Richie home where he belongs."

I shook my head. "I don't think—"

Mrs. Finnerty grabbed my hand. "You have to! I know it's a mistake!"

Mom stood and took her friend by the arm. "Rose, let's sit back down. I'll make us some tea in a bit and we'll talk."

Mrs. Finnerty shoved the telegram into my hands. "Read this. You'll see it has to be wrong."

I didn't want to read it, but I did anyway.

"*THE NAVY DEPARTMENT REGRETS TO INFORM YOU THAT YOUR SON ENSIGN RICHARD EDWARD FINNERTY WAS KILLED IN ACTION IN THE PERFORMANCE OF HIS DUTY AND IN THE SERVICE OF HIS COUNTRY. THE DEPARTMENT EXTENDS TO YOU THE SINCEREST SYMPATHY IN YOUR GREAT LOSS. HIS REMAINS HAVE NOT BEEN RECOVERED AT THIS TIME.*"

There was more about not divulging information about his ship or station to prevent aiding our enemies. To me, that was like pouring salt on an open wound. I felt sick and didn't know what to say. I handed her back the telegram.

"See?" she said. "It's not Richie."

"Mrs. Finnerty," I said. "I hate to say this, but I don't think the navy would send this to you if it wasn't true."

"Irene is right, Rose," Mom said. "You need to telephone Louise, or I can do it for you."

Louise was Mrs. Finnerty's daughter. She was four years older than Richie, and she'd moved to Pittsburgh when she'd married. I'd never known Mr. Finnerty—he'd died in an accident when Richie was a toddler. Mrs. Finnerty had raised her children on her own.

At Mom's mention of Louise, the dam finally broke. While Mom comforted her, I went to the kitchen and made a pot of tea. I couldn't stop thinking about the telegram. In my mind I kept putting Bill's name or Pop's name into a similar one. The teakettle whistle brought me back to reality. I couldn't let myself think about that possibility. I wiped the tears away and poured the boiling water into the pot. I couldn't do anything about Richie's death, but I'd find out what I could about what happened to him and write a tribute for the *Herald*. That would have to be enough.

* * *

I hadn't slept well. Every time I drifted off I had dreamed about a telegram arriving for me or Mom. Once I cried out so loudly I woke Lily. Thankfully, she fell right back to sleep. We had stayed with Mrs. Finnerty until Louise and her family arrived from Pittsburgh. Mom had called Father O'Connor, and he was on his way over when we left.

I went downstairs at five to put some coffee on and found Mom sitting at the kitchen table with a cup of coffee already in front of her. "I see you couldn't sleep either," I said.

"I feel so bad for Rose," she said. "I kept thinking that could have been me sitting there with a telegram in my hand. I try not to think about the danger your father is in, but this brought it home."

"Pop is going to be fine." I poured a cup of coffee and sat down at the table. "He's smart. He won't get too close to the action." I really wanted to believe that was true. And Bill was still in the states, but who knew for how long? He'd eventually be sent overseas. Being in an armored division wouldn't keep him any safer than infantry.

"I pray you're right," Mom said. "I'll check on Rose later this morning and see what I can do to help. I'll notify the members of our group, if they don't know already."

The local Blue and Gold Star Mothers had welcomed Mom to their group even though Pop wasn't a soldier. Although a few other houses in the area had changed their blue stars to gold with the death of a service member, Richie's was the closest to home.

We talked for a while. Mom decided she'd take dinner to Rose and her family tonight. I told her I'd write up something for the paper. I think we both felt better when I left the kitchen to get ready for work. In my case, it helped me push thoughts of what could happen to Bill and Pop aside and focus on the present. The future was out of our hands.

* * *

Peggy arrived at the *Herald* at the same time I did. "I heard about Richie Finnerty," she said. "I just can't believe it." She followed me into my office. "Poor Mrs. Finnerty."

I walked around the desk and dropped my pocketbook into the bottom drawer. "It's horrible." I gave her a summary of the night before.

"I knew there had been a lot of casualties, but I never thought one of our own would be among them," Peggy said. "Every day I realize more and more that none of us are immortal."

Peggy had told me something similar when I'd been investigating Moe Bauer's death last month. She'd been afraid I'd meet the same fate, and I almost had. "I'm going to see if I can get any information on what happened from Pop's friend in the War Department," I said. "I'm not sure how much he'll be able to tell me. I'll write something after that."

She nodded. "I'll go put the coffee on. I think it's going to be a busy day."

It was too early to make that telephone call, so I got to work on a rough draft that I would change when I had more information. I also wrote an editorial about the comments made by Pierre Laval.

It was unconscionable that a Frenchman—or anyone at all—would prefer to be ruled by Hitler. I doubted any reader would disagree with me on this subject, unlike my last editorial a month ago when I had written that it was wrong to remove those of Japanese descent from their homes solely because of their ancestry.

At nine o'clock I dialed the direct number to Pop's friend in the War Department, thankful I didn't have to go through numerous layers of personnel to get to him. He took Richie's information and said he'd call me back. An hour later, he was only able to tell me that Richie had been one of the crew members on a torpedo bomber. From reports of the battle, I already knew that out of forty-one torpedo bombers, only six had been able to return to their carriers. It wasn't much to tell Mrs. Finnerty, and it certainly wasn't the least bit comforting.

After that, I walked out to the newsroom. Rex was writing a follow-up on Roosevelt's ongoing summit with Churchill that had begun on the nineteenth. Ken was out covering a golf tournament at the country club. Frank was the only one unoccupied at the moment, so I asked him to get some local reactions to Richie's death. I grabbed another cup of coffee and went back to my desk to work on some half-finished articles.

Peggy peeked into my office at noon. "Want to grab some lunch? Ken's still at the tournament."

"Sure." I opened the desk drawer and reached for my pocketbook. After a quick discussion, we decided to head to Dempsey's Diner. The diner was owned and operated by Ava and Angela's father, Ned. I was still curious about Angela and why no one—especially Ava—had mentioned her before. It was hard to believe that Ava hadn't been bragging about her younger sister living and working in Hollywood. The Ava I knew would not only have talked about her, she would have embellished Angela's importance. Something about it was strange, and the reporter in me wanted to find out what that something was.

Dempsey's was busy for a Tuesday. There were two empty stools at the far end of the counter. Peggy and I made tracks before anyone else claimed them. Ned Dempsey was pouring coffee for the fellow seated on the next stool. I didn't recognize him, but that wasn't unusual these days, with so many newcomers working at Tabor Ironworks. He gave both of us the once-over and settled his gaze on Peggy's legs. That wasn't unusual either. He opened his mouth to say something to Ned, but closed it when Ned moved over to us.

Ned gave us a big smile. "How are you girls today?"

"We're peachy," I said. "How are you? You look busy today."

"I can't complain. Word must have gotten out about my new beef barbecue sandwich. It's the special today."

"Ooh," Peggy said. "That sounds wonderful."

"If it's as good as your grilled cheese and tomato soup, it's sure to be a hit," I added.

Ned didn't bother to ask for our order. "Two beef barbecues coming right up." He disappeared into the kitchen.

"Well, that was easy," Peggy said. "We didn't even have to look at the menu."

The guy sitting next to Peggy gave us one last look as he dropped a dollar bill on the counter and headed for the exit. There was something familiar about him, but I couldn't place what it was.

"That's a generous tip for just a cup of coffee," Peggy said.

"Maybe that's all he had on him." I grinned. "Or maybe he was paying for that view of your gams."

Peggy rolled her eyes. "That's ridiculous. He was looking at both of us."

"Sure he was."

Ned brought our lunches then. I hadn't realized how hungry I was until I bit into the sandwich. It was delicious. By the time I finished, the diner was emptying out, and Ned came over to chat with us.

"How's the news business?" he asked.

"There's always plenty to keep us busy," I said.

"I heard about the Finnerty boy," Ned said. "It's a real shame."

I nodded. "It is." I changed the subject. "I met Angela yesterday."

Ned's face lit up. "She's a beauty, isn't she? Both my girls are."

"You must be so happy to have them both here," Peggy said.

"You bet I am. I just hope Angela decides to stay here where she belongs and doesn't go back to that two-timing piece of garbage. If I ever lay eyes on him, I'll be the last thing he sees."

"What do you know about her husband?" I asked.

"Nothing, other than he didn't treat Angela right. Anyone who'd walk out on my beautiful girl doesn't deserve her. I've never even seen any of his films."

"You'll be happy to know he's not a very good actor," I said. "I saw his latest and I'd kind of like my quarter back."

Ned laughed. "Good to know." He became serious. "I wish her mother were still around to see how she turned out."

"Your wife died about ten years ago, didn't she?"

"Yep. Second saddest day of my life."

"Second? What was the saddest?"

"Be right back." He went to pour coffee for two customers and returned. "The saddest was when Annabelle left me." He shook

27

his head. "It was my own fault. I don't blame her. I drank a lot in those days, and I was a mean S.O.B. when I did. I never hit her, but I sure wasn't the husband I should have been. It took me a few years to clean up, but by then it was too late. I've been trying to make it up to Ava since she came back here, and now I get a second chance with Angela."

Peggy reached across the counter and patted his arm. "We're certainly glad things are better now."

Ned smiled. "I am too."

I wanted to hear more, but our lunch hour was over and Peggy and I had to get back. I slid off the stool and put fifty cents on the counter. We said goodbye to Ned and left.

"I knew Ned had made it through Prohibition selling bootleg whiskey, but I didn't know he drank a lot," I said.

"I didn't either. I'm glad he straightened out."

As we walked through town, I saw the man who had been sitting next to Peggy on the other side of the street. He stopped old Mr. Cavanaugh and said something to him. Mr. Cavanaugh shrugged and shook his head. The man did the same to two other people walking past him. They ignored him and kept walking. I grabbed Peggy's arm. "Come on. I want to see what this is about."

"Isn't that the man who was sitting next to us?" Peggy asked.

"Yep."

We jaywalked across the street to where the man was standing in front of the A&P. He smiled as we approached. That feeling that I knew him from somewhere returned. I just couldn't place where I'd seen him before.

"Weren't you two in the diner?" he asked.

"Yes, we were," I said. "Do you need some help with something? I saw you talking to Mr. Cavanaugh."

"I don't think the old coot heard a word I said. And those other two? Forget it. Even the guy pouring coffee in the diner wouldn't give me the time of day. I thought this was supposed to be a friendly town."

"It is," Peggy said. "Usually."

"So what can we help you with?" I asked.

"I'm looking for my wife," he said. "She came to town a day or so ago. I just got in late last night. I expected her to be staying at the Excelsior, but she's not registered."

I suddenly realized where I'd seen him before. It was a good thing he hadn't talked to Ned Dempsey. "What's your wife's name?" I asked.

"Angel. Angel Harrison. I'm her husband, Freddie."

Chapter Four

FDR-Churchill Continue Conference, N. Africa Plans

The Progress Herald, June 23, 1942

"The actor?" Peggy said.

"One and the same." Freddie smiled. "I'm surprised no one recognized me sooner."

"It's because no one expects to see a celebrity in Progress," I said. Although I was positive if he was Clark Gable he'd have been recognized. "It's out of context."

"They're going to see a lot of us stars over the next couple of weeks."

Star was a bit of a stretch in his case.

"We're all very proud to be serving our country this way," he continued. "It's an important investment to ensure our fighting men get everything they need to fight the Krauts and the Japs."

With the help of Peggy's father, I'd recently had Donny start a payroll deduction plan for purchasing war bonds. Mr. Reardon owned the Progress Savings and Loan and had set up a payroll deduction for his employees before the war, back when they were called defense bonds. It was less painful to have a small amount deducted from each paycheck. Everyone at the *Herald* had signed up as soon as I'd told them about it.

"So, do you girls know where else my wife would be staying?" Freddie asked.

Peggy and I exchanged glances. According to Angela, she and Freddie were on the outs. Maybe she didn't want him to know where she was.

Freddie must have noticed our hesitation. "Hey, what's the dope? You two know Angel?"

"Not exactly," I said. "We only met her yesterday."

"Where?" Freddie asked. "I have to see her. I have to talk to her." He didn't sound like someone who left his wife for another woman.

"If you want to see her so badly, why did you run off with someone else?" Peggy asked.

"Me?"

If he had been a better actor, I wouldn't have believed he was as shocked as he sounded.

"I didn't leave her," he said. "I would never do that. I love her. Why would you think such a thing?"

"So you didn't take up with another woman?"

"I never said that."

I was confused. "Let me get this straight. You're in love with your wife, but you're having an affair with someone else. And you didn't leave your wife for your—whatever you want to call her—your wife walked out on you."

"Yeah. That sums it up."

"That's not what I heard," I said.

"You talked to Angel? Where is she? I have to see her."

"I'm not sure that's a good idea," I said.

31

Freddie crossed his arms. "Says who?"

"Look," I said. "Angela—"

"She prefers Angel," he said.

"Angel. She was angry that you left her." I held up my hand when he opened his mouth to refute that. "I'll tell her that you want to see her. Where are you staying?"

"The Excelsior."

Peggy and I left him standing in front of the A&P and continued on our walk back to the paper.

"Which one is telling the truth, Angel or Freddie?" Peggy asked.

"I have no idea. I'll telephone Ava this afternoon and give Angel the message."

Peggy opened the door to the *Herald* building. "You should have played dumb. Pretended like you never met Angel."

I agreed, but it was too late to worry about that now. It didn't matter which one was telling the truth. I'd pass on the message and be done with it.

After I finished editing articles that had been turned in, I telephoned Ava's beauty shop. I expected to hear Ava on the other end, but someone with a thick Bronx accent answered instead.

"Is Ava there?" I asked.

"Who may I say is calling?"

"Irene Ingram."

"Oh, hi, Irene." The voice and accent had changed. "This is Angel."

"I didn't recognize your voice at first," I said.

Angel laughed. "I'm practicing for a part I'm auditioning for next month. It's the story of a telephone operator who hears a murder committed on a party line and has to go on the run."

"If it were up to me, I'd give you the part. You were great. I had no idea that was you."

"Thanks," she said. "Ava's busy right now. Can I help you with something?"

I told her about running into Freddie and that he wanted to see her.

"I don't want to have anything to do with him. He broke my heart."

"You should tell him that yourself," I said.

"Wait. Don't tell him that. I don't want him to know I still love him."

I would have rolled my eyes but she wouldn't have been able to see it.

"Is that floozy with him?" Angel asked.

"I don't know. He was alone when I saw him, and he didn't mention anyone but you."

"Tell him—" In the background, the bells on the beauty shop door tinkled. "Sorry. I have to go. Tell him I'll think about it." She hung up.

I dropped the receiver into the cradle. I'd do nothing of the kind. I had delivered Freddie's message as promised. The rest was up to her. Peggy had been right. I should have played dumb.

After dinner, Lily showed Mom and me the posters she'd been working on for the bond drive. The first one had a flag in the background, a sketch of a soldier who looked suspiciously like Frank Sinatra, and a slogan that read *KEEP OUR FIGHTING MEN SUPPLIED—BUY WAR BONDS.*

"Very nice, Lily," Mom said.

In another one, the soldier was the spitting image of Bill. He stood next to a tank. This slogan read *BONDS KEEP OUR LOVED ONES SAFE*. I teared up. "Oh, Lily. This one is beautiful."

"I'll make sure you get one of these for your office," Lily said.

I would have thanked her, but I was too busy swallowing the lump in my throat.

The next drawing featured a stage decorated with red, white, and blue bunting. Mayor Young, Martha Feeney, and Chief Turner were seated at the back of the stage. Standing at the podium was none other than Clark Gable. "I'm still working on it," Lily said. "I haven't come up with a slogan yet."

"You might want to hold off on that one," I said.

"Why?" Lily asked. "Don't you like it?"

"I love it. I'm just not sure you want Mr. Gable on it. And you'll need to add Miss Dempsey's sister and Freddie Harrison."

"Who's he?" Lily asked.

"He's the actor married to Miss Dempsey's sister. He's in town for the bond drive."

"Isn't he a little early?" Mom asked. "The rally isn't until this weekend."

"It's a long story." I didn't want to talk about Angel and Freddie's troubled marriage in front of Lily. I'm sure she knew that all marriages weren't happy, but it didn't feel right to discuss it. I changed the subject. "How was Mrs. Finnerty when you took dinner over?"

"A little better than last night now that she has family there. It will take some time to adjust."

I shook my head. "I just can't imagine." I told her the little I'd found out from Pop's contact in the War Department. "I'm going over to let them know."

I crossed the street to the Finnertys'. Rose and her daughter, Louise, sat side by side on a glider on the front porch. I heard the drone of a radio from inside the house and a little boy making a noise that sounded like a truck engine. Louise stood as I approached. I had told her last night that I was sorry for her loss, but I repeated it.

"Thank you," Louise said. "And thank you for being here for Mother last night. I'm glad she wasn't alone." She gestured to a porch chair. "Have a seat."

I did. "How are you doing, Mrs. Finnerty? Is there anything I can do?" I asked.

Rose Finnerty shook her head. "I'll be all right. I still can't quite believe it."

"I know." There was a long pause before I continued. "I talked to my father's friend in the War Department today to try and get some more information about what happened to Richie."

Rose leaned forward. "Yes?"

"He wasn't able to tell me much." I told her what I knew.

Louise squeezed her mother's hand. "Poor Richie. And those other boys."

Rose wiped a tear from her cheek. "I appreciate you making that effort, Irene."

I stood. "If you need anything at all, please let us know."

"I will," Rose said.

The rest of the evening passed quietly. Mom listened to the radio, Lily worked on her posters, and I made an effort at reading the romance novel I had gotten from the library. My mind kept wandering, and I decided to make an early night of it. I hoped I'd be able to sleep with no dreams of Bill or Pop meeting the same fate as Richie.

* * *

Wednesday was a quiet day at work considering there was a war going on. Most of the news was about the conference between Roosevelt and Churchill. I wrote an update about the pending memorial Mass for Richie Finnerty. Martha Feeney called me later in the day to let me know that the Hollywood Victory Committee spokeswoman said that Mr. Gable would not be coming to Progress. Although I'd thought that would likely be the case, I felt a little let down. Freddie Harrison was no substitute for the movie star. I hoped this fact wouldn't affect the turnout for the fair and deter people from buying bonds.

Everyone on my staff was disappointed, except for Donny-the-know-it-all, who assured each and every one of us that he'd known all along that Gable wasn't coming. I wondered how Ava would take the news. Probably not well. I briefly considered stopping at her shop on the way home but decided it was a better idea to let it sink in first. Besides, I was going to help Lily hang some of her posters after dinner. The ones she'd made for the county fair had been printed by the local shop, but notice had been too short to print the posters for the bond drive. We'd make do with her homemade ones, which were just as nice.

Mom was meeting that evening with the Blue and Gold Star Mothers' group to see what they could do for the Finnerty family, so Lily and I headed out equipped with her posters, a hammer and nails, and some cellophane tape. When we reached the main street through town, Sam Markowicz was just locking up his hardware store. I called out to him.

Sam smiled broadly. "What do we have here?"

"Posters for the bond drive," Lily said. "I made them myself."

"They must be wonderful if you made them," he said. "And for a good cause as well. What can I do to help? We must do everything we can to defeat those monsters." He looked at me. "Thanks to you there are a few less of them."

I felt my face turn red. He'd been thanking me for weeks since I'd discovered who had been targeting him and others in the Jewish community, committing acts of sabotage, and killing my ace reporter. Only a few of us—the chief, his two officers, Katherine Morningside, and the FBI knew the full story. I'd almost lost my life in the process. No one knew that, either—especially my mother. I told Sam once again he didn't need to thank me.

"You are too modest, Irene," he said. He unlocked the door to his store. "Let me put one in my window."

We followed him inside, and he showed Lily where to hang the poster. While she taped it to the window, he drew me aside.

"How is Mrs. Finnerty?"

"As well as can be expected, I suppose."

Sam shook his head. "Such a tragedy. All the more reason for us all to buy many war bonds. Sarah and I have bought several already."

"How is Ben?" I asked. Benjamin Cline had lost his leg in one of the incidents at Tabor Ironworks. He had been staying with Sam and his wife, Sarah, while he recuperated.

"He is getting better every day. He is worried about a job. He's going to start working a few hours here at the store. He is not sure he wants to make that permanent."

"I'm glad he's recovering," I said. "I might be able to find him something at the *Herald*. He should talk to Colleen Lewis at Tabor. I'm sure she would welcome him back." Colleen Lewis was temporarily in charge at the Ironworks until Will Tabor returned to the states after the war.

"I'll mention it to him. You should come and visit. He would be happy to see you."

"I'll do that."

Lily was finished, and we said goodbye to Sam and moved on to the next place. Thirty minutes later, there were posters hanging in Thrift Drug, the A&P, and on a couple of telephone poles. Some of the stores were closed, so Lily and Mom would hang the rest tomorrow. We had one last stop to make before heading home.

Although the dinner hour was over and all you could get at this time of day was dessert and coffee, Dempsey's Diner was busy. Most evenings after Ned left for the day, Lizzie Reynolds held down the fort. Lizzie was in her sixties and didn't tolerate nonsense from anyone. She also made all the pies for the diner. This evening, Lizzie had help.

I waved to Dan Petrie and his wife sitting in a booth at the far end of the diner. Lily and I slipped onto stools at the counter.

"What'll ya have?" Angel said. This time she spoke in a nasal tone and somehow managed to crack her gum at the same time. She was dressed in a pink waitress uniform with a white apron and wore some kind of cap on her head. Her blonde hair was so curly it looked like she had stuck a hairpin into a light socket.

"Hi, Angel," I said. "Rehearsing for another part?"

"You know it, sweetie," she said. "This one's for a comedy starring Bob Hope."

"That sounds good," I said. I introduced her to Lily.

Angel cracked her gum again. "You're the artist, right? I heard a lot about you from my sister."

"I am," Lily said. She unrolled one of the posters. "Can we hang this in your window?"

"Sure, hon. Let me see that." Angel turned the poster around. Her eyes narrowed. "Do you have a different one?"

I looked closer at the poster. Freddie Harrison was front and center on this one. I rolled it back up and told Lily to show her the other one, with soldiers and a buy war bonds slogan.

"I like this one much better," Angel said. She pointed to one of the windows. "Why don't you hang it right there?"

Lily took the tape and poster over to the window.

One of the customers waved to Angel and pointed to his coffee cup. While she refilled his coffee I heard the bells on the door jingle. I glanced over my shoulder. It was Freddie Harrison.

He spotted Angel right away. "Angel! I've been looking everywhere for you!"

Angel set the coffee pot down so hard I was surprised it didn't shatter into a million pieces. "Hello, Freddie." There was ice in her voice.

"Darling, I'm so glad I finally found you." Freddie reached across the counter, and Angel slapped his hand away.

"Don't you dare 'darling' me, you two-timing creep."

"Why did you run out on me like that?" Freddie asked.

Angel put her hands on her hips. "Me? You ran out on me when you took up with that tramp."

All conversation in the diner stopped. No one wanted to miss watching the drama unfold. Lily finished hanging her poster and came back to her seat. Mom would probably have my hide for letting my sister witness this, but I sure wasn't about to leave now.

Freddie leaned on the counter and smiled. He was well aware he had an audience. "Darling, you know Belinda means nothing to me. It's you I'm madly in love with."

"You sure have a funny way of showing it. Are you still sleeping with her?"

There was a loud gasp from someone sitting in a booth. I didn't even have to look to know it was Mrs. Anderson. She elbowed her husband every time he even glanced at a woman in public. His arm must be permanently bruised.

"What does that have to do with anything?" Freddie asked. "You're all that matters to me."

"In other words, you're still sleeping with that hussy and you have no intention of being true to your marriage vows."

"Why does that have anything to do with us?" Freddie asked. "Isn't it enough that I love you and only you?"

Oh, boy. Could he really be that dumb?

Angel slammed both hands down on the counter. Freddie jumped, and so did just about everyone in the diner. "It has everything to do with us! If you don't drop that tramp, you will regret it. You'll be sorry you ever did that to me."

"But—"

Angel shook her finger in his face. "You have until tomorrow or it's goodbye. Permanently."

The sound of someone racking a shotgun got my attention. Ned Dempsey stood by the door to the kitchen with the gun pointing directly at Freddie.

Chapter Five

Eisenhower to London to Head European Theater of Operations
The Progress Herald, June 24, 1942

"**Y**ou have ten seconds to get the hell out of my restaurant," Ned said.

I didn't know Ned all that well, but for some reason I didn't think he'd actually shoot the man. Freddie didn't know that, however. If his eyes opened any wider, his eyebrows would touch his hairline.

"Daddy—"

"That's your father?" Freddie asked.

"Of course it is," Angel replied. "Daddy, I can handle this myself."

"Ten seconds," Ned repeated. "Nine, eight . . ."

"I'm going!" Freddie backed toward the door.

"Seven, six . . ."

Freddie turned his back long enough to yank the door open and run out.

Ned lowered the shotgun. "Sorry for the disturbance, folks. Pie and coffee is on the house."

Angel spun around to face her father. "You should have stayed out of it."

"No one does that to one of my girls and gets away with it," Ned said. "If he comes in here again, I won't give him the ten seconds." He disappeared back into the kitchen.

Customers were lining up at the cash register, probably wanting to get out before Ned picked up the shotgun again. No one seemed to be sticking around for pie. While Lizzie was busy with the paying customers, I asked Angel if she was all right.

"I'm fine," she said. She turned to Lily. "I'm sorry you had to see that."

Lily grinned. "I'm not a bit sorry. That was more exciting than the movies!" She jumped up from her seat. "Can we go now?"

I thanked Angel for letting us put the poster in the window, and we headed for home.

"That was so much fun!" Lily said. "I want to stop at Cindy's. I can't wait to tell her." Cindy was her best friend and was as shy as Lily was outgoing.

"That's not a good idea."

"Why not?"

"If Mom finds out you were there when Mr. Dempsey pulled out a shotgun, we're never going to hear the end of it."

"By my calculation, she's probably still at her meeting. If she's at home, someone has already telephoned her and told her the whole story anyway."

Lily had a good point. In the end, I let her go to Cindy's. I went home alone to face the possible wrath of my mother.

* * *

"I can't believe Ned pulled a gun on Freddie Harrison," Peggy said as we sat in my office the next morning. "I miss all the excitement."

"I don't think he would have shot Freddie. Ned just wanted to scare him."

"I don't know about that," Peggy said. "Remember what he said when we had lunch at the diner. Good thing he didn't know that Freddie had been sitting beside us."

I slid a sheet of paper into my typewriter. "I think it's strange that Freddie didn't know Ned was Angel's father. You'd think he would have made the connection that Ned and Angel had the same last name."

"It doesn't seem like Freddie's a deep thinker."

"Yeah," I said. "And as much as Freddie says he loves Angel, I think his real love is himself. Otherwise, he'd do what Angel wants and stop seeing the other woman."

Ken came into the office and squeezed Peggy's shoulders before taking the chair next to her. The look they exchanged tore at my heart. I was happy they had each other, but I missed Bill more and more every day. How was I going to make it through this war with him so far away? It could be years before I saw him again. Then I thought of Richie Finnerty and felt terrible for being so selfish. If Richie had had a girl, she would never see him again. Surely I could make it however long the war lasted.

"I heard about the incident at the diner," Ken said. "I miss all the fun."

"That's almost the same thing Peggy said."

He laughed. "What do you want me to cover today? There's a tennis match at Tall Pines this afternoon, and a baseball game in Butler this evening. I can cover the game if I don't go with you two tonight to help with setting up the fair."

I'd almost forgotten that was tonight. "Just do the tennis match since that's more local." Tall Pines was the country club a few miles from town. "I think Ellen Petrie is playing." Dan Petrie's wife was an excellent player. "How about writing something up about some of the activities at the upcoming fair?"

Ken grinned. "Like my favorite, the demolition derby?"

"Exactly," I said. "All the metal from the wrecked vehicles will be donated for scrap."

"I'll be happy to write that," Ken said. "I can interview folks tonight and do a follow-up after the event."

"Perfect." We made plans to all ride to the fairgrounds together later.

After Peggy and Ken left my office, I refilled my coffee cup and checked on Rex and Frank. Rex was working on an article on what it meant for the United States and the plans to take on Hitler now that Eisenhower was in London to lead the European Theater of Operations. I would write an accompanying piece on Ike himself. Eisenhower was an excellent strategist and was a good choice to lead us to victory.

The conference in Washington between Roosevelt and Churchill was scheduled to end today and Frank would take care of writing that article.

The first thing for me was to write and follow up on the incident at Dempsey's Diner last evening. I'd go there for lunch and talk to Ned. I still didn't believe he would have shot Freddie in cold blood, but I needed to hear it from him.

The morning passed quickly. When noontime came around, Peggy had errands to run, and Ken had already gone to Tall Pines, so I was on my own for lunch. The diner was practically empty when I arrived. It seemed others weren't as willing to give Ned the benefit of the doubt as I was.

Ned was wiping the counter and I took a seat. "I'm glad not everyone has abandoned me," he said.

"They'll be back," I said. "Once they know you didn't mean it."

"I meant it, all right."

"But you really wouldn't have shot Freddie."

Ned winked at me. "It wasn't even loaded. That rat doesn't know that, though. I'd like to keep it that way. I don't want him coming round here again. And if word got out my shotgun wasn't loaded, it'd kind of ruin my reputation."

I laughed. "What reputation?"

"Well, if you write something for your paper, make sure I look like a crazy old man. I want my daughter to be left alone. No one will do her wrong again."

"I have to print the truth," I said. "But I only have your word that your shotgun wasn't loaded. People will think what they want." I asked Ned if the chief had been in to talk to him.

"Nope."

"Freddie didn't file a report?"

Ned shook his head. "Not that I know of. It would ruin his tough guy image."

I'd check with my future father-in-law. Ned was probably right, though. Freddie wouldn't want it known he'd been run out of the diner by a seventy-some-year-old man.

After lunch, I stopped at the police station. As usual, Jimmy Feeney was behind the desk.

"Well, if it isn't my favorite news hawk," he said.

"I bet that's what you say to all the *Herald* staff."

He smiled and shook his head. "Nope. I reserve the best for you. I can't repeat what I call Rex and Frank. It's not fit for a lady's ears."

I laughed. "Is the chief in?"

"You just missed him. Rally is out too."

Rally Johnson was the third and newest member of the Progress Police Department. When Bill joined up after Pearl, Dad put off looking for another officer as long as he could. Rally was color-blind and, much to his dismay, that made him 4-F and ineligible for the service. Dad hired him a month ago to take Bill's place. It took some getting used to, seeing someone besides my fiancé working with the chief.

"Something I can help you with?" Jimmy asked.

"I was just wondering if Freddie Harrison had reported the incident at Dempsey's Diner last evening."

"No," Jimmy said. "What happened?"

I filled him in. "Ned told me the shotgun wasn't loaded."

"And you believe him?"

"Shouldn't I?"

"Ned's always had a temper," Jimmy said. "It was a lot worse back when he was drinking. He shot up a bar once back in his heyday when the bartender wouldn't serve him another."

"So you don't think he's telling the truth?"

"I didn't say that," Jimmy said. "I've never known him to lie, just that he has a temper. When Rally gets back, I'll go and have a little talk with Ned. Loaded or not, he shouldn't go pointing that thing at anyone."

I went back to work feeling like a tattletale. I should have kept it to myself, especially since Freddie didn't seem to want the police to know. I told myself that it was just a matter of time before someone spilled the beans anyway. I didn't feel any better about that.

* * *

"Where do you want this?" I asked Harold Copeland. I was pushing a cart carrying a large cotton candy machine. Peggy and Ken were somewhere behind me pushing their own carts. One held a popcorn machine and another carried one to shave ice for snow cones. We'd only been at the fairgrounds for fifteen minutes and Harold's wife, Ophelia, had immediately put us to work. Harold and Ophelia had been running the county fair for over twenty years. I'd heard they'd already clashed with Martha Feeney over where she wanted the stage to be set up for the bond drive. I was sure Martha could hold her own against the couple.

"Let me see," Harold said. "How about the cotton candy booth."

The wooden booth he pointed to looked like it had been freshly painted white. As far as I could tell it wasn't labeled. "I don't see 'cotton candy' on it anywhere," I said.

If Harold rolled his eyes any harder, they'd be permanently stuck to the back of his sockets. "Young lady, that is the cotton candy booth. It has always been the cotton candy booth. It will always be the cotton candy booth." He walked away mumbling something about stupid young people.

While I wheeled the cart to the alleged cotton candy booth, I heard Peggy ask Harold where he wanted the popcorn machine. I couldn't help smiling when he told her, the popcorn booth. That one wasn't marked either. It was practically a repeat of the conversation I'd had with him.

When Ken asked him where he wanted the machine for the snow cones, I half expected Harold to run screaming from the fairgrounds in exasperation.

A voice behind me made me jump. "Sheesh, what's with that guy?"

"He doesn't seem to like stupid young people," I said, turning around.

"You're anything but stupid."

The man speaking seemed vaguely familiar. I'd seen him somewhere before, but I couldn't put my finger on it. I'd heard the voice before as well. "How would you know that?" I asked.

He grinned. "You don't recognize me, do you?"

I studied him. He was tall and slender and wore tan trousers with a short-sleeved knit shirt. His skin was tan enough to tell me he spent a good bit of time on the golf course. His dark brown hair was wavy with streaks of lighter brown from being in the sun. Something deep down told me I knew him well, but for the life of me I couldn't place him.

"*Macbeth*. Tenth grade English. Old lady Gilbert made us act it out."

It couldn't be. It couldn't possibly be the same person.

He laughed. "You can pick your jaw up off the ground, Irene."

"Eugene?" Eugene Allen had been one of my classmates all through school. He had been a good fifty pounds overweight, with a bad case of acne. He'd left town after graduation and I'd lost track of him.

"One and the same," he said. "Nowadays, I go by Kirk. Kirk Allen. Same last name. Less confusing that way."

"You look so different," I said. Different didn't even begin to describe it. He'd gone from someone who had never gotten a second glance to an Adonis. "What are you doing back here? Your folks moved away, didn't they?"

Kirk nodded. "They moved to Arizona because of Dad's asthma. I see them often enough since I live in LA. Anyway, I'm here for the war bond rally."

I put it together—the name and physical changes, living in Los Angeles, and the war bond rally. "You're an actor now?"

"Yep. I'm starring in the next Warner Brothers movie. We start filming in a month. I owe it all to *Macbeth*."

I laughed. "Don't forget Mrs. Gilbert."

"How could I forget that old bat?"

"She was definitely memorable," I said. She had been the only person who could diagram a sentence quicker than I could.

"What are you doing these days?" Kirk asked. "With the way you ran the high school newspaper, I expected you to be working at the *New York Times* by now."

"No *Times*, but I am the editor-in-chief of the *Progress Herald*."

"Isn't that your father's paper?"

I told him the story.

"That's great," he said. "I bet you're doing a splendid job."

Peggy and Ken were looking our way, and I waved them over. "You're not going to believe who this is," I said when they reached us.

They had the same trouble I'd had. Finally, Kirk mentioned a playoff game with the Progress High baseball team when he'd hit a grand slam. The score had been tied in the ninth inning and they had two outs. He won the game for them.

Ken laughed and slapped him on the back. "I can't believe it. Peggy, this is Eugene Allen."

"I remember Eugene," Peggy said. "But he didn't look anything like that."

I could tell Eugene—or rather Kirk—got a big kick out of not being recognized right away.

"It's me, all right," Kirk said. He told them about the name change and why he was here.

"So you're an honest to goodness movie star now?" Peggy asked.

"Well, not yet. But I plan to be."

"If anyone can do it, you can," I said.

Kirk looked past me and frowned. "I have to go."

I turned my head. Freddie was walking our way. I was curious. "Don't you and Freddie get along?"

"You could say that. Let's all get together some night while I'm in town."

"That would be great," Ken said.

Kirk began walking away, then turned back to us. "Don't get too friendly with that snake. You'll regret it. I know I will until the day I die. Or he does, which can't come soon enough."

Chapter Six

Second Washington Conference Ends

The Progress Herald, June 25, 1942

"I wonder what that was all about," Peggy said as we watched Kirk walk away.

I didn't have time to speculate before Freddie reached us. Freddie Harrison sure wasn't making any friends, though—if he'd had any to begin with.

"What were you talking to that loser about?" Freddie asked.

"He happens to be a friend of ours," I said. "We went to school with him."

"Sure you did."

"Didn't you know he grew up here?" Peggy asked.

Freddie laughed. "I guess you have some swampland you want to sell me, too."

Ken took Peggy's hand. "I think I hear Harold calling for us."

"It's just you and me, doll," Freddie said.

He reached to put his arm around me and I pushed it away. "Never do that again. And don't call me doll. For heaven's sake, you're a married man. I thought you were in love with your wife."

51

"I am. What does that have to do with having a little fun?"

I shook my head and walked away.

"Wait," Freddie said. "Have you seen Angel? She's supposed to be here."

"I haven't seen her." I spotted Martha Feeney across the fairgrounds where some workmen were constructing the stage for the bond rally and headed that way.

"Irene," Martha said. "You're just the person I wanted to see."

I wasn't sure if that was good or bad.

"We're going to have a run-through for all the speakers tomorrow evening. Can you be here and maybe have Matt take some photographs?"

"Of course," I said. "Can I help with anything else?"

"I don't think so. At least not at the moment." She sighed. "I only hope we have a good turnout. I know everyone was hoping for Mr. Gable, or at least a big name star."

Martha didn't have to add *instead we're stuck with Freddie*. It was implied by her tone of voice. "Maybe Kirk Allen will make up for it. I'm going to write a piece about him. It's so nice to see him again."

"Again?" Martha said.

I filled her in.

"Oh, that's wonderful! I had no idea that boy grew up in Progress. I'll have to let everyone know." She smiled. "I guarantee Ava doesn't know. I have an appointment for a shampoo and set in the morning. I can't wait to see her face when I tell her."

"I wouldn't mind seeing that myself."

The next hour passed uneventfully. Freddie disappeared after Harold asked him to help him hang a sign on one of the booths. Ken, Peggy, Kirk, and I made plans to go to the Starlight after we finished tomorrow night. I went home tired, content, and ready for a fun weekend.

* * *

Matt Redmond, staff photographer for the *Herald*, stopped by my office on Friday afternoon. Matt and I were good friends. He had been a couple of years ahead of me in school and, although he was older, I'd always felt sort of protective of him. He'd been bullied for wearing Coke bottle–thick glasses—at least until he punched out one of the bullies. They mostly left him alone after that.

"Hey, boss," Matt said. He plopped into the chair on the other side of my desk. "What's this I hear about Roosevelt censoring photos?"

"I wouldn't exactly call it censoring. From what I've read he's prohibiting unauthorized photographs or drawings of military properties."

"Like I said, he's censoring photos. Whatever happened to freedom of the press?"

I leaned back in my chair. "So you'd approve of the Japanese or the Nazis getting hold of pictures of, let's say, Carlisle Barracks, and dropping a bomb?"

"No, of course not. But no honest photographer would photograph anything like that anyway."

"The magic word there is honest. There are plenty of people who would do it if the price was right."

"Yeah, I guess," Matt said. "I just don't like the idea of being told what I can and can't take pictures of."

"The president didn't say you can't take pictures. They just have to be approved."

"All right, you sold me." He grinned. "I'll have to remember to never argue with you."

"Since I seem to have won this one, I need you to take some photos at the fairgrounds tonight." I told him about the run-through for the rally and what I wanted in the way of photos.

"You got it, boss."

After Matt left, I gave Rex, Frank, and Ken their assignments for the weekend. I finished the articles I'd been working on and took the final versions down to Donny. For once, he didn't argue with me and actually seemed happy about something. I knew I should have asked him what it was, but I didn't want to interfere with his good mood. I only hoped it lasted. Maybe I'd learn to like the new Donny. I wasn't counting on it, but one never knew.

*　*　*

I drove Mom and Lily in Pop's car and parked near the entrance to the fairground. There were only a dozen or so cars in the field that was being used for a parking lot. Tomorrow the field would be filled with vehicles. It had drizzled off and on all day, but now the skies were mostly clear.

The chief, Jimmy, and Rally all stood inside the entrance. Rally towered over the other two. He was at least six foot five. I still hadn't gotten used to seeing Rally beside the others instead of Bill. I liked Rally well enough, but I missed Bill. I shook off the feeling. There were many more who were in the same situation—or worse. I shouldn't feel sorry for myself.

I nudged my sister with my elbow. "What do you think, Lily? Don't they look like the Three Stooges?"

Lily smiled. "I think you're right."

"Hey, I resemble that remark," Dad said.

Rally made the *whoop-whoop* sound that Curly frequently made and we all laughed.

Dad put an arm around me. "It's a good thing you're marrying my son. Otherwise I'd have to arrest you for making fun of a police officer."

"Since when is that a law?" Mom asked. "You'd have to arrest half the town."

"Touché," Dad said. "I never thought I'd see the day Joan Ingram bested me."

Mom laughed. "Times are changing, Walt. We all need to get used to it."

I think I was more surprised than Dad was. Mom was usually a stickler for decorum. We'd had more than our share of arguments about everything from what I wore to women in the workplace. I was happy that she might be attempting to keep up with the twentieth century. At the very least, maybe she'd stop giving me the stink eye every time I wore trousers to work.

Lily ran off to find Cindy. They would be helping out at the cotton candy booth this weekend, and they were supposed to get instructions on how to work the equipment. It wasn't that hard— I'd manned the booth when I was Lily's age. I'd eaten so much cotton candy at the time I couldn't stomach it anymore, which was probably good for my waistline. I was sure the booth would be popular since sweets were at a premium these days with rationing.

While Mom talked to the chief, Jimmy pulled me aside to tell me he'd had a talk with Ned. "He gave me his word the shotgun wasn't loaded," Jimmy said. "There's been no complaint filed, so I'm going to let it slide."

"That's good," I said. "I don't think he meant any harm."

"I warned him not to do it again."

It wasn't long before Peggy and Ken showed up, followed by Matt, and all of us headed over to the stage, where we gathered with Harold, Ophelia, and a few others. Martha was on the stage talking to a man I didn't recognize. Kirk stood off to the side with Angel. Another woman sat on a wooden folding chair applying blood-red lipstick. Her coal-black hair fell in waves to her shoulders. While everyone else present had dressed somewhat casually—even Angel, who wore beige linen trousers and a white blouse—the newcomer wore a sapphire dress with a deep V-neck that showed off way too much cleavage. It looked so tight, I wondered how she had sat down without splitting a seam. This had to be the woman Freddie was having an affair with.

Matt stood beside me. "Hubba hubba," he said. "Who is that?"

"I imagine that's Belinda Fox. Freddie's paramour."

"Isn't he married to Ava's sister?"

"Yep."

"Lucky guy." Matt snapped a half dozen photos of Belinda.

"Hey. Remember who's paying for that film," I said.

"Gotcha, boss." He took a few shots of the others.

The unknown man shook hands with Martha and picked up a clipboard from the podium. "Look lively, people," he said. "I know most of you have done this before, but we're going to run through it all anyway. Places, please."

Kirk and Angel took their places behind him.

The man looked at the sitting woman. "That means you too, sweetheart."

She folded her compact and dropped it into a small beaded clutch purse. "Freddie's not here yet. I'll wait for him."

"Where is Freddie?" Kirk asked.

She shrugged. "I haven't seen him since this morning." Her gaze settled on Angel. "We had breakfast in bed."

"How lovely," Angel said. "Freddie does like breakfast in bed." If she hadn't clenched her fists, I'd never have known she was upset.

"We don't need Freddie. We'll do it without him," the man said.

"He's not going to like that." Belinda stood and straightened her dress. "I think you should wait."

I glanced at Mom. Her lips were pursed. If she ever got the chance, Belinda would get an earful.

"I don't care what you think," the man said. "Kirk, you can do Freddie's part."

"Be happy to," he said.

Belinda protested. "I insist we wait for Freddie. He's the star."

I turned at a sound behind me.

"Am I late?" It was Ava. "I had some things to finish."

I shook my head. "You didn't miss anything. Freddie's not here yet, and Belinda doesn't want Kirk to fill in for him."

The man in charge ignored Belinda's protest. He moved to the podium and tested the microphone. Finding it worked perfectly, he began. "Welcome, citizens of . . ."—he glanced at his clipboard—". . . Progress, Pennsylvania. My name is Paul Davis, and I run the show here." He smiled. "Although Belinda thinks she does."

He got a big laugh for that one.

"You'll get the full show tomorrow afternoon—this is just a preview. We're going to run through our lines and a few of the songs, among other things. Here we go." He took a deep breath. "Ladies and gentlemen, I'd like to introduce future matinee idol

Kirk Allen. He'll be starring in an upcoming Warner Brothers film. He's been called the next Cary Grant. Let's give a nice round of applause for Kirk Allen!"

Everyone applauded except Belinda, who stood with her arms folded. If looks could kill, both Paul Davis and Kirk would be flat on their backs. Probably Angel, too.

Kirk did a splendid job filling in for Freddie. I was sure Kirk could act rings around Freddie, and it wasn't just because Kirk was a friend. He had that something special that Freddie didn't. After that, they ran through a few songs, and Paul Davis told way too many bad jokes.

Angel spoke about the importance of buying bonds. Belinda followed and mostly said the same thing, but not as well. Davis came back to the podium, thanked everyone, and said he hoped to see us all tomorrow.

I pulled my notebook and pencil from my pocketbook and climbed the few steps to the stage. I introduced myself to Paul Davis.

He gave me the once-over. "What's a pretty young thing like you doing running a newspaper? You should be in Hollywood."

It was different than the usual *Aren't you a little young to be an editor?* Annoying nonetheless. "I bet you say that to all the girls."

He gave me a smarmy grin. "Only the pretty ones."

I got down to business. "I have a few questions, if you have the time."

"How about over a drink?"

I told him I had other plans. I was happy he didn't press the point. I asked him about his background.

"I've been a comedian for the last fifteen or so years," he said. "Did pretty well, too."

I didn't ask him why I'd never heard of him if he was doing well. "Do you like what you do?"

He shrugged. "It beats having a real job. I could do a lot worse."

After a couple more questions, I asked about Freddie. "Does Freddie do this often—not show up?"

"Every so often," Davis said. "But that's Freddie. He thinks he's too good to rehearse. It's gonna bite him in the ass someday. Excuse my French."

It certainly wasn't the worst I'd heard. I thanked him and headed for Belinda, who appeared to be charming the pants off Rally Johnson. Not literally, of course, thank goodness.

"I do so love a man in uniform," Belinda practically purred.

I reached them just in time. Rally's freckled face was flushed, and he mumbled something unintelligible. "Rally, I think the chief is looking for you."

"I—I—have to go," he said to Belinda.

When he was gone, Belinda glared at me. "Why did you do that? We were just getting to know each other."

"That's what I was afraid of," I said. "Besides, aren't you and Freddie an item?"

"Maybe."

"What's that supposed to mean? Either you are or you aren't."

Belinda stuck her nose in the air. "I'm not talking to you. You're friends with Angel. She's no good. Acts like she owns Freddie."

"Well, she *is* married to him."

"Freddie's never going back to her," she said. "Ever." Then she spun around and stalked away.

I shook my head. I didn't understand why in the world Kirk would want to be around these people. None of them seemed to have their feet on the ground. Then again, maybe Kirk didn't either. I watched as Belinda and Paul got into a black limousine and drove away. Kirk got into the driver's seat of another car. I didn't blame him a bit for not wanting to ride with Belinda.

I decided to take a walk around the fairgrounds before joining my friends. It would give me an idea of what aspects of the fair to cover for the *Herald*. I passed the booths with various games of chance and the food booths. I waved to Lily and Cindy, who were practicing their cotton candy–making skills. I kept walking, passing the Ferris wheel and the Tilt-A-Whirl. There was a dunk tank set up beyond the rides, and something caught my eye—a scrap of blue material appeared to be stuck on the inner edge of the tank. I headed that way.

As I got closer I noticed something floating on top of the water. I soon realized it wasn't something—it was someone. When I reached the tank I realized why Freddie hadn't shown up for the rehearsal.

Chapter Seven

Jap Destroyer Sunk by USS Nautilus South of Tokyo Bay
The Progress Herald, June 26, 1942

I ran to where the chief and Jimmy were standing and quietly asked them to come with me.

Dad gave me a puzzled look.

"It's Freddie Harrison. He's dead."

Dad lifted his hand to motion to Rally until he saw he was with Angel and Ava. He lowered it. "I'll fill Rally in later."

They followed me, and I pointed to the dunk tank. "There."

"Wait here," Dad said.

I wasn't about to argue with him. The chief and Jimmy pulled the body out of the water and onto the platform. I was close enough to see that the blue material that had been caught on the edge of the tank was part of Freddie's shirt. There must have been a struggle. The water was shallow enough that Freddie should have been able to stand up. Lost in thought, I jumped when Matt came up behind me.

"What's going on?" he asked. "Is that Harrison?"

"Yep. Keep it under your hat for now. Angel is here, and she shouldn't see her husband like this."

"Gotcha. I'm gonna see if the chief wants me to take any pictures. It'll save him from going back for a camera."

While Matt talked to Dad, Jimmy came over to me. "The chief wants you to find Harold or Ophelia and ask them to make an announcement that everyone should leave—that they want to close up for the evening."

"Should I tell them what happened?"

"As long as Ava and her sister don't overhear. He'll talk to Angel as soon as he can, but we don't want any looky-loos trampling on evidence."

"So it was definitely murder?"

"Yeah. I have to go call Doc Atkins, but it looks like he was hit over the head and pushed into the tank."

I shivered as Jimmy walked away. I had been naïve to think Progress would be spared any more murders after the events of the previous month. I took a deep breath and went to find Harold.

Fifteen minutes later, most everyone had left the fairgrounds. I told my mother I was staying behind to interview Harold and Ophelia, which was partially true. She and Lily rode home with Cindy's parents.

Peggy pulled me aside. "I know something is going on. What is it?"

"Freddie's dead," I whispered.

"Oh no. That's terrible!" Peggy said. "You were the one who found him, weren't you?"

"How did you know that?"

"We've been friends almost all our lives. I can tell by looking at you. Besides, you seem to have a knack for that sort of thing."

"I do not."

Peggy rolled her eyes. "You do. What happened?"

I told her. "Don't let on to anyone except Ken until the chief gives his go-ahead. He'll want to talk to Angel first. And Matt's here taking pictures for the chief."

"What about Kirk? We're supposed to go to the Starlight with him."

"I'm not going to make it. If you see him, just say that something came up."

"Will do." She joined Ken outside the gate and they got into Ken's car.

Ava stood beside her car watching me, probably wondering why I wasn't leaving. To ease her suspicion, I pulled my notebook from my pocketbook and waved to Harold, who was coming my way. It must have worked because Ava and Angel drove away.

Rally joined us as Harold locked the gate. "Jimmy told me what happened. Are you all right?"

"I'm fine," I said.

"Well, I'm not." Harold's key chain rattled as he pulled the key from the lock. "What's going to happen to the fair?"

"That's a question you'll have to ask the chief," Rally said.

"Oh, I will. I'm not shutting down. Those Hollywood people won't like it if we do—not to mention everyone in the entire county."

Rally put his hand out. "I'm going to need that key to let the coroner in."

Harold hesitated like he'd never let the key out of his sight before. Rally didn't budge, and Harold finally slapped it into his hand. "I'd better get that back."

Rally pocketed the key as Harold walked away.

I waited with Rally until Doc Atkins arrived five minutes later. Doc Atkins was a local dentist as well as the coroner. Occasionally he left patients sitting in the dental chair when he was called to a scene. He was also a chain smoker and, for a medical professional, he didn't have the best hygiene. I was glad he wasn't my dentist. I wasn't sure why he had any patients at all.

Rally locked the gate again and took Doc to the dunk tank. I'd need to get statements from the chief and the coroner when they were finished, but the last thing I wanted to do was watch the process.

* * *

Less than an hour later, I had a statement from the chief. When I asked Doc Atkins for one, he said the chief would tell me anything I needed to know. I almost reverted to my ten-year-old self and told him I didn't want to talk to him anyway. It was still early enough to make it to the Starlight, so when I reached the car, I took off the oxfords I'd been wearing and replaced them with the stacked heels I'd brought with me. I powdered my nose, touched up my lipstick, and headed out.

The Starlight was the closest place to go dancing and listen to music. They often hosted local big bands, and occasionally more well-known ones. The building itself wasn't anything fancy. The one-story frame structure had been a roadside tavern. The new owners had spruced up the inside, and the smooth wood floor was perfect for dancing. Since it was Friday evening, the place was packed. It took me five minutes to find a parking space at the far end of the lot.

Inside it was smoky and loud. The band was playing Benny Goodman's "Sing Sing Sing," and even those sitting at the tables were tapping their feet and snapping their fingers. I bounced on my toes to the beat while looking for Peggy, Ken, and Kirk. I'd invited Matt to come along, but he'd passed, saying he wanted to develop the film and get the photos to the police. I finally spotted my friends on the far side of the room.

Ken and Kirk both stood when I reached the table, although Kirk was none too steady on his feet. He grinned and sank back into his chair as I took the seat beside him.

"H'lo, Irene," he said. "Lemme buy you a drink." He stood again and promptly sat back down again.

He was smashed.

I looked at Peggy. "How long have you been here?"

"An hour and a half," she said.

Kirk must have been sucking down the drinks, especially since the booze here was usually watered down. I turned to him. "How much have you had to drink?"

"Not nearly enough," he said.

"What you need is some coffee," I said.

Ken got up. "I'll get some. And I'll bring you a drink, Irene. Rum and Coke?"

"Yes. Thanks."

"I'll have one of those, too," Kirk said.

"No, you won't. You're getting coffee. No argument." Thank goodness I'd gotten used to dealing with obstinate men.

"You're mean," Kirk said.

"It's for your own good."

Kirk slouched in his chair and crossed his arms.

I turned back to Peggy. "Have you told Kirk?"

She shook her head. "Only Ken."

"Told me what?" Kirk asked.

I shifted in my seat. "Freddie is dead."

"I think I'm gonna be sick." He bolted out of his chair for the men's room.

I followed him to the door of the restroom and waited in the hallway. I hadn't expected that sort of reaction from someone who clearly disliked Freddie. What had Kirk said? That he'd regret knowing

Freddie until the day he died. And something about Freddie's death not coming soon enough. Could Kirk have made his wish come true? I didn't want to think Kirk was capable of killing Freddie, but I didn't really know him anymore. We'd been friends in high school, and back then I would have said he'd never kill anyone. But now? He could have changed as much as his appearance had.

Ken came toward me. "I put your drink and the coffee on the table. Why don't you go back? I'll go in and check on him."

"Thanks." Back at the table I took a healthy swig of my rum and Coke, which was more ice than liquid.

"Is Kirk all right?" Peggy asked.

"I don't know. Ken went in to check on him. I didn't think the news of Freddie's death would hit him so hard. I didn't even mention yet that he'd been murdered."

"Well, they did know each other, even if they weren't exactly friends."

"Maybe that's it."

"You think it's more?" Peggy asked.

I shrugged. "I don't know. I'll talk to him when he's sober."

"You don't think he killed Freddie, do you?"

I drained my glass. "Like I said, I don't know."

Peggy gave me a grim smile. "If anyone can find out, you can."

I hoped she was right.

*　*　*

With the events of the previous night, I'd completely forgotten Sylvia was moving into our house until she knocked on the front door at eight o'clock Saturday morning. She was accompanied by Betty Riley, her coworker and friend from Tabor Ironworks. I'd gotten up at seven. Mom had left a note on the kitchen table saying that she'd gone into town to help weed the Victory Garden and would be back soon. I had two cups of coffee while I flipped through a movie magazine, and was about to make some toast before I headed to the police department when I heard the knock on the door. I didn't let on that I'd forgotten. I only told her I was running behind.

"That's all right," Sylvia said. "Betty came to help, if you don't mind."

"Not at all," I said.

Lily bounded down the stairs. She had been looking forward to having a new boarder in the house. She'd been enamored of Katherine and complained daily that life was so boring without her. I had warned her that Sylvia was very different from Katherine. There would be no stories of singing in nightclubs, Frank Sinatra, or much else that Lily found exciting and glamorous.

"Hello," Lily said. "Welcome to our home."

Sylvia smiled. "Thanks."

"Did you bring any records?" Lily asked.

"Lily!" Mom said as she came in the back door carrying a basket of tomatoes and green peppers. "That's no way to greet our guest."

"Well, I did tell her welcome," Lily said.

Sylvia and Betty laughed. "I don't mind, Mrs. Ingram," Sylvia said. "And I'm sorry to say I don't have any records, Lily."

Mom set the produce on the counter and introduced herself to Betty, then put Lily to work helping carry items upstairs. Sylvia didn't have much—it only took two trips. Afterward Mom served coffee and sliced banana bread she'd made the day before.

I kept glancing at the kitchen clock, itching to get into town and talk to the chief. I thought I was being sneaky about it, but Sylvia noticed.

"Got a hot date or something?" she asked.

I shook my head. "I just need to go into town and get some information for tomorrow's paper."

"Anything interesting?" Betty asked.

"You could say that."

I'd told Mom what had happened when I had gotten home last night, but I didn't want to say anything in front of Lily. Mom got up and wrapped the rest of the banana bread in waxed paper. "Lily, run this over to the Finnertys, please."

"Do I have to? I'd rather stay here."

All Mom had to do was give her a look.

Lily sighed loudly and took the package from Mom. "Don't talk about anything interesting until I get back."

I waited until the front door closed. "There was an incident at the fairgrounds last night, and I need to talk to the chief."

"What kind of incident?" Sylvia asked.

"I found Freddie Harrison in the dunk tank."

Sylvia understood what I meant. Betty seemed puzzled. I still wasn't sure if she was just naïve or not full up in the brain department. "What was he doing in the dunk tank?" she asked.

Sylvia elbowed her. "What do you think he was doing there? He wasn't taking a swim."

"The water's not deep enough for that." Betty sounded indignant.

Sylvia rolled her eyes. "Oh, for heaven's sake."

Mom broke in. "What Irene is trying to say is that the man is dead."

I couldn't believe how matter-of-fact she sounded, like I found dead bodies every day. Frankly, it wasn't every day. Just every few weeks lately.

"Oh, my!" Betty said. "That's so sad. He was so good looking. I saw his last picture and I wanted to kiss the screen. He was just wonderful."

She obviously hadn't seen the same movie I had.

I told them what I knew so far. It wasn't much, which was why I needed to go to the police department.

"Who would want to do something like that?" Mom asked. "That poor man. I feel terrible for Ava's sister."

"Freddie wasn't very well liked," I said.

"But he was a movie star," Betty said. "No one kills a movie star."

"Apparently someone did," Sylvia said.

"Will the fair still go on? And the bond rally?" Betty asked. "I hope so. I have a date, and I bought a new outfit for the occasion."

"Probably," I said. "Which means I'd better get moving so I can get my articles written and ready for tomorrow's paper and get to the fair."

Mom said she'd get Sylvia settled, so I retrieved my pocketbook and headed to see my future father-in-law.

* * *

Jimmy wasn't at the front desk when I arrived at the police department. The door to the chief's office was open, so I went around Jimmy's desk and knocked on the doorframe. Dad looked up and motioned for me to come in.

"Are you all by yourself?" I asked.

He nodded. "Jimmy is helping Martha and that Davis fellow with last-minute adjustments to the program since Harrison won't be on the schedule now. Rally is out on patrol. How are you doing?"

I sat down and opened my notebook. "I'm fine. How did Angel take the news?"

"Not how I expected."

"What did you expect?"

Dad's chair squeaked as he leaned back. "I thought she'd be all broken up about it. Instead, she was mad that he'd had the nerve to abandon her. She gave a pretty good speech about it and I had the feeling she was playing a part."

"I've seen Angel do that a few times." I told him about when she answered the phone at Ava's beauty shop and her waitressing gig at Dempsey's Diner.

"Angel didn't like her sister hovering over her either. Ava tried to put an arm around her at one point and Angel pushed her away."

"That sounds very much like the Angel I've seen so far this week. I won't be surprised if she shows up next as the grieving widow. Did Doc give you a time of death yet?"

"He's doing an autopsy this morning, but he said Harrison was killed at least a couple of hours before you found him. He'll know after the autopsy whether Harrison died from the blow to his head or drowning afterward."

I shivered. Neither was a good way to die. "Anything else to tell me for my article? Any suspects yet?"

"I think that's all for now," Dad said. "Right now, everyone who's been in contact with Harrison is a suspect. It's too soon to narrow it down. I'll start checking alibis for yesterday afternoon and go from there."

I closed my notebook and pushed out of my chair. "Will you keep me posted?"

"Of course," he said. "You do likewise."

"I will."

"I mean it. I don't want a repeat of last month."

I nodded. I'd had my reasons for not keeping him informed when my reporter had been killed, but I didn't see that happening this time around. We said goodbye and I crossed the square to the *Herald*. I had work to do.

Chapter Eight

FDR Prohibits Unauthorized Photos of Military Property
The Progress Herald, June 28, 1942

I settled into my office and wrote an article about Freddie Harrison's murder. Matt had left a few photos on my desk that would be appropriate for the paper, meaning there weren't any featuring the victim's body. Without being asked, he'd also left a headshot of Freddie to go along with the article. I'd just finished the article when I heard the front door open.

Rex ambled into my office. "I figured you'd be here. I heard about Harrison."

I passed the article to him and asked him to proof it for me.

He read it quickly. "Looks fine to me. So you were there?"

"Yep. I was the one who found him."

Rex shook his head. "I should have figured that. What is it with you? Pete ran this paper for years without ever finding a body."

"It's not like I go looking for trouble," I said.

"Well, it sure goes looking for you."

I wasn't sure how to respond because it was partially true. I attributed it to my job. Pop hadn't found bodies because he mostly stuck to the editorial side of the business. I was doing double duty.

I didn't look for trouble, but I had to follow it. It was inevitable that trouble would find me occasionally.

"I guess this means we're going to be swamped with out-of-town press," Rex said.

I hadn't thought of that. "Do you really think so? Freddie wasn't very well known."

"He's from Hollywood. He'll be more famous in death than he ever was in life."

I hoped Rex was wrong, but we had to be prepared. "In that case, I want all hands on deck to cover this. We'll beat the big shots at their own game. We need to find out everything we can about Freddie Harrison and who wanted him dead."

"Atta girl." Rex grinned. "That's exactly what your father would have said."

Those words made me happy—especially coming from Rex.

"A friend of mine works for a paper in Los Angeles," Rex said. "I'll telephone him and see what I can find out."

"Thanks," I said. "I'll stop at Ava's and see if I can talk to Angel."

We decided to meet at the fair later, in time for the bond rally at six o'clock. I telephoned Frank and Matt and filled them in. I had made plans to join Peggy and Ken there at three. I looked at the clock on the wall. It was already eleven. I'd better get a move on.

I was just about to take my article and Matt's photos downstairs for Donny when Rex called my name.

"You have to see what just came over the wire," he said.

I looked at what he showed me. The FBI had arrested eight Germans who had come ashore planning to sabotage strategic targets in the eastern United States. A chill went through me. I couldn't help but see the similarities to what had happened here last month—only this was worse. They called it Operation Pastorius after the founder of the first German settlement in Pennsylvania. "Holy cow," I said. "They were going to blow up Horseshoe Curve. Altoona's only a couple of hours from here." Horseshoe Curve was a crucial railroad pass.

"They targeted the Pennsylvania Railroad repair shop there as well," Rex said.

Other major targets were the Niagara Falls hydroelectric plant, Hell Gate Bridge in New York, several factories, and Pennsylvania Station in New Jersey. They also planned to cause panic by planting charges on bridges, water treatment plants, and public places.

"How do you want to do this?" Rex asked.

I folded my hands in front of me so Rex wouldn't see them shaking. I couldn't write the article. I wouldn't be impartial. Not after what had happened. "Would you want to write this up? Unless you think we should just go with the AP article."

"I'll write it. Be happy to."

"Take it down to Donny when you're done. I don't need to see it." I wagged a finger at him. "No sensational headline, though. Keep it simple."

"You're no fun."

"So I've been told."

Rex went to his desk and in seconds he was typing away.

I went to the kitchen and got a glass of water to calm my nerves, then went to see Donny. I heard him whistling an unknown tune when I reached the bottom of the stairs. "You're in a good mood," I said.

"I am," he said. "It's a beautiful day, isn't it?"

I wasn't sure how to deal with my cousin in a good mood. "It is. These will need to go on the front page, but below the fold. Rex is working on something that I want up top." I didn't explain what it was. I handed him the article and photos and waited for the usual complaint.

"Sure thing, Irene," he said with a smile.

I stared at him. "Where is my cousin and what did you do with him?"

Donny laughed. "I haven't gone anywhere."

"Then why are you so happy?"

"Because I've met the most wonderful girl. We've only had one date so far, but I think she really likes me."

"I'm glad," I said. And I really was. I just couldn't figure out what the girl saw in him.

"We're going to the fair later. She wants me to win a teddy bear for her." He stood straighter, as if that was the most important thing in the world.

I smiled. "I hope you do. I'm looking forward to meeting her."

"If I run into you at the fair, I'll introduce you." Donny put the article down on his table. "I'd better get back to work."

I headed back upstairs shaking my head. Whoever this girl was, I hoped she felt the same way about Donny. I liked this new version of my cousin. I retrieved my pocketbook from my office and headed out, thinking of everything I needed to do before three. First would be talking to Angel.

* * *

It came as no surprise that Ava's shop was closed. There was a note on the door stating she was canceling her appointments for the day because of a tragedy in the family. Yesterday, she sure wouldn't

74

have claimed Freddie as family. I hoofed it to the other side of town to her cottage on Dunlap Street.

There was a black wreath hanging on Ava's front door, and the frame was swathed in some sort of black fabric. My guess was this was Angel's doing. I pressed the doorbell button and heard it buzz inside. Seconds later the door was opened by Ava.

"Come in, Irene," she said.

I followed her inside. The front door opened directly into the living room. Ava's home was usually tastefully decorated, but not at the moment. The sofa and two chairs were covered in black fabric, and black gauze was draped over the table lamps. I hadn't realized the fabric store carried this much black.

Before I could ask about it, Ava waved her hand. "Angel had me go and buy all this as soon as the store opened this morning. She's in deep mourning."

"I never would have guessed."

"Sarcasm doesn't become you, Irene."

"I thought she hated Freddie."

Ava motioned for me to have a seat. "One can hate and love someone at the same time."

I didn't have a response to that. It was a ridiculous notion. I didn't believe you could love someone you hated. I also didn't believe Angel really hated Freddie. She was angry with him, and hurt because he'd stepped out on her, but that wasn't hate. "I'd like to talk to Angel if she's here."

"I don't think that's a good idea. She resting at the moment."

"No, I'm not." Angel floated into the living room. She wore a flowing black dress that trailed on the floor behind her. Her hair was covered with a black veil. "Thank you for coming, Irene." She spoke in a British accent and reached out a black-gloved hand.

I had to stifle a laugh. I had thought all the black fabric on the furniture was a bit much, but her costume really took the cake. "How are you?" I asked.

Angel sat on the sofa and arranged the flowing dress around her. "I'm doing as well as can be expected." She sighed, raising her hand and placing the back of it against her forehead. "I don't know how I'm going to live without my Freddie."

"Chief Turner said you were angry when he told you about Freddie," I said. "I thought you didn't want to have anything to do with him."

"I was in shock. I didn't know what I was saying." She began crying. "Freddie was the love of my life. I can't go on without him."

Ava stood. "You need to go, Irene. You're upsetting Angel."

"No," Angel said. "Irene stays. She can find out who did this to my Freddie."

"The police will find the person responsible," I said.

"I don't think Chief Turner likes me," she said.

"Whether he likes you or not, he'll do his job."

"Irene is right," Ava said. "The chief is a good man."

Angel was silent, as if she were thinking it over. "All right," she said finally. "But can't you look into it too?"

I'd been planning to do just that, but I didn't like being pushed into it. I had to stay impartial. I didn't want Angel to believe I was working for her. I only worked for the *Herald*. I told her that.

"I'll be beholden to you no matter what you find out." Angel had switched to a southern accent. She slid the veil off her head and placed it around her shoulders. "Lawdy, look at the time. I must take my afternoon rest before the festivities this evening." She sashayed from the room.

I looked at Ava. "She's not really going to appear at the rally, is she?"

"Of course she is. It's extremely important. The show must go on."

There were more questions I'd wanted to ask Angel, but she wouldn't have given me a straight answer anyway. With the way she became different characters, she would have given that character's answer, not her own. I'd get more from Ava. "I wrote an article about Freddie's death for tomorrow's paper, but I have some follow-up questions, if you don't mind."

"I don't mind at all. I'm happy to help."

I began with preliminary questions like how long Angel had been married to Freddie, and about his work. After that I got to the harder questions. "Do you have any idea who would want to kill Freddie?" I asked.

"Isn't it obvious?" Ava said. "That Belinda woman killed him. She didn't want him to go back to Angel."

"That has crossed my mind. I need to get a few things straight, though. According to Freddie, Angel walked out on him, not the other way around."

Ava crossed her arms. "Wouldn't you if your husband was fooling around?"

"Freddie was right then."

"It's not important who left whom," Ava said. "The important thing is, they were getting back together. Angel said Freddie was going to break it off with that scheming little tramp."

"So Angel and Freddie reconciled?"

Ava nodded. "Angel met with Freddie yesterday afternoon. She stopped into the shop afterward. She was happy. Almost floating on air. She told me Freddie would never hurt her again."

I didn't like the sound of that. "Was that early or late afternoon?"

"Late. She saw Freddie around four and came into the shop around five. Why?"

"No reason. I just want to get all the facts straight."

"That's good," Ava said. "I don't want any rumors spreading about my sister. She and Freddie loved each other and they were going to live happily ever after."

She didn't want rumors spreading about her sister, but she was fine with spreading them about everyone else. I closed my notebook and pushed up from my chair. I thanked Ava and quickly left the house. I paused on the sidewalk. Late afternoon was likely when Freddie had been murdered.

I ran a scenario through my mind. Angel met Freddie on the fairgrounds at the dunk tank. Freddie begged her to come back to him. Angel gave him an ultimatum to dump Belinda, and he refused. Angel became angry, hit him over the head with something, and he fell into the water.

The problem was I didn't know if Angel had the strength to hit Freddie hard enough to either render him unconscious or kill him with the blow. And what had she hit him with? I didn't recall that there was anything at the dunk tank that could have been used as a weapon. It was possible I'd missed it. Once I'd seen Freddie I hadn't stuck around long enough to notice anything else.

I decided to return to the police station and see if Dad had results from the autopsy from Doc Atkins yet. I also wanted to be sure he knew that Angel had met with Freddie. If Doc had narrowed down the time Freddie was killed, it would either put Angel in the clear or make her the prime suspect.

I stepped off the curb to cross the street as a black limousine sped around the corner, ignoring the stop sign. I jumped back to avoid being hit. The car screeched to a stop in front of the Excelsior. I hurried down the street to give the driver a piece of my mind. I reached the car as the limo driver opened the back door.

"Where did you learn to drive?" I asked. "You almost ran me over."

He didn't answer me.

"Didn't you hear me?"

"He heard you perfectly."

A woman stepped from the back seat. She had salt-and-pepper hair in the latest style, and her white suit looked like it was made of silk. Something about her seemed familiar, but I couldn't place her. There seemed to be a lot of that this week.

"You should watch where you're walking," she said.

I didn't care for her tone of voice. "I was watching. Your driver needs to know that we don't drive like maniacs in this town and we obey traffic signs. He ran the stop sign."

She placed a cigarette into a holder and the driver immediately lit it with a Zippo. "I'm sure he just didn't see it. He's a safe driver. He came highly recommended. I wouldn't have it any other way."

"That's no excuse. And why doesn't he speak for himself?"

"I don't permit it."

"You don't permit it."

"That's what I said."

The driver opened the trunk and lifted a half dozen suitcases and placed them in front of the hotel door.

"Find a bellboy, Lonnie," she snapped. "He can carry those in."

He disappeared into the Excelsior.

"I hope they have bellboys here," she said. "This place looks like a dump."

"It's the nicest hotel around, unless you go into Pittsburgh." I wished she would. "You might consider that."

She laughed. "Trying to get rid of me already? It won't work. Besides, I just left Pittsburgh. It's a hell hole. I have a job to do here whether anyone likes it or not."

"What kind of job?" It sure wouldn't be working at Tabor Ironworks. Frankly, I couldn't imagine anyone hiring her for anything at all.

She stared at me. "You don't recognize me? You don't know who I am?"

"No, I don't." It gave me some satisfaction that she was surprised I didn't.

She stuck her nose high in the air. "I am Greta Gray."

Chapter Nine

Nazi Bombers Attack Norwich, England
The Progress Herald, June 28, 1942

"The Queen of Gossip?" It all made sense now. Rex had been right about Freddie's murder being national news. Greta Gray worked for one of the tabloids based in New York City, although she spent most of her time on the West Coast. I'd seen her in pictures with various celebrities—that's why she looked familiar. She was sometimes vicious in what she reported, not caring if it was true or not. If Freddie's affair with Belinda Fox hadn't been headlines before, it would be soon.

Greta Gray sucked on her cigarette holder and blew out smoke. "I don't appreciate that moniker. The queen part, yes. The gossip part, no. I report news, not gossip."

That was worse than Ava saying she didn't like rumors and never gossiped.

"And who might you be?" Greta asked.

"Irene Ingram. I'm the editor-in-chief of the *Progress Herald*."

She ignored my outstretched hand and laughed instead. "Oh, that's so quaint! I should have known a little girl would be running a newspaper here."

I mentally counted to ten. "I am a grown woman, not a little girl. The *Herald* is a well-respected newspaper. You might want to read it before making fun of it."

"Darling, I only read important newspapers. I don't need to know the price of feed for the pigs or whether Maybelle's rheumatism acts up when it rains."

The bellboy exited the hotel with a cart to retrieve her bags before I had time to respond with something I might regret later. I continued on my way, listening to her instructing the bellboy on how to place her bags on the cart. By the time I reached the police station, my blood pressure had almost returned to normal.

The chief hung up the telephone when I entered his office. "I was just going to call you. Doc finished the autopsy."

I took a seat and opened my notebook. "Was he able to narrow down the time of death?"

"No, only that it was late afternoon."

That still wouldn't let Angel off the hook. "What else?"

"Are you sure you want to hear this?" he asked.

"Dad, I'm a newspaperwoman, not some delicate flower that wilts at every little thing."

"Of course you're not. It's just that after last month . . ."

I knew what he was getting at. "Speaking of that . . ." I told him about the FBI arrests.

"Are you sure you're all right?" he asked.

"It was a shock, but I'm fine. Rex is going to write it up. I didn't think I could be impartial."

The chief nodded. "Anyway, Doc said that there was water in Harrison's lungs, but that he would have died anyway from the blow to his head."

"Does that mean whoever hit him had to be strong enough to cause that much damage?"

"Maybe. But I'm not ruling anything out yet. Why?"

"Have you talked to Ava or Angel today?"

He shook his head.

I relayed what Ava told me about Angel meeting Freddie.

"Hmm. I'm going to have to have another talk with both of them. Neither one mentioned that last evening."

"I'm not sure how much you'll get from Angel." I told him about the living room draped in black and how Angel seemed to be acting a part again.

He gave me a grim smile. "It's hard to believe she's Ava's sister and Ned's daughter."

I'd almost forgotten about Ned. Despite Angel's strangeness, it seemed to me Ned was a more likely suspect. He'd actually threatened Freddie. "Have you interviewed Ned?"

"I stopped by the diner early this morning, but it was too busy to say more than a few words over coffee. I'll go back later."

I was glad Ned hadn't permanently scared off his customers. "Do you know what the killer hit Freddie with?" I asked.

"Doc Atkins said he thought the wound looked like it was made by a crowbar. We haven't found anything yet."

I couldn't imagine Angel lifting a crowbar or even knowing what one was, and I didn't think she'd have her wits about her enough to carry it off the fairgrounds to dispose of it. If she had murdered Freddie in the heat of the moment, she'd have dropped the crowbar where she stood.

Dad's phone rang then, so I waved goodbye as he answered it. I started walking home, then changed my mind and turned around. The lunch rush at Dempsey's Diner should be over by now. Maybe I'd have better luck talking to Ned.

* * *

Instead of Ned, Lizzie was at the counter in the almost empty diner. "I'm surprised to see you here this early," I said. "Where's Ned?"

"He wasn't feeling well and went home to rest for a bit. He'll be back for the dinner rush."

I slid onto a stool. "Is he sick?"

"Just tired, I think. What can I get you?"

I hadn't eaten lunch and realized I was famished. "How about a cherry Coke and a ham sandwich?"

"Coming right up."

I watched as Lizzie expertly filled a glass at the soda fountain, added some cherry syrup, and gave it a stir. She placed it in front of me, then disappeared into the kitchen. I sipped my Coke and wondered about Ned. I couldn't remember him ever taking the afternoon off. Was it because he was getting old or because he'd murdered Freddie? I hated to think the killer could be someone I'd known all my life.

Lizzie returned with my sandwich, and I bit into it with relish. At this moment nothing was better than a chunk of ham on homemade bread slathered with mustard. When I'd demolished half the sandwich, I asked Lizzie if she'd heard about Freddie.

"It's all anyone talked about today," she said. "It's such a shame. He was too young to die."

"I guess Ned didn't think it was much of a shame."

"That's not true. He seemed sort of shook up about it." Lizzie picked up my empty plate and put it in a bin with other dirty dishes. "After what happened with the shotgun, I think he's afraid Chief Turner will think he did it."

I wanted to say, *well, did he?* I figured I'd better be more subtle than that. "That shouldn't be a problem. Ned was here late yesterday afternoon, wasn't he?"

"Is that when that man was killed?"

"Yes."

"Ned was here when I came in around six."

"What about before that?" I asked.

Lizzie shrugged. "I don't know, but I don't believe Ned would close the diner to go kill someone. He just wouldn't."

I hoped she was right, but I wasn't so sure. I thought about it more on the walk home. Angel had met with Freddie around four. She could have gone to the diner to tell her father the good news. Ned wanted Freddie to stay away from Angel. He might have been angry enough to close the diner for an hour, then confront Freddie at the dunk tank. Freddie refused to leave Angel alone, Ned picked up a crowbar lying there and whacked Freddie over the head. He then disposed of the crowbar outside the fairgrounds. But where? Until the police found the murder weapon it would be almost impossible to narrow down the suspects.

It was close to three by the time I got home. The house was empty. Mom and Lily were at the fair already—they'd gotten a ride from Cindy's parents. It was possible that's where Sylvia was too, since it was her day off. I washed my face and changed my clothes, and after running a brush through my hair, headed out myself.

* * *

Peggy and Ken were waiting by the entrance gate when I arrived. "Sorry I'm late," I said. "I got tied up with a few things."

"That's all right," Peggy said. "What have you found out?"

"How did you know I was investigating?" I asked.

She laughed. "Maybe because we've been friends our entire lives."

"She's been driving me crazy," Ken said. "She insists you've figured it all out by now."

"I wish I had," I said. "I'll tell you about it later."

We paid our admission fees and walked through the gate. The fair was in full swing. It didn't appear as if a murder on the premises had diminished attendance at all. If anything, it seemed like more people were here than normal. I hoped that boded well for bond sales. I knew most people in town were probably contributing already, but there was something about buying bonds after being asked to by a celebrity that made people open up their wallets even further.

The line for the Ferris wheel didn't seem overly long, so I suggested we ride that first. I liked the Ferris wheel, but I also wanted a bird's-eye view of the fairgrounds. Ken's arm around Peggy made me wish Bill was here. We'd always done things together as couples and I often felt like the third wheel now. They always insisted that wasn't true, but that's how I felt. They'd be together on the ride, and I'd be alone. I was sinking low into feeling sorry for myself when Kirk slipped into line beside me.

"Mind if I join you?" he asked. "I'd hate to have to ride by myself."

"I'd be happy if you joined us." It wasn't the same as having Bill ride with me, but at least I'd have company. It would also give me a chance to ask him about Freddie.

"Thanks."

"You look better than you did last night," Ken said.

Kirk smiled. "Sorry about that. I'm good as new now, thanks to some aspirin and a little hair of the dog."

"Glad to hear it," Ken said.

It was our turn to get on the Ferris wheel. We were soon seated and the ride operator closed the bar in front of us. We lifted into the air and stopped for Peggy and Ken to board the next car.

"I really am sorry about last night," Kirk said. "I don't usually drink that much."

"Why did you, then?"

The last car was filled and the ride began moving. "I guess I was celebrating my good fortune."

"Good fortune?"

"It was the first time I got to headline one of these things. Freddie was late for rehearsals before—usually showing up just in time to push me to the rear again. He always made sure to rub my nose in the fact that he was well known and I wasn't. Not yet, anyway. I was glad he didn't show up."

"He was dead."

"How was I supposed to know that?"

"I didn't say you were."

I took in the view as we went around. The fairgrounds covered several acres. In addition to the rides, there were booths featuring games of chance, various food stands including the cotton candy one where Lily was working. There was an area set up with picnic tables where families could bring baskets of food if they didn't want to buy from vendors. Wooden barricades had been placed around the dunk tank, and a few people were standing nearby and pointing to it. I wondered if it wouldn't have been better to remove it. The fair was only a week long and even if the chief let them open it, I couldn't imagine anyone volunteering to sit on that seat and get dropped into a tank. Even though there'd be fresh water in it, a man had died there. They should keep it closed. It wasn't much of a money maker anyway.

"Frankly, I'm glad he's dead," Kirk said. "I'm not going to deny it. Freddie Harrison made my life a living hell."

"I know he wasn't the nicest person, but living hell might be a stretch."

"You have no idea, Irene. Let's talk about something else. What's the war news today?"

I told him about the Nazis arrested today.

"That's really something," Kirk said. "It's so hard to believe. Out west, everyone worries about Japanese spies. No one thinks twice about Germans."

The ride was over and we disembarked. Within minutes, Peggy and Ken joined us. I attempted to push everything out of my mind other than having fun, with limited success. Every once in a while my thoughts went back to Freddie's murder. I didn't want to, but I added Kirk to my list of suspects. He certainly had a motive if Freddie had been making things difficult for him. Plus, he was now the main attraction for the bond drive. Kirk actually had a double motive. Neither Angel nor her father had alibis for the time Freddie was killed. Did Kirk? I'd have to find out.

"Hey, I'm hungry," Kirk said. "If I remember right from the old days, they have the best hot dogs here. How about we get some? My treat."

"I'll never turn down free food," Ken said. "I'll help you carry everything."

Peggy and I gave him our orders, then found an empty picnic table nearby.

"So what did you find out today?" Peggy asked.

I filled her in, including what Kirk had just told me, and I needed to find out if he had an alibi.

"My money's on Angel," Peggy said. "I like Ava and all, and I know she's her sister, but there's something not right with her. Normal people don't play a part all the time."

"I don't know. Would she have the strength to hit Freddie that hard?"

"Maybe she had help."

"What do you mean?" I asked.

"Her dad obviously hates Freddie. What if he went with her to meet him?"

"I don't know. Ava's the one who said Angel met with Freddie. She never mentioned Ned. Wouldn't Angel have told her that Ned went along?"

"Considering Angel seems to live in a fantasy world, maybe not."

I had a horrible thought. "I think we need to consider another suspect."

"One of the others on the tour?"

"They're certainly possibilities and I haven't ruled them out, but that's not what I was thinking."

"Who then?"

"Ava."

Chapter Ten

Actor Freddie Harrison Found Dead at County Fair

The Progress Herald, June 28, 1942

"You can't be serious," Peggy said.

"I don't like the idea any better than you, but it's possible. Ava is very protective of her sister. She goes out of her way to make sure Angel is taken care of. Look at the way she fussed over her in my office the other day."

"But murder?" Peggy said. "I don't think Ava has it in her to kill anyone."

"If she thought Freddie was going to hurt Angel again, she might." I spotted Kirk and Ken heading our way, loaded down with hot dogs and bottles of Coke. "We'll talk more later when Kirk isn't around."

"So what were you girls talking about while we were gone?" Ken asked. He set four bottles of Coke down on the table.

Peggy smiled. "Just about how handsome you two are."

Kirk gave Peggy and me each a hot dog and he and Ken had two apiece.

"Really, what were you talking about?" Kirk asked.

Now was my chance to see what Kirk had been doing yesterday afternoon. "We were talking about you."

"Me?" Kirk bit into his hot dog.

"Your rehearsal last night looked seamless, even with the change of plans."

Peggy jumped in. "It was impressive how you were able to take over like that."

"If it were me, I'd have been up on that stage all afternoon trying to get that speech straight," I said.

Kirk wiped mustard from the corner of his mouth. "Nah. The basic speeches don't change much. We just put our own touch on it."

"So you didn't have to practice all yesterday afternoon?" I said.

"Nope. I stayed in my room and took a nap. I only got here about fifteen minutes beforehand."

That wasn't much of an alibi unless someone at the Excelsior had seen him. Even then, he could have slipped out and killed Freddie. The more I thought about it, his motive was a little thin, unless there was more to it.

"I wish I could take an afternoon nap," Ken said. "My boss won't let me."

Kirk laughed. "But you get to work with these lovely ladies. That has to make up for it." He stood. "I'd better get changed and ready for the real thing. I'll see you all later."

When he was out of earshot, Peggy said, "He doesn't have much of an alibi, does he?"

"I knew you two were up to something," Ken said. "You really think Eugene—I mean Kirk—killed Harrison?"

"To use a baseball phrase, we're just covering all the bases," I said. "Peggy can fill you in. Frankly, I'm tired of talking about murder. Let's go and have some fun."

* * *

I had set aside two dollars to play games, which I spent in less than half an hour. Ken won Peggy two Kewpie dolls and a stuffed bear by knocking down milk bottles until someone squealed that he'd been a star player on the Progress High baseball team. Ken insisted he was rusty and hadn't thrown a ball since then, but the man running the game didn't buy it.

Peggy and Ken went to the parking lot to put her winnings in the car. I said I'd meet them by the stage before the speeches began. I spotted Sylvia and Betty sitting at one of the picnic tables, so I headed that way.

Betty held up a large teddy bear. "Isn't he just the cutest thing?"

"He is," I said. "I thought you had a date."

She giggled. "I do. He went to get some lemonade. I'm parched."

I asked Sylvia if she had gotten settled in all right.

"I did," she said. "Your mother's been great. I really appreciate all you've done for me."

"We're happy to help."

Betty jumped up and pointed behind me. "Here he comes now. I can't wait for you to meet him."

I turned around and got quite a surprise. "Donny?"

My cousin seemed as shocked as I was. "Irene?"

Sylvia said, "Do you two know each other?"

"Not only that, we're related," I said. "Donny is my cousin."

Betty clapped her hands together. "That's wonderful!"

92

Donny set Betty's lemonade down and took the seat beside her. "How do you all know each other?" he asked.

Betty began telling him. Sylvia broke in and finished after Betty got off track for the third time. While she talked, I watched Betty and Donny. They obviously adored each other. If I had known they'd be a perfect pair, I would have introduced them to each other weeks ago. It had never crossed my mind. I hadn't been able to see my cousin as anything but a thorn in my side.

"I knew you two worked at Tabor," Donny said, "but I didn't remember you were the ones Irene wrote that article about. Wasn't there another girl too?"

Sylvia and I exchanged glances.

"She doesn't work at Tabor anymore." I changed the subject. "How did you two meet?"

Betty laughed. "We literally ran into each other. I was going into Thrift Drug, and Donny was coming out. He almost knocked me over." She leaned her head on his shoulder. "He was so sweet about it and insisted on buying me a Coke over at Woolworth's."

"We've been seeing each other since," Donny said.

I noticed my future father-in-law walking past the food vendors. I excused myself and caught up to him near the funnel cake booth.

"Enjoying yourself?" Dad asked.

"I am. How about you?"

"More or less. I'm on duty, so I'm leaning toward less."

"You're always on duty, even when you're not."

"True," he said. "I guess I'll get a day off when I retire someday."

"I hope that's not for a long time." I couldn't imagine anyone else doing the job, except maybe Bill.

He smiled. "I'm not going anywhere. I wouldn't know what to do with myself."

"Good. Anything new with the investigation?"

"Speaking of always working . . ."

I shrugged. "Looks like we're in the same boat."

"Let's go over there." We walked to a grassy spot away from the activity. "There's really nothing new since earlier today," he said. "I haven't had a chance to talk to Ava or Angel. I'm going to try and corral them after the rally. Have you learned anything?"

"Not much. I stopped at Dempsey's Diner, but Ned wasn't there. Lizzie said he'd taken the afternoon off and gone home to rest."

"That's not like Ned," Dad said.

"I know. Lizzie said he's worried you'll think he killed Freddie because of how he threatened him with the shotgun."

"He's certainly high on the list, but if he didn't kill Harrison, he has nothing to worry about. Anything else?"

I told him about Kirk.

Dad nodded. "I've asked everyone who knew Harrison to stop at the station tomorrow, so I'll talk to him then."

He continued on patrol, and I went to find my staff before the rally began. It was almost showtime.

*　*　*

More than thirty minutes had passed by the time Mayor Young gave his usual long-winded speech welcoming everyone to the fair, and Evelyn Quinn shattered eardrums with her version of "The Star-Spangled Banner." I was standing near the front with Peggy, Ken, and Matt. Rex and Frank were milling through the crowd. Evelyn was about to launch into another song. I nudged Matt. "Want to go backstage with me and snap some behind-the-scenes photos?"

"Please," he said. "I'm bored to tears. I've heard the same speech from the mayor at least a dozen times. I'm sure by now everyone in the tri-state area knows old Ralph rode with Teddy Roosevelt and the Rough Riders."

I laughed. "At least the Hollywood folks haven't heard it before."

"If they're even listening," Matt said.

We rounded the edge of the wooden stage. There was a trailer parked behind the stage that hadn't been there yesterday. A long table was set up in front of the trailer decorated with red, white, and blue bunting. This was where bonds and stamps for stamp books that could be converted to bonds would be sold. Mom would be helping Martha and Sarah Markowicz here after the rally. There were two boxes on the table as well as a large ledger type book. A beefy security guard stood next to the boxes. I asked Matt to get a couple of shots of the setup while I talked to Mr. Security.

I introduced myself. "Do you mind if my photographer takes a few pictures?"

He nodded.

I wasn't sure if that meant Matt could or not, but he didn't budge when Matt started snapping away. I asked the guard a few questions, but gave up when I couldn't even get him to tell me his name. He wasn't exactly the friendly sort.

There was a second trailer on the other side of the stage, so Matt and I headed that way. Belinda Fox exited just as we reached it. "Miss Fox," I said. "Do you have a moment?"

She seemed about to say no until she saw the camera. "Of course I do." She tugged at the bottom of the jacket to her scarlet suit, then reached up and smoothed her perfectly styled hair.

Matt raised his camera. "Keep your hand right there on that gorgeous mane," he said.

Belinda beamed at him. "Anything for the press," she purred.

Anything for publicity was more like it. "How are you holding up?" I asked.

She changed her pose. "Holding up?"

"Freddie's death must be stressful," I said. "Many people are surprised the rally wasn't canceled."

Her expression changed to one of sadness. It looked well practiced to me.

"It's tragic, of course, but the show must go on," she said. "We owe it to Freddie, and to our fighting men. No sacrifice is too big." She tilted her head back and gazed into the camera. "Freddie and I were going to be married, you know."

That was news to me. "I was under the impression he was going back to his wife."

Belinda stopped posing. "Is that what that shrew told you?"

"Yes."

"She's delusional," Belinda said. "Freddie loved me."

If that were the case, Freddie wouldn't have been searching all over town for Angel when he first arrived. Freddie wanted both of them. That could have been what had gotten him killed. Before I could ask anything else, Paul Davis rounded the corner.

He took a drag on his cigarette, then tossed the butt on the ground. "Let me guess. You're talking about Harrison."

"You guessed right," I said. "Want to give me a statement for the paper?"

"Sure. Freddie Harrison will be missed by many."

"I get the feeling you won't be one of them," I said.

"You got that right. I'm glad I don't have to deal with him anymore. Harrison was a worm."

"He was not," Belinda said. "You didn't know the real Freddie."

That sounded a lot like how Angel described him.

"Actually, he was lower than a worm, if that's possible," Davis said.

"Why do you think that?" I asked.

Davis shrugged. "It's not important now." He turned to Belinda. "It's almost showtime, Toots. I suggest you join the others."

"And I suggest you stop talking about Freddie that way. Besides, I know when I have to be on," she said. "Stop nagging me."

"Suit yourself," he said. "But don't be late." Davis went back the way he came.

"He shouldn't talk that way about Freddie," Belinda said. She glared at me. "I'd better not see any of that in your paper. I don't want his name dragged through the mud."

"I never sling mud," I said. "I write the facts."

Belinda suddenly turned to Matt and touched his arm. "You'll be sure to get me copies of those pictures, won't you?" Her tone would turn most men to mush.

It sure worked on Matt. He stared as she walked away swinging her hips.

I elbowed him twice before he even noticed. "How about putting your eyeballs back in your head. We have work to do."

* * *

After the Progress High School band played a marching tune that sounded vaguely familiar, Martha Feeney strode to the podium. "Thank you all for coming and taking time away from the rides and games to participate in this most important event. I especially want to thank the Hollywood Victory Committee for sending these wonderful performers to us."

From where I stood with Peggy and Ken at the far right of the stage, I could see Belinda and Paul Davis standing side by side. It surprised me, considering their recent exchange. Kirk stood away from them. Angel, accompanied by her sister, was only now climbing the steps behind the stage. Angel had traded the black garb from earlier for a black suit with a matching hat. It was quite a contrast to Belinda's red one.

"Before we go on to our featured guests," Martha continued, "I want to mention one reason why buying these bonds to support our men in uniform and supply what they need to fight our enemies is so important. Just this week we lost one of our own Progress boys. I'm sure most of you know by now that Richie Finnerty was killed when he was shot down by the Japanese during the Midway battle. Buy a bond, or if you can't afford it right now, purchase some stamps. Every dime helps. Do it for our boys, but especially do it for the Finnerty family. And now I'd like to ask for a moment of silence in memory of Richie."

I looked around as the crowd quieted. Jimmy Feeney stood beside the chief and Rally in front of the stage at the opposite end from where I was. Jimmy was beaming. He was so proud of his wife. Backstage, I noticed Davis and Belinda were quietly arguing about something. Probably continuing their disagreement over Freddie's character. Davis grabbed her arm, and Belinda tore it away. Angel and Ava stood beside Kirk doing their best to ignore Belinda. I expected Kirk to intervene, but he stayed put, just shaking his head. It seemed like arguing was a common occurrence between Davis and Belinda. It was obvious they didn't like each other.

Martha finished and turned the stage over to Paul Davis. He bounded to the podium. "Hello, hello, hello, Progress!" He went into his spiel, which included some jokes, earning him a few chuckles from the audience. A few groans as well. They weren't any funnier than when I'd heard them the day before. Davis then introduced Kirk the same way he had in rehearsal. "Ladies and gentlemen, I'd like to introduce up and coming matinee idol Kirk Allen. He'll be starring in a new Warner Brothers picture and has been called the next Cary Grant. Let's give a nice round of applause for Kirk Allen!"

Kirk strolled to the microphone like it was a Sunday walk in the park. His hands were tucked into his trouser pockets. His suit jacket was unbuttoned, and he'd loosened his tie just enough to look casual. His smile as he reached the podium would have the women in the audience swooning. Davis calling him the next Cary Grant wasn't entirely accurate. Kirk was Cary Grant, Jimmy Stewart, and Tyrone Power all rolled into one. It was hard to believe he was really Eugene Allen from Progress, Pennsylvania.

"Wow," Peggy said. "How does he do that?"

"Do what?" Ken asked.

Peggy and I laughed. "You wouldn't understand," she said.

Ken shook his head. "I'll take your word for it."

I watched the audience as Kirk spoke. I knew it was a rehearsed speech because I'd heard it already, but the way he delivered it made it seem like he was talking to his friends. Men and women alike were captivated. There was thunderous applause when he finished.

Backstage, Angel hugged him and Ava shook his hand. As Davis returned to the podium to introduce Angel, I caught a glimpse of Belinda. The look on her face was hard to gauge— a cross between jealousy and something else. I just didn't know quite what.

Chapter Eleven

FBI Arrests 8 in Nazi Sabotage Plot
The Progress Herald, June 28, 1942

At Mass on Sunday morning, Father O'Connor announced that the memorial service for Richie Finnerty would be Tuesday morning at ten o'clock, with a brunch in the church basement following the service. After Mass, Mom gathered with the other women to plan the menu and who would bring what. While Lily and I waited for her, we chatted with others. All anyone could talk about was the rally the night before. For a small town, a record number of bonds had been sold.

On the walk home from St. Michael's, all Lily could talk about was Kirk. "He's so handsome," she said at least a dozen times.

"What about Sinatra?" I said. "I thought he was your true love."

"Oh, I still like him and his music, but Kirk is a dreamboat."

I couldn't disagree, although I remembered him as Eugene. I couldn't quite erase that picture from my mind. I had a sudden thought. "Maybe Kirk would want to come for dinner tonight before he has to be at the fair."

Lily practically jumped up and down. "Oh, I would just faint! Please, Mom, can he come for dinner? Please?"

Mom smiled at her indulgently. "Only if you promise not to faint." She looked at me. "Can you arrange it? It's very short notice. What about his folks?"

"His parents don't live in the area anymore," I said. "I'll stop by the Excelsior before I go into the *Herald* and ask him."

With that settled, Lily walked on clouds the rest of the way home.

*   *   *

The Excelsior wasn't as grand as the William Penn Hotel in Pittsburgh, but it was certainly grand for Progress. It was conveniently located next to the train station, so travelers didn't have far to go, unless they wanted to, of course. The doorman held the heavy brass and glass door open, and I entered the lobby. The marble floor was polished to a shine. The marble continued up the wall as wainscoting, and the walls above were creamy white and gold. Crystal chandeliers hung from the coffered ceiling. There were chairs and sofas upholstered in a plush red fabric. A grand piano sat in the middle of the room.

As I headed for the front desk, I spotted Greta Gray seated in one of the chairs. She had a tablet on her lap and a cocktail on the table beside her. I walked past her, then changed my mind and turned around. I hadn't thought about it until now, but I realized she hadn't been at the rally last night. "Good afternoon, Miss Gray," I said.

She looked up. "If it isn't the little paper girl. What brings you to this dump? Not that I really want to know."

I refused to let her get under my skin. I sat in the chair beside her. "I missed seeing you at the bond rally yesterday. I thought you'd be there."

Greta laughed. "Oh, darling. How quaint. I don't go anywhere there are masses of people trying to catch a glimpse of second-rate actors—third-rate in some cases."

"Isn't that your job? How can you write about it then?"

"I get impressions," she said. "I don't need to be there."

"What do you mean by impressions?"

Greta put a cigarette in her holder and a bellboy immediately appeared at her side to light it. She put a dollar in his hand. No wonder he'd been so quick. "Tell me if I'm correct. Since Freddie Harrison is dead, Kirk Allen took his place and did a splendid job. Angel Harrison played the grieving widow, and Belinda Fox was, well, Belinda Fox."

"Someone must have told you all that."

"Anyone could figure out that Allen would do a better job than Harrison. He's a better actor. Angel always plays what suits the moment best, and Belinda never changes. She's too full of herself." She took a sip of her cocktail. "So you see, I know everything that you know without wasting my time traipsing through the dirt, mingling with nobodies, and being bored to tears."

How dare she call us nobodies. "Not everything," I said. "You don't know that the crowd was enthralled by Kirk and Angel. You don't know that for a town this size, a record number of bonds and stamps were sold." The more I spoke the angrier I became. "And you sure as heck don't know anything about Richie Finnerty."

Greta's surprise only showed on her face for a split second. I didn't think too many people dared speak against her. They were probably afraid she'd write something nasty about them. I was small potatoes, so I didn't care. I probably wasn't worth of one of her gossip pieces.

"Who in the world is Richie Finnerty?" she asked. "I've never heard of him."

I got up. "Ask at the front desk for copies of the *Herald* from last week. Richie was front page news." I walked away before she could tell me that reading my newspaper was beneath her. It took everything in me to not snap her cigarette holder in two. I'd wanted to ask her if she'd uncovered anything about Freddie's death, but was glad I hadn't had the chance. It would have been one of her *impressions* and would have had nothing to do with facts.

The clerk at the front desk didn't want to give me Kirk's room number until I explained I was the editor of the *Herald*. I'd even had to show identification. Apparently, girls had been trying to visit him all morning. The clerk had to have a bellboy physically remove two of them.

"I don't understand kids these days," he said. "Before that other fellow died, we had the same trouble with him."

"Girls were trying to get into Freddie Harrison's room too?"

The clerk nodded. "One even made it past us. Miss Fox was in the hallway and complained when the girl pounded on Mr. Harrison's door. Miss Fox was mad as a hornet."

"I'm sure."

"After that, the boss insisted we keep a better eye out. That's why I needed to see ID. You're awfully young to be the editor of the paper."

I smiled. "I hear that a lot." I had an idea. I asked if Freddie's room was near Kirk's and if I could take a look around.

"Why would you want to do that?" he asked.

"Freddie's wife, Angel, is a friend of mine. She has to remove his belongings, so I thought I'd see what she needs to do so the hotel can use the room again."

My explanation seemed to work. I would let Angel know, although that wasn't the reason I wanted to see his room. Freddie hadn't been killed there, but maybe there was some clue as to who had had it in for him. I knew Dad had been there already, but maybe he'd missed something. It wouldn't hurt to check. The clerk gave me Freddie's key and Kirk's room number. They were both on the fourth floor at opposite ends of the hallway. I decided to check Freddie's room first, only because it was closer to the elevator.

The room had a Do Not Disturb sign hanging from the doorknob. Not that it mattered. There was no one there to disturb. Once inside, I locked the door behind me and surveyed the room. It was a mess. Either Freddie had been a horrible slob or someone had tossed the place. My guess was the latter. The bed covers were on the floor. Dresser drawers had been opened, and Freddie's suitcases had been emptied onto the floor. I made my way to the bathroom. His shaving kit was in the sink, but nothing else was out of place.

What had someone been searching for? Money? Valuables? Freddie hadn't worn any jewelry—not even a wedding ring—and he would have had his wallet with him. The bigger question might be *who* had been searching? Maybe it hadn't even been a search. Angel, or even Belinda, could have been angry enough to come in here and tear everything apart. I wondered where Belinda's room was. There were two doors on the other side of the room. I assumed one was a closet. It was possible the other led to an adjoining room.

I crossed the room and opened one of the doors. It was a closet, as I suspected. Two suits hung from the bar, as well as a bathrobe. I closed the closet, then tried the other door. It was locked. I took the room key from my pocket, inserted it into the lock and turned it. I heard a click as it unlocked. I slowly opened the door a crack, hoping I didn't run into anyone on the other side. The room was empty and neatly made up. I was just about to go in when I heard a key in the lock. I backed up and pulled the door almost closed. I wasn't surprised to see Belinda enter the room. So she and Freddie did have adjoining rooms—awkward if he'd managed to get Angel to come back to him. If Angel had found out Belinda was on the other side of the door, that would certainly have made her angry enough to destroy the room. And maybe angry enough to kill Freddie.

I locked the door to the adjoining room, took one last look around, then went down the hall to Kirk's room. I knocked on the door.

"Did you forget some—" Kirk stopped mid-sentence as he swung the door open. "Oh. Irene. I thought . . . never mind." He stepped back. "Come on in."

He'd thought someone else had been at the door. I wondered who. "I hope I'm not intruding," I said.

"No, not at all."

"It sounded like you were expecting someone."

"Not really. The maid was just here, and I thought she forgot something."

From the looks of the room, the maid hadn't been anywhere near it. The bed was unmade and there were two wineglasses and plates on a small table. Someone had been here, but it sure wasn't housekeeping. I was curious, but it was really none of my business if he'd had company.

He pulled his robe tighter around him. "Sorry I'm not dressed. I had a late night."

"That's all right. I just stopped to see if you wanted to come over to our house tonight for dinner. Mom's making a roast."

"It's nice of you to ask." He smiled. "I haven't had a home-cooked roast for years."

"So that's a yes?"

"Sure. Why not?" He looked at his watch. "I have an appointment in an hour. I'm not sure how long it will take."

"With Chief Turner?"

"How did you know about that?"

"He's talking to all of you. It's part of the investigation."

"He's Bill Turner's dad, right?"

I nodded. "And my future father-in-law."

Kirk nodded and changed the subject. "I wasn't sure about coming back to Progress, but I'm glad I did. It's nice to be with old friends again. I really appreciate your hospitality. Thank your mother for me."

"You can thank her yourself when you come over. I do have to warn you about something, though."

Alarm showed on his face. "Warn me? About what?"

I grinned. "My little sister, Lily."

"I remember her. How old is she now? About eleven or twelve?"

"She's fourteen, and as of last night, she's madly in love with you."

Kirk laughed.

"I'm serious." I told him she'd thrown over Frank Sinatra for him.

"Well, that's a first. Someone dumping Sinatra for me. I'm honored. I'll try not to break her heart."

I considered telling him about Freddie's room being tossed, but decided not to. Whether I liked it or not, Kirk was a suspect. Instead, I mentioned I had run into Greta Gray in the lobby.

He made a face. "I managed to avoid her when I came in last night. Remember Mike Weaver?"

"Maybe. I think he was in one of my science classes."

"He's the clerk at the night desk. He showed me how to slip in the back. Greta's been asking around about Freddie. I'm not sure why. All of Hollywood already knows he slept around. Angel is probably the only one in the dark. At least until recently."

"Maybe she's trying to get the scoop on who killed him."

Kirk shook his head. "That's not her usual style. She doesn't care who killed him, or for that matter even that he's dead. She's looking for dirt. That's what she's best at."

I had a lot on my mind as I walked to the *Herald*. Why would someone toss a dead man's room unless they were looking for something? But what? Had Freddie been hiding something? If Greta Gray was looking for dirt on Freddie, she might have been the one who tossed his room, or sent her chauffeur to do it. If she already knew about Freddie and Belinda, what else was she looking for? If there was more, that opened up at least another motive for his murder. I had been thinking it was a crime of passion, but it was possible it was more than that.

And what about Kirk lying about who had been in his room? I didn't know what to make of that. What did it matter who his visitor was? Unless . . . Belinda entered her room just before I went to see Kirk. If Belinda had been with Kirk, I understood why he wouldn't tell me that. Belinda and Freddie were supposed to be an item. I doubt that Freddie would have tolerated Belinda seeing someone else, even though he was doing the same thing. Maybe he had confronted Belinda about it, they fought, and she killed him. The same scenario could have happened if he'd fought with Kirk about it.

My head was spinning by the time I settled at my desk. I pushed it all out of my mind for the moment and concentrated on getting articles written and ready for tomorrow's newspaper. After all, there was still a war going on.

Chapter Twelve

Fighting Resumes on North African Front
The Progress Herald, June 28, 1942

"Lily Marie, stop daydreaming and get the table set," Mom said. "Our guest will be here any minute."

Lily spun around and put a plate on the table. "I can't believe an honest to goodness movie star is eating dinner with us." She spun and placed another plate.

"At the rate you're going, you won't have the table set by tomorrow morning," I said. "Kirk does have to go back to the fairgrounds after dinner."

"So do I." Lily set the last two plates.

I handed her the napkins I'd just folded. "How's the cotton candy business?"

Lily made a face. "I used to like eating it, but not anymore. I think Cindy and I ate a little too much of it yesterday."

Mom and I both laughed just as the doorbell rang. I went to answer it.

Kirk held a large bouquet of flowers. "I brought these for your mother."

"That's nice of you," I said. Kirk followed me to the kitchen, and I introduced him to Mom and Lily.

"I remember you from the high school plays, although you certainly look different now," Mom said. "Even back then you were very talented."

"Thanks." He turned to my sister. "It's nice to meet you, Lily."

"It's nice to meet you, too," Lily said. "I've never met a movie star before. The closest I came to that was Katherine. She's friends with Frank Sinatra and she sings with him too. I still like Frank's music—"

"Lily, you're rambling," Mom said.

Kirk smiled. "That's all right, Mrs. Ingram. I don't mind a bit."

Halfway through dinner, Lily must have realized Kirk was a normal human being like everyone else, especially when they began discussing movie artwork. By the end of dinner, Lily had decided she would move to California after high school and be an artist for one of the movie studios.

Kirk and I sat on the front porch while Mom and Lily cleaned up. "Your sister is charming," he said. "Your mother, too."

"I'm glad you think so. Lily is very enthusiastic when she gets talking about art and drawing."

"That's how I was with acting," Kirk said. "I wasn't just Eugene Allen. I could be anyone I wanted to be. I always preferred being on stage to just about anything else. Still do."

"It shows. I can tell you do it because you love it and not because you need the adulation. That's why you'll be successful."

"I hope I will be. The last few months have been a challenge."

"Because of the bond rallies?"

"Among other things. Where is Bill stationed? Will he be going overseas?"

Kirk was really good at changing the subject. Whatever the other things were, he didn't want to talk about them. "Bill's in Louisiana with the Third Armored. He heard they're being transferred to another camp soon, but that's all he knew. He'll be going overseas eventually, but he doesn't know whether it will be Europe or Africa."

"I've been thinking of enlisting," Kirk said. "I'm under contract for that movie with Warner, but maybe after that wraps up. Jimmy Stewart's in the Air Corps, and even Gable is thinking about it."

"You're already doing your part with these rallies and keeping people entertained."

"That's what I've been told," he said. "It doesn't always feel like enough. Look at what happened to Richie Finnerty."

"You heard about that?"

Kirk nodded. "We were good friends. I always knew he'd be a pilot. In fact, I encouraged him. I wish I hadn't now."

"You can't look back," I said. "You both did what you were meant to do."

We were quiet for a minute, then I asked him about his appointment with the chief.

He shrugged. "He asked a lot of questions and fingerprinted me. I assume he's doing that with everyone who knew that son of a bitch. Excuse my language, but I hated Freddie Harrison and I'm not sorry he's dead."

"I hope you didn't express that to the chief."

"Not in those words, but he knows we weren't on the best of terms. Frankly, no one liked Harrison, except maybe Angel."

"What about Belinda?"

"Not even her. She saw him as a stepping-stone to better her career."

And maybe now she was using Kirk to do the same. I kept that to myself. If Kirk had wanted me to know who he'd been with, he would have told me.

Kirk smiled suddenly.

"What?" I said.

"Belinda went in to see Chief Turner as I was leaving. I should have stuck around to see her reaction when he said he wanted to fingerprint her."

That would have been something to witness. Mom and Lily came out to the porch and we chatted for ten minutes until Kirk had to leave. Mom drove Lily to the fairgrounds right after that. I considered going along but decided to stay home. The events at the fair would be the same as last night and I doubted I'd miss anything. I settled into the living room and turned on the radio.

It was quiet and peaceful in the house, even with the radio on. It was a perfect time to write to Bill. I filled him in on the fair and the bond rally without mentioning anything about the murder. I told him about Eugene Allen's transformation into Kirk Allen and meeting Greta Gray. Most importantly, I told him how much I missed him and how I couldn't wait to see him again. I addressed the envelope, added a stamp, and placed it on the telephone table by the front door to mail tomorrow. I went to bed early and slept soundly, only waking once when Lily came in and got ready for bed. It was a nice change.

* * *

Mondays were always busy at the *Herald*, and today was no exception. I'd already written my weekly home and fashion columns for the Wednesdays in June. There were five Wednesdays in July, and I could have written an extra one for this week but decided to skip it. It was hard enough coming up with ideas for the four columns, let alone a fifth. Instead, I focused on writing more about the fair and the bond drive. In war news, the Germans had begun a new offensive on the eastern front. I assigned Frank to cover it. Peggy was busier than ever with advertisements. It was definitely a good thing, because most of our revenue came from the ads. Peggy had managed to keep up so far, but it looked more and more like I'd need to hire another person to assist her. If we continued to grow, we might even need an advertising department like the larger newspapers had. I'd also been planning to hire another reporter. I had thought we could get by without replacing the one who was killed, but it was becoming too much of a strain. It would be a nice surprise for Pop to come home to a few new employees.

By ten o'clock I was ready for a break, so I thought I'd stretch my legs and walk over to the police department. I needed to pick up the weekly blotter, and I could check on Dad's investigation of Freddie's murder while I was there.

Jimmy was at the front desk as usual when I arrived at the police station. "Good morning, Irene." He yawned.

"Morning," I said. "Late night?"

"I'll be glad when the bond drive is over. Martha and I didn't get home until midnight. We're too old for this."

I smiled. "You? Old? I'll never believe that."

"You're too kind," he said. "I have a copy of the blotter for you." He passed a sheet of paper across the desk.

"Thanks. Is the chief busy?"

"Always, but go ahead in anyway."

I walked around the desk, knocked on the closed door, and went into Dad's office. He put aside the report he was reading.

"I was wondering if you were going to stop in today," he said.

"I thought I'd see if there was anything new."

"Nothing much," he said. "I interviewed Eugene Allen—"

"You mean Kirk Allen."

"Eugene Allen is still his legal name until the courts say otherwise."

I hadn't thought of that.

The chief continued. "I also talked to Belinda Fox—believe it or not, that's her real name. And I fingerprinted both of them. Miss Fox was not pleased about either the interview or the fingerprinting."

"Speaking of fingerprints, were there any on the dunk tank? Wouldn't the killer have had to touch something there?"

"The problem is there were too many, and some had probably been there for years. We'd have to fingerprint everyone ever associated with the fair, plus everyone who'd even visited the fair. Even if we could locate them all, it would be an impossible task."

"Have you talked to Angel again?"

"Briefly. It was hard to get any kind of an answer with Ava hovering over her. I hate to say it, but I'm not counting Ava out either. She's very protective of her sister. And she has a temper. If she thought Harrison was going to hurt Angel, she could have hit him in the heat of the moment, then covered it up."

"I guess," I said. "Or since Angel met with Freddie that afternoon, Ava might think her sister killed Freddie and is trying to protect her."

Dad leaned back in his chair. "I haven't been able to establish alibis for any of the others. Angel is the only one who can actually state what she was doing that afternoon, and that doesn't bode well for her. Eugene says he was napping. Miss Fox says she was in her room on a telephone call, which I haven't been able to verify.

Mr. Davis says he took a walk and stopped for a drink but doesn't remember where. And Ned Dempsey was home alone."

"What will happen if you don't know the killer by the end of the week?"

"Then it gets messy," he said. "I can't very well demand that they all stay in town. I'll still be able to make an arrest, but it'll be more complicated."

I held back telling him about the condition I'd found Freddie's room in. He wouldn't like that I'd finagled the key out of the desk clerk. Heck, he wouldn't like that I'd gone there at all. Instead, I asked if he'd found anything in Freddie's room.

Dad shook his head. "Nothing at all. I told the hotel this morning they can let Angel know she can pick up her husband's belongings so they can use the room again."

I couldn't very well ask if it had been torn apart when he checked it without giving myself away, so I let it go. Maybe I'd volunteer to help Angel clear it out so I could take another look. I said goodbye and headed back to the paper. It was disappointing that he wasn't any closer to finding the killer. I wondered if he ever would.

* * *

Peggy and I bought sandwiches and bottles of Coke at Woolworth's for lunch and took them to the park. We headed for the bench in the shade of a large oak tree near the town's Victory Garden. Dan Petrie was rolling up the hose attached to the water spigot near the fountain.

"The garden looks like it's doing well," I said.

"It is," he said. "I thought I'd give it a little extra water since it's going to be hot for a couple of days."

"I hadn't thought of that," Peggy said. "Anything we can do to help?"

Dan shook his head. "I don't think so."

I asked if he'd been to the fair yet.

"Ellen and I went on Saturday." He smiled. "We saw you hobnobbing with those Hollywood folks."

Peggy and I laughed.

"We bought a bond and a stamp book to save up to buy another one."

"They sold a lot," I said.

"So I heard. We're helping with the sales tonight. I don't expect it to be as busy as it was over the weekend. It's a shame about Ava's brother-in-law—the actor who was killed. Does the chief know who did it yet?"

"Not yet."

"It's funny," Dan said. "I delivered the flowers for the stage that afternoon, and I saw him talking to Angel near the Tilt-A-Whirl."

Chapter Thirteen

USS Nautilus Sinks Jap Minesweeper South of Tokyo Bay
The Progress Herald, June 29, 1942

D an saw Angel and Freddie together? The dunk tank was right behind the Tilt-A-Whirl. I nudged Peggy to keep her from asking a question and waited for him to continue—a trick Pop taught me. It kept people talking because they felt they needed to fill the silence.

Except Dan didn't fill it. So much for that trick. "Were they arguing?" I asked.

"I don't know. I figured it was none of my business so I left."

"Did you run into anyone else while you were there?"

"No one in particular. Some of the workmen were still setting things up. Harold and Ophelia were there, Martha, that announcer, and a couple of others." Dan finished rolling up the hose and wiped his hands on the front of his trousers. "I'd better get back."

Peggy and I said so long and sat down to eat our lunch. "What do you think of all that?" Peggy asked.

"I don't think it's good news for Angel." I bit into my egg salad sandwich.

"I was afraid of that," Peggy said. "It's going to be hard on Ava if Angel gets arrested."

I swallowed and took a swig of my Coke. "Angel has already said she met with Freddie, but she didn't seem aware that her admission was important. I don't know if she's really innocent and that naïve, or if it's all an act." I told Peggy about running into Greta Gray in the lobby of the Excelsior, then getting the key at the front desk to check out Freddie's room yesterday and how Kirk thought I was someone else when he'd opened the door.

"Who do you think he's fooling around with?" Peggy said.

"What makes you think that? It could be perfectly innocent."

Peggy rolled her eyes. "Come on now. He's wearing a robe, there are dishes and wineglasses on the table from the night before, and he asks if whoever it was forgot something."

I grinned. "I'll make a detective out of you yet. I think it might be Belinda." I filled her in.

"I don't know," Peggy said. "Kirk is too smart and too nice to fall for her."

I crumpled up the paper my sandwich had been wrapped in. "I hope you're right. I don't like her much."

On the way back to the *Herald*, I told her that I planned to call Angel to see if she wanted company to retrieve Freddie's belongings from the hotel. Even though I'd been there already, Angel might know if something of his was missing.

"Let me know and I'll go with you," Peggy said.

As soon as I was back at my desk, I dialed Ava's beauty shop. I half expected Angel to answer as one of her characters, but Ava picked up the receiver instead.

"Oh, Irene," Ava said. "I'm so glad it's you." She didn't sound like her usual self.

"Is something wrong?"

"I tried to talk her out of it."

I didn't like the sound of that. "Out of what?"

"That awful Greta Gray telephoned an hour ago. She wanted to talk to Angel about Freddie. I warned Angel not to go, but she went anyway. I just know that horrible woman is going to twist everything around and make it seem like my sister killed her husband."

I didn't think she'd have to twist much, but if Angel was innocent it would be the end of her career.

"I was just going to call you," Ava said. "You're the only person I know that can put a stop to that woman."

"Me? Why do you think I can stop it?"

"Because you and that woman are in the same profession." Ava made it sound like I was stupid for even asking the question.

"We are not in the same profession. I'm a reporter, she's a gossip columnist. They're not even similar."

"Regardless, there's no one else to ask. Chief Turner will tell me it's not his business . . . I don't know what else to do."

Ava sounded so frantic, I relented.

"Thank you, Irene," she said. "I'll never be able to repay you."

That was an understatement if I ever heard one.

*   *   *

The desk clerk at the Excelsior pointed me to Morrison's, the restaurant next to the train station. Morrison's was the town's fancy restaurant where everyone went for special occasions or if they had a little extra moolah to spare. I was positive it wasn't up to Greta Gray's standards. She'd call it a dump. The last time I'd been there was over a month ago, and it hadn't been a pleasant experience, but not because of the food. I pushed that thought out of my mind.

"Party of one?" the hostess asked.

I shook my head. "I'm meeting Miss Gray and Mrs. Harrison. Have they arrived yet?" I suddenly became more important.

The hostess smiled. "Right this way, Miss . . ."

"Ingram. Irene Ingram." I said it in the most hoity-toity tone I could muster. Fortunately, she hadn't noticed I was wearing a cotton dress and sandals. I shouldn't have worried. Angel was dressed much the same way, except my dress was a nice floral and hers was a drab charcoal. It looked like a matron's dress from a prison movie. I wondered briefly where she was getting all these clothes. They certainly hadn't all fit in a few suitcases. She must have planned to stay for longer than a week and had trunks shipped to Ava's.

"Good afternoon, ladies." I sat on the edge of the booth and nudged Angel over with my hip.

"Oh, hi, Irene," Angel said. "I didn't know you would be here."

Greta stared at me as if she'd like to burn a hole through my head. "You were not invited. This is a private conversation."

"Private until you twist everything Angel says out of proportion and smear her good name."

Greta laughed. It sounded like broken glass. "What good name? Who needs one? I'll make her famous."

"Infamous is more like it," I said.

"There's no difference in my book." Greta sucked on her cigarette holder and blew smoke out through her nose. "I only want to hear this poor child's story."

"And I have swampland I'd like to sell you." I turned to Angel. "What have you told her?"

Angel didn't answer my question. "What do you mean by infamous?"

"Miss Gray can explain it better than I, but I'd bet she plans on publishing all the sordid details of your relationship with Freddie, his affairs, and end up making her readers believe that you killed him."

Angel's eyes opened wide. "Is this true?" she asked Greta.

"Darling, I only want my readers to know the truth—what a cad Freddie Harrison was. You had every reason to kill him."

"But . . . but . . . I didn't kill him. I loved Freddie with my whole heart and soul."

"You ran out on him because you finally found out he was sleeping with Belinda—although I can't fathom how you didn't know before now. It's been going on for a year. He refused to part ways with her. You argued and pushed him into that thing with water, knowing he couldn't swim."

I was gratified Greta didn't have all the details. I was not about to correct her.

"That's a terrible thing to say." Angel began crying. "I loved Freddie. He was coming back to me. He promised. He was going to break it off with Belinda that very day."

"Darling, he was never going to do that and you know it," Greta said.

"I think that's enough." I took Angel by the arm and helped her stand. I walked her to the foyer of the restaurant and sat her down in a plush upholstered chair. I told her I'd be right back and returned to Greta's table.

"You again," she said. "What do you want now?"

"I want to give you a warning."

She laughed that broken glass laugh again. "You can't be serious."

I clenched my fists at my sides so I wouldn't pummel her. "If you so much as print one word of whatever Angel told you, or any insinuation that she killed Freddie, you'll regret it."

"Little girl, I will print whatever I like, and you can't stop me. I don't know why you even care. It has nothing to do with you. Besides, she's guilty as sin."

"Even if she is, that's for the police and a court of law to decide, not you. And if you try to talk to her again, I'll have her file a complaint for harassment." I didn't like to use my relationship with the chief, but I did it this time. "My fiancé's father is the chief of police, and he won't take kindly to your tactics." I spun around and marched to the door before she said anything else.

I walked Angel back to Ava's shop and left her in good hands. Ava said she'd relay the message about clearing out Freddie's room and let me know when Angel decided to tackle the job. I went back to the *Herald* still steaming about Greta Gray.

* * *

The war news that afternoon was mixed. Six more U.S. ships had been sunk by U-boats off the coasts of North Carolina, Florida, and near the Virgin Islands the day before. It was becoming an almost daily occurrence. In more encouraging news, the USS *Stingray* attacked a Japanese convoy in the Philippine Sea, and a navy squadron had attacked Tulagi in the Solomon Islands. I had Rex write something about this and asked him to include maps so readers would know where the Solomon Islands and the Philippine Sea were. I had to say my knowledge of geography got better every day.

I'd just finished typing my local news article with items from the police blotter when Peggy came into my office and sat down.

"Ava just called. Angel wants to pack up Freddie's things from the hotel tomorrow afternoon if you're available. I told her you would be."

"Thanks. I should be able to make it." Richie Finnerty's funeral Mass was in the morning and I'd have to write something on it, but that wouldn't take much time. "Do you still want to go with me?"

"If I can talk Ken into answering the phone for me."

"That shouldn't be too hard."

Peggy grinned. "Unless by magic some emergency golf tournament materializes."

"I'll just have to make sure that doesn't happen. I am the boss, after all."

We were still laughing when Ken came in. "What are you two plotting now?"

"Nothing much," I said, "other than you're manning the telephone tomorrow afternoon while Peggy and I help Angel pack up Freddie's belongings."

"Sure, I'm happy to," he said.

"See how easy that was?" I said to Peggy.

"Peggy and I are going to see *Mrs. Miniver* tonight," Ken said. "Want to go with us?"

As much as I wanted to see the movie, I didn't want to tag along. I felt like I did that too much already. I made the excuse that I was helping my mother and Lily at the fair. It wasn't entirely false. While I had worked on the local news article, I thought about Dan Petrie seeing Angel and Freddie talking near the Tilt-A-Whirl. If Angel was telling the truth and they were getting back together, it was possible someone else had heard or seen them talking. Maybe even someone who hadn't been happy about that—like

Belinda. Returning to the fair tonight would give me a chance to ask around. It might amount to nothing, but it was worth a try.

At the end of the day, I checked the layout for the morning paper with a still very cheerful Donny, then headed home. On the way, I thought about something Greta Gray said—that she didn't know why I cared. I knew she'd meant why I cared what she wrote, but I was now wondering why I cared who killed Freddie. It shouldn't matter to me. I didn't even like him. Dad would discover who killed him, and I'd write an article for the *Herald*. I didn't have to be involved. But then I thought of Ava. As much as she annoyed me with her gossip at times, I knew she loved her sister and her father. Angel was the prime suspect, with Ned a close second. Ava would be devastated if either one of them were charged with murder. I tried to convince myself that I was looking into this for Ava, but that wasn't the whole story either. Just as with some of last month's events, part of me would have felt compelled to get involved even if Ava hadn't asked for my help. Just like Pop, I couldn't tolerate any injustice even when it didn't directly affect me. I remembered the editorial I'd written after the last residents of Japanese descent had been evacuated from San Francisco. I made the point that it wasn't right to treat citizens that way no matter their nationality. I'd gotten threats afterward, but I had to speak up at the injustice. It was part of who I was. If that meant investigating another murder, so be it.

Chapter Fourteen

Germans Begin New Offensive on Eastern Front
The Progress Herald, June 29, 1942

There wasn't a rally scheduled for this evening—the actors had tonight and tomorrow night off, since attendance at the fair usually wasn't as big on Monday and Tuesday. On Wednesday they'd be in Butler for a rally at the county courthouse, then back here on Thursday. Friday was the big demolition derby that usually drew a large crowd. And Saturday the fourth would be the final rally and celebration for Independence Day. Although there were no celebrities tonight, sales of war bonds still went on. Mom and Martha Feeney were stationed at the table near the empty stage in front of the trailer. I promised them I'd check back later and help out if they needed me.

I walked with Lily to the cotton candy stand. Her friend Cindy was already there spinning sugar for a little boy and his mother. The line was five deep, so I left them to their work. I took my notebook and pencil from my pocketbook and wandered around talking to fairgoers for the next hour. Mostly everyone was enjoying the fair. One man grumbled that he thought the games were rigged, and a woman complained that the funnel cakes didn't have enough powdered sugar on them because of "that unfair rationing." When I asked for her name so I could quote her, she quickly moved on.

I strolled past the rides until I reached the Tilt-A-Whirl. This was where Dan Petrie had seen Angel and Freddie talking. I turned around and looked toward the other rides and the booths. The stage and trailers were in the distance to my left. In the far distance was an area with some bleachers where the demolition derby would be held. The food booths were straight ahead beyond the rides, and the games were to the right of the food booths. The area near the stage was open for fairgoers to gather around to watch the rally. There had been no large crowds the day Freddie was killed like there were now, so anyone who'd been near the area that day would have had a view of Angel and Freddie talking.

I turned around again. The dunk tank was maybe a hundred feet away and hadn't been visible until I'd almost reached the Tilt-A-Whirl. I took a deep breath and headed toward the tank. The barricades had been removed, so there were no obstacles in my way other than my reluctance to relive finding Freddie's body.

The dunk tank sat on a wooden platform with wheels. There was a hose attached to a spigot on a water pipe sticking up out of the ground. It looked like the tank had been filled here because of the water supply. I guessed the tank and platform would have been hitched to a tractor or truck and moved to somewhere near the games if Freddie hadn't ended up in it. I walked around the tank looking for I don't know what. The area had been thoroughly searched, and I didn't find anything either. I looked toward the rides again. The only ones visible from here were the Tilt-A-Whirl in front of me and the Ferris wheel at the far end. There was no way anyone could have witnessed Freddie's murder. Except the killer himself.

* * *

I bought a funnel cake for a snack. There was plenty of powdered sugar on it—the proof was all over my blouse. I was dusting off when I spotted Harold coming down a wooden ladder holding a light bulb. I caught up with him as he folded the ladder. "Looks like your work is never done," I said.

Harold smiled. "Or yours either. I saw you walking around with that notebook." He tossed the light bulb into a nearby garbage can. "So, will I like what I read in the paper about my fair?"

I liked how he called it his fair. "Everyone I talked to is having a wonderful time." I didn't mention the guy who thought the games were rigged. "How about you? Are you enjoying yourself?"

"I wouldn't know what to do with myself if we didn't put this on every year. It takes all year to plan it, organize everything, schedule entertainment . . ." He paused. "I feel real bad about the fellow that got killed. This might sound selfish, but I was relieved we could open up anyway."

"It's not selfish at all. Everyone looks forward to this every year." I got my notebook out again. "Would you mind answering a few questions?"

He looked at his watch. "As long as it don't take more than five minutes."

"Did you see anything out of the ordinary the day Mr. Harrison was killed?

"Chief Turner already asked me that."

"I know," I said. "But I'd like to hear it firsthand. Maybe you remembered something else since you talked to him."

"It was business as usual. There were men finishing setting up some things and working on the rides—you know, making sure they were greased and safe for everyone."

This might be something. "Were they working on all the rides?" Harold nodded.

"What about in the late afternoon? Around five or so?"

"That would have been the merry-go-round. They saved that one for last."

The merry-go-round wasn't anywhere near the Tilt-A-Whirl. "So none of them would have been near enough to the dunk tank to see or hear anything."

"Afraid not," Harold said. "But that security guard—the one that's been watching the bonds—he saw that fellow talking to that pretty blonde actress."

Freddie and Angel. "Near the Tilt-A-Whirl?"

"He didn't say. You'll have to ask him."

"I will." If it was the same guard I'd tried to engage in conversation the other day, I didn't think I'd get far. It had been like talking to a statue.

Harold glanced at his watch. "I'd better skedaddle. It'll soon be time to turn the lights on." He smiled. "It's a pretty sight to see them from the Ferris wheel. I always take a ride before we shut down for the night."

"I might have to do that one night. Thanks, Mr. Copeland."

I went straight to where Mom and Martha were selling bonds. I was happy to see Mr. Talkative watching over them. There was no one in line, and Mom had just finished a sale. "Are you two ready for a break?" I asked.

"Are you sure you don't mind?" Martha said. "I'm parched. I'd like to get something to drink."

"So would I," Mom said.

I told them I didn't mind at all, and Martha took a few minutes to show me how to record any purchases. When they were out of sight, I turned to the security guard. "There's an extra chair here, why don't you have a seat?"

He shook his head. "I'll stand."

Two words. An improvement on the last time. "Don't your feet get tired?"

"Sometimes."

"Do you travel with this group to all the bond rallies?"

"Yes."

"Do you like it?" I asked.

He shrugged. "It's all right. The pay is good."

I was thrilled I got two sentences out of him. "Are the actors nice to you?"

"Most of them."

I smiled. "Let me guess. You'd rather not say which ones aren't."

Unbelievably, I got a smile in return. "I'd lose my job."

"Can you tell me about the nice ones?" I asked.

He glanced around like he wasn't supposed to be talking to anyone. "Mrs. Harrison reminds me of my baby sister. Sweet as can be. Mr. Allen is nice enough."

"What about Mr. Harrison and Miss Fox?"

"I'd better not say."

He didn't have to. His non-answer was enough. "It's a shame what happened to Mr. Harrison."

"Is it?"

"What do you mean?"

"Lady—"

"My name's Irene. What's yours?"

"Clyde. Clyde McAllister."

"Nice to meet you, Clyde. What were you going to say?"

"I really shouldn't be telling you this. I shouldn't be talking to you at all."

"I won't tell anyone if you won't."

"But aren't you a reporter?" he asked.

"Right now I'm just sitting in for my mother. Anything you tell me is off the record."

Clyde was silent for a bit, and I was afraid he was going to clam up again. "I was going to say that you don't know the half of it. Mr. Harrison is—was—a mean son of a gun. The way he treated his poor wife was terrible. And that Miss Fox is even worse. She'd do anything to get her name up in lights. Those two belonged together. Mrs. Harrison deserves someone better. Someone who appreciates her."

Like you, I thought. It sounded like Clyde might have a crush on Angel. Enough to kill for her? "Angel—Mrs. Harrison—said that she met her husband here the afternoon he was killed and that they were getting back together. Have you heard anything about that?"

"I saw them talking, and Mrs. Harrison was happy when she left."

"You saw her leave?"

Clyde nodded. "We talked for a while when she stopped to say goodbye to me on her way out."

"Did she say anything about her husband?" I asked.

"Nope. And I didn't ask."

I asked him if he had seen Freddie after that.

"No. Miss Fox was looking for him, though."

"What time was that?"

"Around five. Mr. Davis was with her, and he had me take my dinner break then."

Our conversation ended when a couple came up to the table. Clyde went back to being a statue while I sold my first war bond. Mom and Martha returned, and I didn't get to talk to Clyde again. I sure had a lot to think about, though.

* * *

I spread some of Mom's homemade apple butter on a slice of toast. It was after midnight and I was still wide awake. I kept turning over what I'd learned from Harold Copeland and Clyde McAllister. In all honesty, it wasn't much, but it felt like progress anyway. I poured a glass of milk and sat down at the table.

The front door opened and seconds later Sylvia came into the kitchen. "You're up late," she said. "Is that apple butter?"

"Yep. Help yourself."

"Thanks. I will." She sliced the bread and put it in the toaster. "We were busy as usual tonight, and I ate dinner so fast I didn't even taste it."

I was glad to hear business was booming at Tabor Industries.

"You'll be happy to know they finished rebuilding the box shop," Sylvia said.

That section of the plant had burned down the previous month. The official story had been that a disgruntled employee had set it on fire. The unofficial story was much more complicated. "That was quick."

"Thanks to Miss Lewis. When the war is over, Tabor Junior should really let her stay in charge."

Colleen Lewis had worked at Tabor her entire career as Wilfred Tabor's secretary. She knew the place better than anyone. "I agree. Unfortunately, she'll be relegated back to her former status."

"I hope not. It's not fair." Sylvia's toast popped up, and she slathered apple butter on it. "Maybe she won't want to go back to being a secretary. I sure wouldn't." She poured a glass of milk and sat down across from me. "I'm not giving up my job after the war, that's for sure."

"I thought you were only there for the money."

"I am, and that's why I'm not giving it up. I'm not going back to being a waitress or shop clerk." She grinned. "Although if that Kirk Allen wanted to whisk me off to Hollywood, I'd leave in a heartbeat."

I laughed. "You and a million other girls." I drained my glass and pushed it aside. "And Lily might have something to say about it. She's got her sights set on him now."

"I'm shocked," Sylvia said with a smile. "I thought Frank Sinatra was the love of her life. She showed me that autographed picture that Katherine sent her."

"And next month she'll be in love with someone else. I guess you don't remember being fourteen years old."

"I'm not sure I was ever fourteen."

I took my dishes to the sink and then sat back down.

"So what's keeping you up?" Sylvia asked. "You looked lost in thought when I came in."

"I'm just trying to figure out a few things."

"Like what?"

"Do you really want to hear?"

"I wouldn't have asked if I didn't," Sylvia said.

I told her what I'd been doing, and what I'd been thinking. "I haven't learned much other than what I knew already, that Angel and Freddie met that afternoon."

"But you did," Sylvia said. "That guard told you that Belinda Fox was looking for Freddie. She could have found him and killed him."

"It's not enough. There are no witnesses and no proof. Besides, I'm not sure it's Belinda's style. She's the sort who would hire someone to do it for her."

"Unless he made her mad enough."

That was possible. She could have picked up the crowbar in anger. "Maybe."

"It's got to be hard figuring out if actors are telling the truth," Sylvia said.

"So far it's been impossible." I thought of how Angel seemed to play a different character every time I saw her. The only two suspects who weren't actors were Ava and Ned. If either of them murdered Freddie, they'd done it to protect Angel. If Ned had killed him, I had a feeling he'd confess. Ned hadn't hesitated to say he meant it when he brandished the shotgun and warned Freddie he'd use it. I honestly didn't think Ned had killed Freddie, but he would certainly cover it up if one of his daughters had. I needed to talk to Ned first thing tomorrow.

Chapter Fifteen

British Bombers Attack Bremen, Germany—Factories Damaged

The Progress Herald, June 30, 1942

Dempsey's Diner opened at seven, and I arrived shortly after Ned unlocked the door. Ned's early morning business was usually brisk, but not at the moment. Maybe everyone had had a late night at the fair. Even my mother was sleeping in this morning—a rare occurrence.

Virgil Curry sat at the counter. He was a fixture in Progress and spent most of his time on a park bench in the town square when he wasn't in the bar up the street. Virgil was a veteran of the previous war, and from what Pop once told me, he'd never been the same afterward. He was almost always pleasant—as long as you didn't sit on what he considered *his bench*. Virgil looked up as I came in and smiled. "Morning, Newspaper Lady."

"Good morning, Virgil," I said, taking a seat at the counter.

"It's gonna be a hot one today."

"How do you know that?" I asked. It was a little on the muggy side, now that he mentioned it.

133

"I can feel it in my bones," he said. "They ain't hurting today. They like the heat."

Ned came through the swinging door to the kitchen. "I thought I heard voices. You here for breakfast, Irene?"

"That and a few questions if you don't mind."

Ned smiled. "I figured you'd have questions sooner or later. Lizzie said you'd stopped by the other day." He turned the mug in front of me right side up and filled it with coffee. "What can I get you?"

I ordered scrambled eggs and toast and told him to bring the same for Virgil.

"You don't have to do that, Newspaper Lady," Virgil said.

"I want to. And please, call me Irene."

"Irene's a pretty name, Newspaper Lady."

Apparently I wasn't going to win this one. That was all right.

In no time at all Ned came out of the kitchen with two plates. He placed one in front of Virgil and refilled his mug. Ned asked if I wanted to move to a booth and he'd join me for a cup of coffee. I agreed.

Once we were situated he said, "For the record, I didn't kill that poor excuse for a human being. I'd be bragging about it if I had."

"That's not something to brag about."

"Says you."

I didn't argue the point. "What have you told Chief Turner? I assume he wanted to know where you were when Freddie was killed."

"I was right here. There were no customers. I stayed in the kitchen and cleaned."

In other words, no one saw him. It wasn't much of an alibi. "Did you leave at all?"

"I did not. I'd tell you if I did."

The bells on the door jingled and Ned stood. "I'm not sorry he's dead, but I didn't do it." He took a few steps and turned. "If you find out who did, I'd like to shake his hand."

I finished my breakfast and left fifty cents on the table. It would more than cover both breakfasts.

I was the first to arrive at the *Herald*, so I went to the kitchen and put the java on to percolate. By the time it finished, Peggy had arrived. We each grabbed a cup and took them back to my office.

"How was *Mrs. Miniver*?" I asked.

"It was so good," Peggy said. "You have to see it. How was the fair?"

I sipped my black coffee. "Interesting."

She grinned. "You weren't helping at all. You were investigating."

"Well, I did sell a bond."

"One bond is not helping." She leaned forward. "So spill. What did you find out?"

"Not a whole lot." I told her about talking to Harold Copeland and Clyde McAllister.

"I don't know," she said. "It sounds like a lot to me. You have more than one witness now who saw Angel talking to Freddie."

"That's what I'm worried about. I don't think Angel did it, even though everything is pointing to her right now."

"What about that guard?" Peggy asked. "If he likes Angel as much as you say, he might have killed Freddie. He could have said Belinda was looking for Freddie to throw suspicion off of himself."

"It's possible, I guess. He did say that Paul Davis was with Belinda, so I can verify what he told me. I'd definitely prefer it to be him rather than one of the people we know."

"Me too."

"Another thing that bothers me is motive. There's no doubt a lot of people disliked Freddie, but is that enough reason to kill him?"

I heard the door open and voices in the newsroom as the others arrived for work.

Peggy got up. "It's something to think about. If I come up with any ideas, I'll let you know."

"Same here." I pushed our discussion to the back of my mind. It looked like I wasn't going to find a killer this morning. At the rate I was going, it was possible I never would.

*   *   *

The news for the Allies in Africa wasn't good. Tobruk in North Africa had fallen to the Axis last week, and now, after a three-day battle, so had Mersa Matruh. The Allies were forced to retreat. All the news wasn't bad, however. British bombers had attacked Bremen in Germany, damaging the Focker-Wulf aircraft factory as well as a submarine shipyard. Frank would follow up with any new details on the situation in Africa, and Rex would do the same with the Bremen attack.

At a little after nine, I went home and donned a hat, then Mom and I drove to St. Michael's for Richie Finnerty's Mass. I'd been to funerals before, but this was the first I'd attended without a coffin—Richie was in the sea thousands of miles away. It was only the second funeral I'd attended for someone around my own age. Years ago, a classmate had died from some rare blood disease. Our entire third grade class attended the funeral. The only things I remembered about it were her parents crying and that we'd gotten a half day off school. At eight years old, I really hadn't understood death, but I certainly did now. It was sad. It was brutal. And it was permanent.

Inside the church were many of those same classmates—at least the ones who hadn't moved from the area or joined the military. I nodded to a few as I followed Mom halfway down the aisle. I genuflected and made the sign of the cross, then slipped into the pew after her. Peggy, Ken, and Peggy's mother were in the row in front of us. After saying a prayer, I looked around the church. Matt was sitting toward the rear, and as I started to turn to face front again, I saw Kirk enter and slip into the last pew. Before I could get up to invite him to sit with us, the organ music began and the Finnerty family processed up to the front row.

The Mass was solemn, and in his sermon Father O'Connor assured everyone that we'd see Richie again someday. I wasn't always sure I believed that, but Father O'Connor presented a good case. Richie's sister Louise got up and sang a beautiful "Ave Maria" after communion, which made almost everyone reach for their handkerchiefs. When Mass was over, the family went to the sacristy with Father O'Connor while everyone else went downstairs to the church hall.

My mother and Mrs. Reardon went to the kitchen to help the other ladies on the hospitality committee finish up preparations for the luncheon. I made the rounds saying hello to people I knew. I was finally cornered by Roger Eckel's ninety-year-old mother, who kept asking me questions but didn't hear any of my answers because she was so hard of hearing. I looked around the room hoping someone would rescue me. My gaze settled on Kirk, who was standing alone in a corner. I caught his eye and mouthed *help*, and he headed my way. He took my elbow and I excused myself, even though Mrs. Eckel couldn't hear it.

"Thanks for saving me."

"Any time," Kirk said. "That was a nice send-off for Richie."

"It was." We crossed the room and joined Peggy, Ken, and Matt. By this time, Rose Finnerty and her family had come downstairs and the hospitality ladies had set out the buffet. The five of us got in line behind everyone else. Peggy nudged me.

"We're being stared at," she said.

"You mean I'm being stared at," Kirk said. "No one recognizes me and they're all wondering what I'm doing here. I shouldn't have come."

"Nonsense," I said. "You were friends with Richie too."

"I know. It just feels strange, that's all. I shouldn't complain. Even when I was Eugene I felt out of place unless I was performing and could be anyone but myself."

"I still feel out of place most of the time," Matt said. "Everyone knows me as the goofy kid with the thick glasses. I'd rather be Matt Redmond, famous photographer." He said the last part in the deep voice an announcer on the radio would use.

We all laughed and got a few raised eyebrows in response.

"You're the best photographer around," I said. "Pop wouldn't have hired you otherwise."

"You must be good or Irene would have fired you by now," Ken added.

Matt gave him a friendly punch on the arm. "Thanks a lot, pal."

It was finally our turn at the buffet, and we filled our plates and went to an empty table to eat. We'd just finished when I noticed Wanda Wilkins coming toward us. I groaned.

"What?" Peggy said.

"It's Wanda." She had never forgiven me for being elected secretary of the Progress High student council instead of her. I had avoided her ever since.

"Maybe she'll be nice for a change," Peggy said.

"I'm not counting on it."

"If I remember right, Wanda doesn't know the meaning of the word nice," Kirk said.

"She doesn't know the meaning of a lot of words," Matt said.

I held in a laugh as she reached the table.

"Well, if it isn't Irene Ingram," Wanda said. "I know you have to sell papers for that terrible newspaper of your father's, but I'm shocked you would stoop low enough to cover a funeral."

"I was a friend of Richie's," I said. Wanda hadn't been. "Why are you here?"

"To offer my condolences to the family, of course." She looked around the table and her gaze settled on Kirk. "Aren't you one of those people with that war thing? What are you doing here?"

Before I could tell her that Kirk was a friend, he stood and came around my chair. He took Wanda's hand and kissed it. She looked as surprised as I was.

"I'm Kirk Allen," he said. "I'm pleased to make your acquaintance."

"Same here. I mean I'm not you, of course. I'm Wanda Wilkins. Well, Wanda Reynolds now. Wilkins was my maiden name." She was flustered, and rightly so. Kirk was making Cary Grant seem like an amateur.

"Any friend of Irene's is a friend of mine." Kirk still held her hand.

"Oh, thank you," Wanda said. "Irene and I have known each other forever."

And hated each other forever, I thought.

Wanda's husband was crossing the room toward us. "Here comes Wayne," I said.

Wanda whipped her hand from Kirk's, spun around, and rushed toward him. I'd never seen her move so fast.

"Kirk, old boy, that was splendid," Matt said.

He grinned and shrugged. "She had it coming."

Peggy and Ken stood. "We'd better get going. Frank and Rex have been holding down the fort long enough. They'll never forgive me," Peggy said.

Matt got up as well.

I nodded. "I want to say goodbye to Louise and Rose. I'll meet you back at the paper." Mom was staying to help clean up and would get a lift from one of the others. I turned to Kirk. "Thanks for taking care of Wanda."

He smiled. "It was fun. Like I said, I don't feel out of place when I'm acting. It wouldn't have gone as well if she'd have known I was Eugene."

"Probably not."

"Do you mind if I come with you to say goodbye? I'd like to give them my condolences."

"I don't mind at all." I didn't see Rose, but Louise was standing near the exit and had just said goodbye to one of the mourners. We headed that way.

Louise gave me a hug. "Thank you for coming. You were a good friend to Richie."

"He will certainly be missed."

She reached for Kirk's hand and shook it. "Thank you as well. I don't believe I know you."

"Actually, you do," Kirk said. "I was a good friend of Richie's in high school."

Louise seemed puzzled. "I know all of Richie's friends. You don't look familiar at all."

He smiled. "I've changed a bit, including my name. I go by Kirk Allen now, but back then my name was Eugene Allen."

Her eyes opened wide, and a look I couldn't quite fathom appeared on her face. "You!"

"You do remember me, then."

"You bet I do," Louise said. "You have a lot of nerve. How dare you show up here." There was venom in her voice. "Get out. Leave now."

Why was Louise acting like this? I glanced from one to the other. Pure hatred showed on Louise's face. Kirk seemed shocked. I didn't understand what had happened. "What's going on?" I asked.

Louise turned to me. "I'll tell you what's going on. If it wasn't for Eugene Allen, my brother would still be alive."

Chapter Sixteen

Mersa Matruh in N. Africa Falls to Axis
The Progress Herald, June 30, 1942

What in the world was she saying? "That doesn't make any sense, Louise. Richie died at Midway. The Japanese navy killed him. Kirk had nothing to do with it. He was Richie's friend."

"Some friend. Richie wouldn't have joined up if it wasn't for him."

"Let's go, Irene," Kirk said. "We're upsetting her."

"You bet I'm upset," Louise said. "I want both of you to leave right now."

I wanted to get to the bottom of this. "I'd like to say goodbye to your mother first."

"Stay away from her," Louise said loudly enough that a couple of people looked our way. She continued more quietly. "I don't want her knowing about this."

"Knowing about what?" I said.

Kirk took me by the arm. "Let's go."

"But—"

"Let's go."

I had trouble keeping up with Kirk as he pulled me through the doorway and up the stairs to the parking lot. Once we were outside, I yanked my arm from his grasp. By this time I was the angry one—angry enough to swear. "What the hell was that all about? That woman is nuts! Why would she say something like that? You and Richie were friends and she treats you like that? Why didn't you stop her? Why didn't you make it clear she was wrong?"

"Because maybe she wasn't wrong."

He started across the parking lot and I followed. "Now you're as wacky as she is."

Kirk stopped beside his rental car. "It makes sense." He got in.

I blocked the door so he couldn't close it. "No, it doesn't. You're not leaving until you tell me what you mean. What Louise meant."

"I can't," he said. "Leave it alone. Please."

"No."

He turned the key in the ignition. "You'd better move."

"You'd rather run me over than talk to me?"

Kirk didn't answer. He put the car in gear. "Please." His voice broke. "I can't."

The pain in his voice went right through me. I took a few steps back from the car. He slammed the door shut and I watched him drive away.

* * *

Back at the *Herald*, I wrote a brief article about Richie's funeral for tomorrow's paper, but I couldn't get the conversation with Louise and Kirk out of my mind. I couldn't concentrate on anything else. When Peggy came into my office an hour later, I was tapping my pencil on the top of my desk, lost in thought.

"Are you ready to go?" she asked.

"Go where?"

"To meet Angel at the Excelsior. Remember?"

It had completely slipped my mind. "Oh. I forgot." I opened my desk drawer and picked up my pocketbook.

"Ken's all set to answer the phone," she said. "Rex and Frank are out, but Ken will let them know if anything comes in."

I thanked her for taking care of it. On the walk to the hotel, Peggy asked me what was on my mind. My best friend could always tell when something was bothering me. I told her about what happened with Louise.

"That's really strange," Peggy said. "And Kirk won't tell you anything?"

I shook my head. "I can't figure it out, and it's going to bother me until I can."

"Well, you can't very well force him to spill the beans."

"I know," I said. "Whatever it is, he's really torn up about it. The way he sounded broke my heart."

Peggy gave my arm a squeeze. "Give him some time. Maybe he'll come around."

We reached the Excelsior and the doorman held the door open as we went inside. Greta Gray was holding court again in a prominent spot in the lobby. I thought we'd made it safely past her when I heard, "Little girl!"

"Crapola," I said. "Don't turn around. Pretend you don't hear her."

Of course Peggy turned around. "Is that Greta Gray? I want to meet her."

"You won't like her. I guarantee it."

"I don't care." She grabbed my arm. "Come on."

"Whatever you do, don't tell her anything. And I mean anything. She'll twist it all around to suit herself." Peggy nodded and we crossed the lobby.

"I see you've brought a friend with you today." Greta gave Peggy the once-over.

"I'm Peggy Reardon." She reached her hand out, which Greta ignored.

"How nice," Greta said. "I hear you were at a funeral this morning."

I didn't ask how she knew that when she probably never left the hotel. Despite saying she knew what was going on using her "impressions," I suspected she paid people to get information for her. "A friend from high school was killed at Midway."

"Why was Kirk Allen there?"

I shrugged "He's a friend."

Greta waved a bellboy over to light her cigarette. "Darling, you know that's not the whole story."

"I don't understand," Peggy said. "What more could there be?"

"I heard there was an argument of some sort."

"Really?" I said. "I didn't see any argument." I turned to Peggy. "Did you see anyone arguing?"

"Nope. Everything was copacetic."

Greta stared at us. I think she knew we weren't telling her the whole truth. Finally, she waved her hand in dismissal. "Never mind."

When we reached the elevator, Peggy said, "You're right. I don't like her. How in the world would she even know about the funeral? And what was that about with her asking about an argument?"

"Well, someone told her about it, and told her about Louise throwing Kirk and me out. I'd love to know who."

"Me too."

"I have a feeling she has little spies everywhere." We were quiet in the elevator, and the attendant let us off on Freddie's floor. I knocked on the door when we reached his room.

Angel opened the door. "Please do come in. I'm so glad you could make it." She sounded like she'd invited us for tea.

The room was still a mess. "Have you been here long?" I asked.

"I actually just arrived. Kirk told me how to come in the back way to avoid the Dragon Lady."

"If Greta Gray is going to be in town for long, I might need to know how to do that too."

"It's easy," Angel said. "You just knock on the kitchen door."

I wondered how the kitchen staff would feel about more people traipsing through. Angel and Kirk could get away with it, but I wasn't sure I could. "What can we help with?"

Angel looked around. "Freddie wasn't the neatest person in the world, but I didn't know he'd throw everything around like this. He must have been very upset. Oh, my poor Freddie." Tears filled her eyes. "What will I ever do without him?"

Peggy put an arm around her. "You'll go on. Freddie would want it that way."

Angel dabbed her eyes with a handkerchief. "He would, wouldn't he?"

While Angel composed herself, I thought about her saying that she didn't know Freddie would toss things around like this. I'd had an inkling before that someone had been in here searching for something, and now I was sure. I hoped Angel would know if anything was missing.

There were several suitcases on the floor. I picked two of them up and opened them on the bed. "Angel, why don't you help me pack Freddie's clothes?" She'd have to decide what to do with them. I had another thought but didn't want to ask—what was she going to do with Freddie? He was still in the morgue in Doc Atkins's basement. I'd leave that question for the chief.

After thirty minutes, we'd only packed half of Freddie's things. Angel had to sniff every piece of clothing and sigh before slowly folding it and passing it to Peggy or me to place in a suitcase. We'd be here until tomorrow if she didn't hurry up. I was ready to suggest she let me do the rest when she picked up a white shirt, sniffed it, and threw it violently across the room.

"That witch!"

Peggy and I looked at each other.

"How dare she!" Angel said.

"Who are you talking about?" I had a good idea, but I asked anyway.

"Belinda Fox. Her perfume is all over that shirt. How could she do that to my Freddie?"

I was pretty sure Freddie had something to do with it too.

"I don't want that shirt. It goes in the garbage."

Surprisingly, no more pieces of clothing were thrown across the room. We packed the remainder quickly because Angel was still angry and had stopped sniffing and sighing. I took the suits out of the closet and checked the pockets. In one of the inside jacket pockets there was a folded piece of paper. I opened it. There were several dates on it, the last being Friday, the twenty-sixth— the day he died. I showed it to Angel. "Do you know what this is?"

"It's a bunch of dates," she said. "It's probably trash. You can throw it away."

I went over to the dresser and slipped it into my pocketbook instead. I'd learned how important slips of paper could be sometimes. Granted, these were only dates, but you never knew.

Angel opened the drawer in the bedside table. "That's odd," she said.

"What?" Peggy said.

"Freddie had a book he almost always carried with him and kept in the bedside table. It's not here."

"Maybe he didn't bring one this time," I said. "He wouldn't have had much time to read." Especially if he'd been fooling around with Belinda.

"Not that kind of a book," Angel said. "This was a book with a black cover that he kept notes in."

"Notes?" Freddie hadn't seemed like the note-making type. A black book with women's telephone numbers was more his style. "What kind of notes?"

Angel sat on the bed. "I'm not exactly sure. Freddie wouldn't let me see it. I picked it up and opened it once and . . . well . . . he wasn't happy about it."

"Did you get a look at what was in it?" Peggy asked.

"I only saw that there were names and some numbers."

"Telephone numbers?" I asked. It could very well have been what I'd thought.

Angel shook her head. "It didn't look like telephone numbers. More like lists of numbers next to names, and some were crossed off."

I couldn't make heads or tails of what could have been in it. It must have been important enough to Freddie to not even let Angel see it. Whoever had tossed the room must have taken it. Belinda? She and Freddie had adjoining rooms, so she could easily have gained access. The problem with that was that if she had been sleeping with Freddie she might have known where he kept the book. All she would have had to do was wait until he wasn't here and take it from the nightstand. It had to be someone else. Someone wanted that book. Had that same person killed Freddie?

"Do you remember any of the names in the book?" I asked.

"No. Freddie took it from me before I had a chance to read any of it. I only got that quick glance." Angel looked around the room. "I wonder where it could be."

I didn't want to say that I thought it had been stolen. "I'm sure it will turn up eventually."

"You're probably right," Angel said.

"Maybe he even forgot to bring it with him this time," Peggy said.

"That's right," I added. "He was so upset about possibly losing you that he couldn't think of anything else."

Angel sighed. "Poor Freddie. I shouldn't have upset him so."

I didn't know how to respond to that. Freddie was two-timing her and she was worried she'd upset him. "You shouldn't blame yourself."

"But I do. Freddie had his faults, but he really did love me."

I knew by now that Freddie only loved himself. I took one last look around the room. "I think we have everything."

Angel called the front desk and they sent a bellboy up with a cart. He loaded it and took it down to the lobby. When we were in the hallway, I took Peggy aside and told her I'd meet her downstairs, that I wanted to check on Kirk.

After the attendant closed the elevator door, I went down the hallway to the other end where Kirk's room was located and knocked on the door. Three knocks later, the door swung open.

"I said I din't wanna be dishturbed."

Kirk was drunk as a skunk.

"Oh. Ish you." He stumbled back, almost falling.

"Peggy and I helped Angel clear out Freddie's room, so I thought I'd stop and see how you were."

Kirk plopped onto the bed. "I'm fine. Wanna drink?" He reached for a half-empty bottle of whiskey on the nightstand.

"No thanks," I said. "You don't look fine to me."

"I'll be even better when this bottle is gone." He poured whiskey into a glass, most of it sloshing onto the table.

I snatched the bottle out of his hands, picked up the glass, and headed to the bathroom.

"Hey!"

"You've had enough." I poured all the booze into the sink.

"That's mine."

"Too bad." I tossed the empty bottle into the trash can and left the glass on the sink.

"I'll jus' get another."

"Not if I have anything to say about it." There was a telephone on the nightstand and I picked up the receiver. "I'm calling room service. The only thing you're drinking for the rest of the day is coffee."

Kirk stuck his tongue out at me like a five-year-old. "You're not my mother."

"Thank goodness for that." I'd planned to ask him more about Louise's comments, but it would have to wait. He was in no condition to talk about that—or much of anything.

"What were you doing in Freddie's room?"

"I told you. Peggy and I were helping Angel pack up his things."

"Why?"

"Angel asked for help."

"Freddie was a jerk, you know," Kirk said. "I woulda helped Angel." He stretched out on the bed and closed his eyes. "I'm glad he's dead, but it doesn't matter. It'll never stop."

"What will never stop?"

"It'll . . . never . . ."

I started to ask again, then realized he'd passed out. I waited for a few minutes until the coffee arrived. He'd have to drink it cold when he woke up. I covered Kirk with the blanket at the foot of the bed, then went downstairs to meet Peggy, still wondering what he meant.

Chapter Seventeen

Memorial Service for Local Boy Killed at Midway
The Progress Herald, June 30, 1942

B y the time Peggy and I got back to the *Herald*, it was late afternoon and almost time to put tomorrow's issue to bed. The articles I'd assigned Rex and Frank were on my desk, as well as a few Ken had written on various sports events, including interviews with drivers participating in Friday's demolition derby. We'd run that one the morning of the event. I quickly read through everything, then took it all downstairs to my cousin.

Donny was whistling. It was slightly off key, but I recognized it as a Harry James tune. He stopped when he saw me. He looked embarrassed, if that was possible for him.

"Don't stop on my account," I said. "I like happy employees."

He smiled—another rare occurrence—and pointed to the papers I held. "You're cutting it a little close."

A month ago I would have gotten a lecture on how hard he worked and how he should be running the paper instead of me. I really hoped he and Betty were a permanent thing. "I'm sorry about that. It couldn't be avoided."

He took the articles from me and quickly looked through them. "I know just where these will go."

"How is Betty?" I asked. "Did you have a good time at the fair?"

He smiled again. "She's perfect. And we had a great time. She's on the daylight shift this week so we've been seeing each other every night."

"I'm happy for you," I said. And I meant it. We chatted like two normal people for a minute or two—something we never would have done before.

Miracles do happen.

*　*　*

Mom and Lily were off to the fair again that evening. I opted to stay home. I needed the peace and quiet. It had been a long day. I had borrowed Peggy's copy of *Frenchman's Creek* a couple of weeks ago and figured an evening of reading was exactly what I needed. I'd enjoyed Daphne du Maurier's *Rebecca* and hoped I'd like this one as well. I was halfway through the second chapter before I realized I didn't recall anything I'd read so far. It wasn't Miss du Maurier's fault. My thoughts were elsewhere. I closed the book and put it aside. I'd try again another day.

I still couldn't get over Louise's behavior earlier. I didn't understand what could have made her act that way toward Kirk. He and Richie had been friends. Maybe not best friends, but they'd had a lot in common. Both had been in the drama club and on the baseball team with Ken. Maybe Ken would know if there had been any problems between the two of them. Even if there were, Louise's statement that her brother wouldn't have enlisted, and he'd be alive, if it weren't for Kirk made absolutely no sense. I needed to talk to Louise.

It was only eight o'clock, so I pushed out of my chair and slipped on the sandals I'd left in the hallway. I crossed the street and saw Rose and Louise sitting on the front porch. Rose greeted me. Louise studied her fingernails.

"I didn't get to say goodbye to you today, so I thought I'd stop over and see how you were," I said.

"My mother is fine," Louise snapped. "You can go back home."

"Louise!" Rose said. "That's no way to treat a guest."

"That's all right," I said.

"No, it isn't," Rose said. "Come and sit. Would you like some lemonade?"

"That would be lovely."

Louise stood. "I'll get it."

I was pretty sure she just wanted to escape and avoid me.

Rose put a hand on her arm. "I will do it. You sit here and talk with Irene." She disappeared into the house.

Louise glared at me.

I decided to ease into what I wanted to know. "Where's Carl and the boys?"

She wouldn't even look at me. "At the fair," she said.

"They'll have fun. There's a lot to do there. Lily is working at the cotton candy stand this year."

"They wanted to ride the merry-go-round."

Not much, but at least she was speaking to me. I had to get to the point before Rose returned with our lemonade. "Louise, I don't understand what happened this afternoon."

"Nothing to understand," she said. "I don't want Eugene anywhere near my family."

"I don't understand why. Kirk . . . Eugene was only there to pay his respects. He and Richie were good friends. Frankly, nothing you said to us made any sense."

Louise had tears in her eyes when she looked at me. "I can't talk about it. There's no point now. Richie's dead."

"But—"

"Ask Eugene."

"I have. He won't tell me either."

"Then let it go," she said. "But keep him away from my family."

Rose carried three glasses of lemonade on a tray and pushed the screen door open with her hip. "Here we go." She passed us each a glass and sat down. "What were you girls talking about?"

At the same time Louise said, "Nothing," and I said, "Eugene Allen."

"I remember Eugene," Rose said. "He was such a nice boy. I wonder whatever happened to him."

Louise gave me a don't-you-dare look, which I ignored.

"He's an actor now and lives in California," I said. "He's in town for the war bond rallies."

"Oh my!" Rose said. "I should have known that boy would make something of himself someday. He and Richie used to act out scenes from those plays for school. Sometimes they'd even make up their own."

"That's enough, Mother," Louise said. "Irene doesn't want to hear all that."

"But I do," I said.

Louise stood. "I'll leave you to it then. I can't listen to it." She went inside.

"I'm sorry about my daughter," Rose said. "She's taken Richie's death very hard. They were very close. She was always so protective of him, and she was beside herself when he enlisted before the war. She stopped talking to him, and now that he's gone . . ."

"I understand." I got up. "I should really be going."

"I'm so glad you stopped by. If you see Eugene, tell him to stop and see me."

"I will." I didn't add that it would have to be when Louise wasn't around. It might do Kirk good to talk to Rose.

Back home, I switched on the radio, turning the dial until I heard music. Visiting the Finnertys hadn't been productive, but at least Louise seemed to be somewhat over her anger toward me, not that it mattered. There was a tangled thread of something tickling the back of my brain that I couldn't quite unravel. Whatever it was, Louise wouldn't talk about it. Neither would Kirk. I'd talk to Ken tomorrow and see if he remembered anything. And then I'd talk to Kirk again. I only hoped he'd be sober when I did.

* * *

It turned out I didn't have to go to the Excelsior to talk to Kirk. He was waiting for me outside the *Herald* at seven the next morning when I arrived. "What are you doing up this early?" I asked. "I thought you Hollywood types slept until noon." I unlocked the door and we went inside.

"I couldn't sleep, and I have one hell of a headache."

He followed while I dropped my pocketbook on my desk and went to the kitchen to make a pot of coffee. "There's aspirin in the cupboard there if you want some."

"Thanks." He shook two aspirin into his hand.

156

I filled the percolator with water and measured coffee into the basket.

Kirk turned the faucet back on and washed the pills down by drinking straight from the stream of water. I would have choked on them doing that.

"I'm sorry about yesterday," he said.

"Come on back to my office and we'll talk while the coffee is brewing." When we reached the office, I went around my desk and sat down.

Kirk took the seat across from me and leaned forward. "I really am sorry."

I nodded. "I went over to the Finnertys' last night."

"You shouldn't have done that."

"I wanted to see Rose. I didn't get a chance to tell her goodbye."

"Because of me."

"No, because of Louise. She wasn't happy to see me. She still wouldn't tell me anything. She said to ask you."

Kirk was silent.

"Why are you here, Kirk?" I asked. "You didn't come here just to tell me you're sorry. You could have telephoned to tell me that." That tangled thread was tickling me again.

"You won't understand. No one understands."

"You don't know that."

"I don't want to lose you as a friend now that we've found each other again. If I tell you, it could change everything."

I got up. "When I come back with coffee, you're going to talk and I'm going to listen." I was half afraid he'd disappear before I returned, so I was glad he was still seated in my office when I got back. He was looking at the photograph of Bill and me I kept on my desk.

"How is Bill?" he asked.

"He's doing well."

"I bet you miss him."

"More and more every day. In his last letter he said he might get home on leave before the summer is over."

"I hope he does," Kirk said. "Bill's a good guy. You're lucky to have each other."

There was a long silence while we both sipped our coffee. Finally I broke it. "Please talk to me."

Kirk took a deep breath. "You'll hate me, just like Louise."

"No, I won't. We've been friends a long time. You should know me better than that."

"I'm just going to say it then. I'm a homosexual."

Maybe I should have been shocked, but I wasn't. The thread finally untangled. I think part of me knew this about Kirk already. Being a homosexual wasn't something anyone talked about. Even in this day and age, it had to be kept a secret. One of Peggy's aunts had lived with another woman for more than twenty years. They told everyone they were good friends, but anyone with a brain or a heart could tell that it was more than that. No one spoke about it. Ever. There were laws on the books in most states, including Pennsylvania. "I'm glad you told me," I said.

"I'll leave if you want me to."

"Don't be ridiculous. You're my friend, no matter what. It doesn't change anything. You are who you are."

The relief on his face almost brought tears to my eyes. "I've always felt different," he said. "That's one reason I fell in love with acting. I could be someone else for a little while." He set his mug down on my desk. "I never wanted to be like this, you know. If I could have changed it, I would have. I've tried. Believe me."

"It must be difficult."

"I've come to accept that it's the way I am. Most of the time I'm all right until I run into someone like Louise."

"How did Louise find out?"

Kirk sighed. "I don't know. Maybe Richie told her."

"What about Richie?"

"He wasn't like me, if that's what you're asking. We were close all through high school and I thought . . . maybe . . . but I was wrong. He never treated me the same after I told him. I think that's why he enlisted as soon as we graduated. He had to prove he wasn't like me. So Louise is right—it's my fault he was killed."

"No, it's not," I said. "The blame is squarely on the Japanese who shot him out of the sky. You knew he always wanted to fly airplanes. When we were kids he was always running around with his arms outstretched, pretending he was flying."

"That's beside the point. He didn't have to join the military to do it."

"Maybe he wanted to do both."

Before Kirk had a chance to rebut that, the door to the newsroom opened and Ken and Peggy entered.

Kirk stood. "I'd better go. Thanks for the coffee and for listening." He lowered his voice. "You'll keep all this to yourself, right?"

"I won't tell a soul."

My friends came into my office. "Don't leave on our account," Ken said.

"I have things to do," Kirk said. "We have the rally later in Butler in front of the courthouse, and I have to get ready for that."

I walked him to the door, then followed Peggy and Ken to the kitchen to refill my mug.

"That was a surprise," Ken said.

"Is he all right?" Peggy asked. She knew about the condition I'd found him in the previous afternoon, and she'd probably told Ken.

"He'll be fine," I said. "He wanted to apologize to me for yesterday. I told him that he didn't have anything to worry about, that everything was hunky-dory."

And it was. At least I thought so.

* * *

At lunchtime, I grabbed my umbrella and took a walk over to the police department. I hadn't talked to my future father-in-law for a couple of days, and I wanted to see if he had an update on the murder investigation. Rally was at the front desk instead of Jimmy. "Don't tell me you and Jimmy switched duties today," I said.

Rally laughed. "Not a chance. Sarge had a doctor's appointment, so he took the afternoon off."

I'd never known Jimmy to visit a doctor. "I hope it's nothing serious."

"I don't think it is," Rally said. "He's been complaining about his gout lately, so the chief and Mrs. Feeney ganged up on him and made him go get it checked. Sarge wasn't happy about it."

"I can imagine. Is the chief in?" I turned when I heard the door behind me open. It was Dad. "I was just asking if you were here," I said.

"I am now."

I followed him into his office. "Rally said you made Jimmy go see a doctor."

Dad sank into his ancient chair. "The old coot's been limping more lately and complaining about his feet. Martha's been after him for years to go to the doctor." He smiled. "Jimmy seems to think doctors still use leeches instead of modern medicine."

160

"I hope his doctor will prescribe something for it," I said. "And that he takes it."

"Oh, Martha will make sure of that."

I asked if there was anything new in the investigation.

"As a matter of fact, there is."

"And?"

"I believe we've found the murder weapon."

Chapter Eighteen

Axis Troops Reach El-Alamein
The Progress Herald, July 1, 1942

"Where?" I asked.

"The stream behind the old Pell farm."

The Pell place hadn't been farmed since long before Raymond Pell passed away five years ago. There were no heirs, and the farm had been abandoned since his death. "That's a good half mile from the fairgrounds, isn't it?"

"Yep."

"Who found it? Was it a crowbar like Doc thought?"

"It was. A couple of kids were fishing in the stream and noticed something in the mud, which turned out to be the crowbar. Their parents telephoned yesterday afternoon."

"How did they know to call?"

The chief smiled. "Apparently they read the *Herald*. They knew the weapon might be a crowbar. I just dropped it off at the state police lab. They're better equipped to see if there are any fingerprints on it besides the ones left by the kids who found it."

"A half mile over farmland isn't an easy trek for someone not familiar with the area. Whoever killed Freddie took a good bit of effort to dispose of it. This should narrow down the suspects." I wasn't sure I liked this option. That left Ava, Ned, and Kirk as suspects. Angel wasn't familiar with the area, unless she had assistance from her sister. But both Ned and Kirk would have known the location of the stream.

Dad shook his head. "Not necessarily. The road cuts through the middle of the Pell farm. The killer didn't need to walk. He—or she—could have put the weapon in their car and disposed of it later. Unfortunately, we're not any farther ahead than before—at least until I hear from the state police."

Everyone at the fairgrounds that day would have driven, or ridden with someone. Angel had borrowed Ava's car to meet Freddie. Kirk had a rental car. Belinda and Paul Davis rode in a limousine. Then there were all the workers and handymen who had been setting things up. If anything, the list got longer. It was possible Freddie's murder had nothing to do with his personal situation. Maybe he said the wrong thing to a workman who lost his temper and whacked him over the head. It was a stretch, but certainly within the realm of possibility.

"What's your next step?" I asked.

"I'm going to re-interview everyone who had contact with Harrison that day. I'll mention finding the murder weapon and see if it shakes anyone up."

"Anything I can do?"

He shook his head. "Just keep me posted if you hear anything."

I got up to leave and remembered something. "I almost forgot to tell you. I helped Angel pack up Freddie's belongings yesterday.

She mentioned Freddie carried a book with him that had names and some numbers in it, but we couldn't find it. Did you see anything like that when you searched his room?"

"Nope. Did Angel say what it was exactly? Were they telephone numbers?"

"That's what I thought at first, but Angel said no—and some of the numbers were crossed off. She said it had a black cover. Freddie would never let her see what was in it. She only got a quick glimpse once before Freddie took it from her. Apparently he took it everywhere."

"I'll keep my eyes open," he said. "If it turns up, I'll let Angel know. I'll see if she can tell me more about it when I talk to her again."

* * *

When I got back to the paper, Frank had the *New York Times* open on his desk. "Still reading the competition?" I couldn't help ribbing him.

"They buried a story again," he said. "Come here."

I went over to his desk. He pointed to a story on page seven of yesterday's paper. It was a report from London from the twenty-ninth of June. It stated that Hitler had massacred over one million Jews since the war began. The *Times* had done something similar last month with a United Press story about what was happening in the Baltic states. I knew there was a lot of anti-Semitic sentiment, even in this country, but it seemed to me this deserved more than page seven. "Would you follow up on this, please?" I asked.

"That's my plan," Frank said.

"I want something for tomorrow's paper. Can you manage that?"

"You got it." He reached for the telephone before I even took a step.

I remembered Pop saying something before he left for the Pacific about how even in Europe newspapers had been hesitant to report on any atrocities because of what had happened in the previous war. Apparently, papers had published stories of carnage similar to this, and many turned out to be untrue. It was different now. These were firsthand reports from reliable sources that could easily be verified. I didn't understand the hesitancy.

In other war news, a U-boat had been sunk off the coast of Bermuda and Axis troops under Rommel had reached El-Alamein. The Allies' campaign in North Africa was foundering, and I wondered if that was where Bill would be heading eventually. I didn't like the idea—heck, I didn't like the idea of him fighting at all—but if the desert was where he had to go to beat Hitler, so be it. I didn't see much of anything on the wire on how we were faring in the Pacific. Maybe Pop would send an update soon, which reminded me I owed him a letter. I'd write one tonight.

In between editing articles and going over ads that Peggy had worked on, I thought about everything that had gone on for the last week and a half—from Angel coming to town last Monday, to Kirk's revelation this morning. Other than recovering the crowbar, the chief was no further ahead in solving Freddie's murder. And what had been in that black book that Freddie carried with him?

I suddenly remembered the slip of paper I'd taken from Freddie's suit jacket when I was helping Angel pack. I opened my drawer and took the paper from my pocketbook. The only things written on it were some recent dates; the latest was Friday, the day Freddie was killed. I looked at the calendar. The other dates were also Fridays. Was it some kind of reminder for Freddie? Why wouldn't he have just looked at a calendar like I just did? I wondered if it had any connection to the black book. If that were the case, he probably would have written the dates in the book instead of carrying around a slip of paper.

Other than asking a few questions, I really hadn't done much in the way of investigating Freddie's murder. There were too many suspects and very little evidence. If there were no fingerprints on the crowbar, or if the fingerprints didn't match the suspects, I didn't think there was much chance of finding the killer. Angel would live with the shadow of being the last person to have seen her husband alive, and the suspicion that she had killed him would follow her everywhere. Ava would be the subject of whispers that she was the sister of a murderer. I needed to do more to help the chief solve this.

I had an idea. I finished checking Peggy's ads and took them back to her desk. "What are you doing tonight?" I asked.

"Nothing. Ken and his dad are going golfing. I was just going to stay home and read a book. Why?"

"How would you like to go snooping?"

* * *

"Are you sure about this?" Peggy asked for at least the third time.

We were outside one of the trailers parked near the empty stage at the fair. Everyone involved in the war bond rally was in Butler, including Clyde McAllister, who would be guarding that haul.

"Of course I'm sure," I said. "This is the perfect time to take a look around."

"But isn't this breaking and entering?"

"Only if we get caught. Which we won't. Besides, there's no lock on the door."

"I'm not sure I like this," Peggy said.

I opened the door. "Wait out here then." Peggy paused for a moment, then followed me inside.

I expected the trailer to be more utilitarian than it was. It was more like a lounge car on a train. To the right was a table with two benches. Several magazines were on top of the table. And I was happy to see a copy of the *Herald*. To the left were a sofa and chairs covered in a blue fabric.

"This is nice," Peggy said.

Beyond the sofa and chairs was a curtained area. That seemed like the most promising place to search. I headed that way with Peggy right behind me.

"What are we looking for anyway?" she asked.

"I don't know. I'll know it when I see it." At least I hoped I would.

I slid the curtain aside. The area appeared to be a small dressing area. There was a clothes rack—empty now except for a few neckties. There was a full-length mirror leaning against the wall and a small table with a chair. I imagined this was used for makeup touch-ups. There were some shelves on the opposite wall. One shelf contained a stack of papers. I pointed to it. "That might be worth a look."

"Does it seem to you we're always searching through papers?" Peggy asked as she handed me some.

"Maybe because we are." The papers she'd given me were bound together on one side. It was a script for something called *Paris Undercover*. I scanned the first couple of pages. "This isn't half bad," I said. "I wonder who it belongs to."

Peggy took a look. "My guess would be Freddie or Kirk. It's some kind of spy picture and the hero is a man. Of course, Angel or Belinda could be auditioning to be a femme fatale."

"That wouldn't be much of a stretch for Belinda." I put it back on the shelf. We didn't find anything in the other papers until I came across one with dates on it in the same handwriting as the one I'd found in Freddie's room. The dates on this page were from a month ago, and like Freddie's, they were all Fridays. I told Peggy.

"I wonder what the significance of Friday dates is," she said. "And why would you even need to write them all down like that? Just pick up a calendar."

I thought about that for a minute before it hit me. "Fridays are paydays."

"For most people, yes," Peggy said. "But do actors get paid like regular people?"

"I don't know. It's the only thing I can come up with, though."

The rest of the search didn't turn up anything, so we moved on to the second trailer. This one wasn't as fancy, containing only a cot and a table and chairs. It looked like this was where Clyde spent most of his time when he wasn't standing guard. There were no papers or magazines, and a quick walk-through didn't turn up a thing—not even spare bullets for his gun. I guess he didn't expect to use any. Probably a good thing.

Peggy and I left the trailer and we both decided we needed a funnel cake before we went home. We sat down at one of the picnic tables with our snack. I'd just taken a bite when I saw Wanda Wilkins and her husband Wayne coming our way. It was too bad Wayne's last name was Reynolds. Without the alliteration, Wanda Reynolds just didn't have the same ring to it.

"I know why you're here," Wanda said when she and Wayne reached us.

"I'm here for the funnel cakes," Peggy said. She could be a smart aleck at times, which was one reason why we were best friends.

Wanda ignored the comment. "I saw you go into that trailer over there."

"So?" I said.

"Who gave you permission to do that?" she asked. "I have half a mind to call the police."

Half a mind was right.

"You can't do that," Peggy said.

"And why not?" Wanda placed her hands on her hips.

I had a feeling Peggy was about to beg for mercy, but I had a better idea. I kicked her under the table. "Aren't you forgetting something?"

Wanda tilted her head. "I don't forget anything."

"You seem to have forgotten that Kirk Allen is a friend of mine."

"What does that have to do with you breaking into that trailer?" she asked.

I wiped powdered sugar from my fingers. "The trailers belong to the Hollywood Victory Committee and travel with the actors and actresses. Kirk is one of the actors. We were checking on it for him since they're in Butler tonight for their rally." It was only a little fib.

"Mr. Allen asked you to check it?" Wanda asked.

"Of course he did," I said. This time Peggy kicked me under the table. That was a bigger fib, but it beat explaining to the chief what I was doing. "The security guard went to the rally too. There was no one else to ask."

"He could have asked the police," Wanda said.

"Dad is much too busy," I said.

"Dad?" Wanda's memory wasn't as good as she claimed.

"Chief Turner. Bill's dad. My future father-in-law."

Wanda didn't seem to know how to respond. She couldn't very well say she forgot about Bill. We had always been together.

Wayne finally spoke up. "Let's go, Wanda."

"But . . ."

He took her by the elbow. "It was nice seeing the two of you." He led Wanda away.

When they were out of earshot, I started laughing and Peggy did too.

"I shouldn't be laughing," Peggy said. "What if she finds out Kirk didn't ask us to check the trailer?"

"She won't. She'll be too tongue-tied if she sees Kirk again. Besides, I'll tell him first. He'll back us up."

Peggy stopped laughing. "Do you really think you should tell him?"

"Why not?"

"Well, I like Kirk and all, but he's still a suspect."

"I know he is, but I don't think he killed Freddie."

"But you don't know that for sure."

Peggy could always bring me back to reality. I couldn't go by what I felt or what I thought. The fact was Kirk *was* still a suspect. And just like with Angel and Ava, I needed proof he wasn't a murderer. I intended to find it.

Chapter Nineteen

U-Boat Sunk West of Bermuda

The Progress Herald, July 1, 1942

It was only around nine when I got home. Lily was still at the fair manning the cotton candy booth with Cindy, and Cindy's parents would bring her home later. Since there were no bond sales tonight, Mom had the evening to herself. I found her sitting at the kitchen table with her good stationery writing a letter to Pop.

"Tell Pop I said hello," I said. "I owe him a letter."

"Why don't you sit here with me and write one now?" Mom slid a blank piece of paper across the table.

I'd planned on trying to read *Frenchman's Creek* again, but writing to Pop was a better idea. I poured a glass of milk and retrieved a fountain pen from the table in the hallway and sat down. I filled Pop in on the goings on at the *Herald* and about the fair and the bond drive. I described the actors and asked if he remembered Eugene Allen. I told him about Richie's death at Midway, but I didn't mention Freddie's murder. In Pop's last letter he said he was settled and would start sending more firsthand accounts to publish in the *Herald*. I told him I was looking forward to them. By the time I finished, I had written three pages.

Mom was still writing, and she had tears in her eyes. I reached over and squeezed her hand. "Pop will be fine," I said.

"I know." She wiped a tear away. "He says he's not in any danger—at least none that he'll tell me about. I just miss him."

"I do too."

Mom folded the pages of her letter and slipped them into an envelope. "Did you and Peggy have fun tonight?"

I nodded. "At least until we ran into Wanda Wilkins and her husband. She's still a pill."

"Wasn't she at Richie's funeral?"

"She was." I told Mom how Kirk had charmed her practically speechless.

"Louise seemed to be upset with Eugene for some reason," Mom said. "What was that all about?"

I shrugged. I wasn't sure she'd understand. Plus, I had made a promise to Kirk. "Louise wouldn't say. It's not important, though." I didn't think Mom believed me, but she didn't pursue it.

We moved to the living room and listened to the radio until Lily came home smelling like spun sugar. It wasn't the first time I thought someone should make a cologne of that scent. It would remind people of happier carefree days and take their minds off the war for a little while.

* * *

I was almost asleep when Lily got into the other twin bed in the room we shared.

"Are you still awake?" she whispered.

"Sort of. Why?"

"Do you think Kirk is too old for me? I don't mean now—I mean when I graduate in a few years."

I smiled in the dark. "He's the same age as me. When you're eighteen he'll be twenty-six."

"So he won't be too old," Lily said.

"No, but I'm sure by then you'll have met someone else."

"Like you and Bill?"

"Yep."

She sighed. "All the boys I go to school with are such . . . such . . . children. It's terrible. All they want to do is make armpit noises and shoot spitballs."

I laughed. "It wasn't any different when I was your age. Bill hit me with one of those spitballs."

"He did?"

"Of course. Girls just mature faster. It will be a whole different story in a year or two."

"I still think Kirk and I would make a nice couple."

I couldn't very well explain why that wouldn't work. "Should I let Kirk know you have it all planned?"

"Don't you dare!" she said. "I would be mortified if he knew I liked him."

"Your secret is safe with me. My lips are sealed."

"Good." Lily yawned. "I'm glad you're my big sister."

"I'm glad you're my little sister." I lay awake with a smile on my face for a long time—well after Lily fell asleep. I finally did the same myself. For the first time in several days I had no thoughts of murder on my mind. If only that would last.

*   *   *

The good news that came over the wire on Thursday was that Churchill had easily survived a no-confidence vote in the House of Commons. The final tally was 475 to 25 in favor of Churchill's leadership. The whole situation had been ludicrous. John Wardlaw-Milne, a Conservative Party politician, wanted to oust Churchill, nominating the Duke of Gloucester to take his place. I couldn't imagine anyone but Churchill leading England's war effort, especially not the duke.

Rex had covered the rally in Butler the previous night, and he had turned in his article before nine AM. I made a minor change in his headline and set it aside to send down to Donny later. Frank was investigating a report of counterfeit gas ration stamps. Just that morning I'd talked to someone who wanted to know why there would be a demolition derby when gas and rubber were being rationed. I explained that the vehicles were being donated as scrap for the war effort and the drivers were using their own ration stamps. It wasn't anything like the Indianapolis 500, which had been suspended until the war was over. Our derby was barely even a race. Even so, it would probably be the last one unless there were more who wanted to donate their old vehicles. The manufacturing of automobiles had stopped, so it was more likely people would hold on to them. I wrote an article for tomorrow's paper explaining the issue. Between my piece, Frank's article on gas stamps, and Ken's on the derby itself, we had all angles covered.

I'd brought a sandwich with me and ate an early lunch at my desk while I worked. By noon I was all caught up and could afford to take a few hours out of the office. I took a walk up to Ava's beauty shop to see how Angel was doing. And ask a few questions, of course. I was surprised to see Ava sitting at the front desk in her shop reading a *Photoplay*. When I opened the door she perked up until she saw it was me.

"Oh," she said. "I thought it was a customer."

I closed the door behind me. "Having a slow day?"

"A slow week. Hardly anyone has come in, and a few canceled their appointments." Ava put her magazine aside. "No one wants their hair done by the sister of a possible murderer."

"That wasn't the case the last time I stopped by."

"That was before that piece of—before that Freddie Harrison was murdered—and deservedly so, I might add."

"I didn't realize that was before he was killed."

"You have a terrible memory for someone so young."

I didn't argue with her. "What can I do to help?"

"You can find the killer and clear Angel's name," Ava said. "Especially since Chief Turner isn't doing his job."

"He's doing the best he can. There's not much evidence. Whoever killed Freddie covered their tracks very well."

"That fact right there should clear Angel," she said. "I don't mean to speak ill of my sister, but she's not the sharpest knife in the drawer. She wouldn't know the first thing about covering up a crime."

I couldn't help thinking she might if she was playing a part. Angel was smarter than Ava gave her credit for. "Who do you think killed him?" I asked.

"How should I know?" she snapped.

"Come on, Ava. You know and see most of what goes in Progress. Surely you've heard something."

"Angel thinks it was Belinda Fox."

"I know that," I said. "I want to know what you think—or what you've heard from someone besides your sister."

Ava hesitated before answering. "This has to stay between you and me. And I'm not saying I think he did it, but it's possible. I'm worried that he might have. He's always had a temper. It was worse when he was drinking. And if he was provoked . . . well . . . he could have."

"You're talking about your father, aren't you?"

She nodded. "I feel awful for even thinking it. I know he has to be at the top of Chief Turner's suspects after he threatened Freddie with the shotgun."

"He is." I mentally searched for something to set her mind at ease and didn't come up with much. "If your father killed Freddie, would he have covered it up?"

"I don't know."

"When I talked to him about pulling the shotgun on Freddie, he didn't hesitate to say he wasn't sorry about it."

"If that's supposed to make me feel better, it's not working," Ava said.

"Wouldn't he have done the same if he was the one who killed him?" I asked. "Wouldn't he just admit it?" Ned had been near the top of my suspect list too, until now. He wouldn't have hesitated to turn himself in. He wouldn't have gone out of his way to get rid of the crowbar. He certainly would never let Angel take the blame for something he did.

Relief showed on Ava's face. "Oh, thank goodness. He didn't do it either. If my dad was a cold-blooded killer, he'd be the first to admit it."

As strange as that sounded, I had to agree. "So where does that leave us?"

Ava folded her arms. "With exactly who Angel said—Belinda Fox."

I'd learned the hard way that the most obvious suspect wasn't always the correct one. Belinda could very well be a murderer, but then so could Kirk. As much as I'd like to, I couldn't rule him out. I also couldn't rule out Angel yet. There was also Paul Davis. I'd hardly had a chance to speak to him at all. I knew almost nothing about him other than it seemed he and Belinda didn't get along. And what about the security guard, Clyde McAllister? I only had his word that he had seen Angel leave and that Belinda had been looking for Freddie. I needed to verify this with Paul Davis since he'd been with Belinda at the time. It would give me a chance to ask him a few more questions. I was about to mention these other suspects to Ava when Ellen Petrie entered the shop and asked about getting her hair done.

Ava was thrilled to have an actual customer. I said goodbye to both of them and left to do some sleuthing.

* * *

I'd forgotten to ask Ava how Angel was doing, so I decided to stop at Ava's house and see for myself. I had questions for her anyway. The house was a short walk from the beauty shop, and when I arrived Angel was sitting on the front porch. The black wreath was no longer hanging on the front door. There wasn't a trace of black in her clothing, either. She wore pink shorts and a sleeveless pink and white polka dot blouse tied at the waist. Her blonde hair was pulled back in a loose chignon. I wondered again how she managed to bring so many clothes with her.

"Hi, Irene," she said. "This is a nice surprise."

"I just stopped to see your sister and thought I'd check on you." I took a seat in the wicker chair beside her. "How are you?"

"I'm doing all right," she said. "I wish they'd find Freddie's killer, though. Everywhere I go people stare at me. No one believes that I didn't do it. I loved Freddie."

I'd been trying to determine if she was playing a character or being herself for a change and I decided on the latter—at least for now. "It's just a matter of time. The chief won't let anyone get away with murder."

"I hope so. Chief Turner told us he found the murder weapon. That should help."

He was probably trying to see if it rattled her. I wondered who else he'd told. "Have you found that black book you were looking for?"

Angel shook her head. "No. I think Freddie must not have brought it with him."

I didn't pursue it. It was either that or whoever had searched his room had it. I doubted he'd forgotten it. Angel said she wanted to donate Freddie's clothes to charity, and I suggested she call St. Michael's. Father O'Connor would know who could use them. She had also decided to have Freddie's body sent to Los Angeles for burial. After that, I asked her how the rally in Butler had been.

"It would have been lovely if it wasn't for *her*," Angel said. "The way she flirted with those reporters was disgusting. If she'd hiked up her dress any higher—well—you know."

Angel now sounded like a schoolmarm from a western movie.

"It was indecent. And before the rally, she just about draped herself over one of the city councilmen. He was old enough to be her grandfather! I told Paul he needs to rein her in before she gives someone a disease."

I hid a smile with my hand. "What did Paul say about that?"

Angel shook her head. "He said he would, but I'm sure she won't listen. They hate each other. Kirk said I should ignore her,

178

but it's hard—especially when she talks about Freddie. She makes it sound like they were Romeo and Juliet."

I wondered if she knew how that story turned out.

"Freddie really was going to end things with her. He promised. He planned to tell her the news right after I left."

"Clyde McAllister said he talked to you when you were leaving that day."

Angel smiled. "He did. Clyde is so nice, and he's a good listener. He knew all about that witch getting her claws into Freddie. I told him Freddie and I were getting back together."

"What did he have to say about that?" I asked.

"He was very happy for us."

He may have told her he was happy about it, but when I had spoken to him, it was apparent he didn't like Freddie. He thought Freddie and Belinda deserved each other. It would be a good idea to find out more about him.

When I left Angel, I walked back to the *Herald*. I hadn't learned much at all. I still had the same suspects as before. I hadn't quite ruled out Angel or Ava, although it was looking less and less likely that either of them had killed Freddie. Kirk was still in the running as well. It seemed more and more likely that Belinda Fox had killed her lover. If Freddie had ended their relationship, I could see her being angry enough to hit him with the crowbar and cold-blooded enough to cover it up.

As I neared the Excelsior, Greta Gray's limousine pulled up to the curb. I stopped walking so I wouldn't have to speak to her. Her driver rounded the vehicle and opened the back door for her to exit. Greta wasn't alone. Much to my surprise, Belinda Fox stepped out of the limo right behind her.

Chapter Twenty

First B-17 Flying Fortress Arrives in England
The Progress Herald, July 2, 1942

I f birds of a feather flocked together, these two had to be birds of prey. I'd been told that Belinda would do anything to advance her career, and this seemed like proof to me. Although Greta Gray was known for nasty gossip, if an actor or actress could manage to stay in her good graces, it often resulted in better roles and more press. It also often backfired. One tiny little thing, and Greta would turn quicker than a propeller on an airplane. I wanted to know what they were up to.

I walked to the corner and back to give them enough time to enter the hotel and go up to their respective rooms, hoping Greta didn't decide to park herself in the lobby as usual. I went inside and Greta was indeed in the lobby complaining about something to the front desk clerk. I hightailed it past her and into the elevator without being seen.

The elevator attendant recognized me from the last time I'd been there, and I didn't even have to give her the floor number. Outside Belinda's room, I raised my hand to knock on the door. I stopped when I heard her voice on the other side and leaned closer to the door.

"I don't want to hear it," Belinda said.

I expected to hear another voice responding. Instead there was a pause.

"You didn't have a problem with it before," Belinda said.

She was either rehearsing something or talking on the telephone.

"Nothing has changed except it's me now," she said. Another pause. "I don't care. I'll expect it on schedule. Tonight. No excuses."

She hung up the receiver so hard I heard the bell inside the telephone ding. I knocked on the door.

Belinda opened the door a few inches. "What do you want?"

I should have had some kind of plan in mind, but I didn't. It was fortunate I could think on my feet. I gave her my biggest, friendliest smile. "I'd like another interview," I said. "I know we got off on the wrong foot, but my readers are clamoring to know more about you. The telephone calls have been endless."

That seemed to do the trick. She opened the door the rest of the way. "Come in. I don't have a lot of time, but I'm happy to answer a few questions for my fans." She pointed to one of the chairs. "Have a seat."

I sat down and retrieved my notepad and pencil from my pocketbook so she'd think this was a real interview. Well, it was—just not the kind she thought.

"Can I get you anything? I can ring room service."

"No thank you. I don't want to keep you long. I know how busy you must be."

Belinda sat in the other chair. She smoothed her navy skirt in a practiced motion. I'd bet a nickel if I had been a man she would have adjusted it upward to show more leg. I'd bet she didn't have a shortage of stockings like the rest of us, either. Personally, I didn't mind going bare-legged in the summer, but I'd be wearing trousers more often once the weather got cold again.

"I appreciate your consideration for my time," she said. "Not everyone does. But it goes with the territory."

"I guess it does. It must get tiring," I said. "Do you get much time for yourself?"

Belinda let out a dramatic sigh. "Very little. But that's the sacrifice I must make to keep the public happy. That's all I ever want to do."

Oh, brother. I opened my notebook to a blank page. "Tell me a little bit about yourself." I jotted down a few things as she talked. She grew up in Peoria, Illinois, only child, starred in every school play, and she left home for Hollywood at seventeen. With all that established, I asked her how she met Freddie.

"We met at a party at Greta Gray's."

Now that was interesting. "I didn't realize you knew Miss Gray."

"Everyone knows Greta," she said. "Or at least knows of her. We're very good friends." I wasn't sure I believed that. "As a matter of fact, she has me to thank for getting her a new chauffeur when her last one quit suddenly. Blake was hauling our trailers and now he's her private driver. It worked out for both of them."

We were getting off track. "Let's get back to how you met Freddie."

"You know Greta has two places—one in Manhattan and one in LA."

I didn't, but I nodded anyway.

"Freddie's whimpering wife couldn't make it to the party, so Greta paired us up."

Angel didn't whimper. At least not that I'd heard.

"We fell in love." Belinda paused, then burst into tears. "Oh, Freddie, why did you have to die?"

She wasn't a very good actress. Even I could tell the tears were manufactured.

Belinda dabbed at her eyes with a handkerchief. "I just know Angel killed him. She didn't want us to be together."

"According to Angel, they were getting back together," I said.

"She's a scheming little liar. Freddie loved me. He told me he'd left her for good."

"Did you see Freddie the day he was killed?"

"Of course. We had breakfast in bed."

"What about after that?" I asked.

"Freddie said he had some business to attend to. He planned on meeting me at the fairgrounds later."

"What kind of business?"

Belinda shrugged. "I really don't know. Freddie had many . . . investments."

"What kind of investments?" I asked.

She looked down and picked at a fingernail. "He didn't talk about it."

Belinda was lying. I was sure of it. I'd have to ask Angel if she knew about any investments. Maybe it had something to do with the black book with names and numbers. "So he met you at the fairgrounds later—"

"I didn't say that. I said he was supposed to meet me. I got to the fairgrounds right before we were set to rehearse. That's when he didn't show up."

According to Clyde, she was there much earlier than that. I didn't want to give away that I'd caught her in two lies, so I kept it to myself.

She started crying again. "Oh, Freddie. What am I going to do without my Freddie?"

I was out of questions for the moment. I would have loved to ask her about the telephone call I had overheard, but that would be showing my hand. "You'll be fine," I said. "You have your whole career ahead of you."

She smiled suddenly. "I do, don't I? I owe it all to Freddie."

I closed my tablet and slipped it into my pocketbook. "Thank you for talking to me," I said.

"When will you publish the article?"

"I'm sorry to say it won't be until next week. You'll be gone by then. I can send you a copy if you'd like." Now I was the one telling whoppers. There would be no such article. Belinda walked me to the door and, as we passed the table with the telephone, I noticed something I hadn't seen on the way in. There was a book with a black cover beside the phone. It had to be the one Angel had been searching for. I couldn't think of a way to ask about it, but at least I knew where it was.

I left the hotel and headed back to the *Herald* with that black book on my mind. If Freddie had been so secretive about it, what was Belinda doing with it? More importantly, what was in it?

*   *   *

Peggy followed me into my office and closed the door behind her. "How was Angel? Did you find out anything?" She sat down in the chair across from me.

I told her what Angel said about Clyde.

"So you don't think Clyde told you the whole truth?"

"Either he didn't or Angel didn't. My money's on Angel. I think she only sees what she wants to see. She could very well think that

184

Clyde was happy for her when he wasn't. For all we know, Angel might think she and Freddie were getting back together when the opposite was true."

I filled her in about Belinda Fox and Greta Gray, my talk with Belinda in her hotel room, and the black book. "I'm sure it's the book Angel was looking for when we helped her pack up Freddie's belongings."

"Tell me more about the telephone call you overheard."

"There's not much more to tell," I said. "Belinda was insistent that whoever she was talking to give her something before the day is over."

"What do you think it is?"

I shrugged. "I don't know. Could be a lot of things. Whoever was on the other end must have balked at whatever it was. Belinda said something like 'you didn't have a problem before,' so the person had done it before. Maybe a favor of some kind? She's an actress, so it could be something to do with a part in a film. Honestly, I have no idea."

"If we could figure out who was on the other end of the call, we could ask them," Peggy said.

"The problem is, it could be anybody," I said. "What I need to do is get hold of that book somehow."

"And just how do you propose doing that? Belinda isn't just going to hand it over."

"I know that. I need to get into her room when she's not there."

"The front desk isn't going to let you in there," Peggy said.

I thought for a minute. "If Freddie's room is still empty, we could reserve it for the night. Belinda's room adjoins it. We might be able to get in that way."

"What's this *we* stuff?" Peggy said.

"I thought you liked adventure."

"Adventure, yes. Getting caught by a possible murderer, no."

"You're forgetting Belinda won't be there tonight. She'll be at the fair."

"I still don't like the idea." Peggy's telephone rang and she pushed out of the chair. "She could still find out. She'll know someone was in there when she sees that book is missing."

Peggy was right, but that was a chance I had to take. I picked up the receiver and dialed the number for the Excelsior. Five minutes later I hung up disappointed. Freddie's former room was occupied as of thirty minutes ago. I'd have to figure out another way to get into Belinda's room.

* * *

I was still trying to figure it out after dinner. Mom and Lily had left for the fair and I was sitting on the front porch. I was so lost in thought, I jumped when the screen door slammed. Sylvia had worked the daylight shift at Tabor and came outside to join me.

"I didn't mean to startle you," she said.

"That's all right."

Sylvia took a seat. "What's on your mind?"

I shook my head. "I'm just trying to come up with an idea for something and I'm at a loss."

"An article for the paper?"

"Definitely not."

"Maybe I can help you figure it out," she said.

I hadn't known Sylvia for long, but I knew she would keep anything I told her to herself. "I'm trying to figure out how to get into someone's hotel room without them knowing it."

"That's not what I expected to hear. I know plenty of ways to get into someone's room, but usually he's with me."

"That's not what I mean!"

"I know. I'm only teasing. Why do you need to get into the hotel room?"

I told her.

"That's some story," she said. "And you think that book has something to do with that actor's murder?"

"It has to," I said. "I could tell Angel where it is and let her deal with Belinda, or tell the chief, but I want a good look at it. The only way to do that is if I get my hands on it first."

Sylvia grinned. "You're in luck then. Did I ever tell you I used to work for a locksmith?"

Thirty minutes later, we were outside Belinda's room at the Excelsior.

"Stand guard," Sylvia ordered.

"Are you sure you know how to do this?" I was nervous and excited at the same time. If we got caught, the chief would not be happy with me.

"Of course I do," she said. "These locks have to be twenty or thirty years old. A baby could open them. This skeleton key has never failed me."

"I'm amazed that locksmith let you have a skeleton key."

"He didn't. Not exactly anyway," Sylvia said. "He owed me three days' pay and refused to give it to me. I took this and went back later to get my money." The door unlocked and she straightened. "I kept the key. I don't even think he missed it. He never came after me anyway."

"Not even for the money?"

Sylvia pushed the door open. "Nope. He was a good locksmith, but a lousy bookkeeper. I doubt he even knew what was in the cash register."

I took a handkerchief out of my pocketbook and wiped the doorknob. I knew enough about fingerprints to know not to leave any—especially Sylvia's. I'd already been in the room, so I wasn't as worried about mine. "Don't touch anything you don't have to."

Sylvia gave me an *I'm not an idiot* look. "What do you think Belinda will do when she finds the book missing?"

I shrugged. "I really don't care. It doesn't belong to her. I doubt she'll report it to the police or she'd have to admit she had it." The book was right beside the telephone where I'd seen it earlier. I picked it up and dropped it into my pocketbook.

"Aren't you going to look at it?" Sylvia asked.

"Not until we get home." I didn't want to take the chance that anyone would see me with it.

Sylvia locked the door with her skeleton key and I wiped the doorknob again in case Belinda reported the theft, as unlikely as that was. We managed to get out of the hotel without incident, and I was more than relieved Greta Gray wasn't in the lobby. Once we arrived home, we went to the kitchen and sat down at the table. I got Freddie's book out of my handbag and placed it on the table.

"Mind if I get something to drink?" Sylvia asked.

"Not at all. You don't have to ask. Always help yourself. Nothing in the kitchen is off limits. It's your home too."

"Thanks."

I opened the book while Sylvia poured a glass of orange juice. The inside of the book wasn't anything like I'd pictured. I had imagined scribbled names and numbers, but this looked more like an actual ledger. There were maybe a dozen pages filled in. The rest of the book was blank. Angel had told me she had spotted names before Freddie took the book from her, but if these were names, I didn't recognize them. They were either nicknames or some kind of code name. Each page had one name at the top. There was Blue Lou, Roman Legion, Old Gray Mare, The Professor, Pink Lady, Scarlett O'Hara, and a half dozen others. I showed Sylvia. "How am I supposed to figure out who they are—if they're even real people?"

"Maybe his wife will know," Sylvia said.

"It's possible, I guess. She only got a quick glimpse of the inside, but maybe Freddie talked about some of these people and used those names."

"What do you think those numbers mean?" Sylvia asked.

"They actually make more sense to me than the names." I pointed to Blue Lou's page. "See how almost all the numbers are the same and there's a dollar sign in front?"

Sylvia nodded.

"I think either Blue Lou was paying Freddie or Freddie was paying him. My guess is Freddie was the one collecting."

"What do you think he was collecting for?"

"I'm not sure," I said. "Maybe he was a bookie? That would explain how he had enough lettuce to own a home next to Clark Gable. All the roles he had were in lousy movies. He'd have to supplement his acting income somehow."

We paged through the rest of the book. If these were indeed payments, he had collected a small fortune. One entry—The Elephant—had paid him over a hundred thousand dollars. If Freddie had been a bookie, though, he'd have had to pay out once in a while, but nothing on these pages showed anything like that. I wondered if Angel and Freddie had a joint bank account. If

Freddie had been hiding this from her, it was more than likely he had a separate account that she didn't know about. I'd ask when I turned the book over to her.

I closed the book, and Sylvia and I chatted for a while. When Mom and Lily came home we all sat in the living room. We listened to the radio and my mother and sister told us about their evening at the fair. War bond sales were still going strong. We laughed when Lily said she was sick of cotton candy and swore she'd never eat it again.

When I went to bed I was still thinking about those names and numbers. I'd almost drifted off to sleep when it hit me. I sat up and pulled the book out from under my mattress. I didn't want to wake Lily by turning on a light so I took the book over to the window and pushed the curtain aside. The street light was bright enough to see the pages. Although the amounts varied from person to person, they were consistent for each individual. Between that and the fact it didn't appear as if Freddie had been making any payments, I came to the realization that Freddie hadn't been a bookie.

He'd been a blackmailer.

Chapter
Twenty-One

Churchill Easily Survives 'No Confidence' Vote 475-25
The Progress Herald, July 3, 1942

That had to be it. It made perfect sense. It also opened up a big reason why someone would want him dead. Anyone listed here was a suspect—provided they were here in Progress, which meant it had to be someone with the bond tour. I needed to find out who these nicknames belonged to. I hoped Angel would be able to help. It was already after eleven—much too late to talk to her now. I got back in bed. I'd make time tomorrow.

As usual, I was the first one into the *Herald* in the morning. I put coffee on to percolate and went back to my office. I opened Freddie's book on my desk. The more I thought about it the more I was sure that these entries were Freddie's way to record his blackmail payments. I wished he had used actual names, though. Blue Lou, Roman Legion, Old Gray Mare, The Professor, Pink Lady, and Scarlett O'Hara could be just about anybody. I paged through the rest of the book, but none of those nicknames rang a bell either.

The dates of the payments were consistent. They were all on Fridays, but they varied from person to person. Some were monthly, some biweekly, and others weekly. I wondered how the victims got the money to Freddie. Had he insisted on cash? Or money orders? Checks could be traced, but maybe that hadn't been a problem. I was sure he'd have come up with some kind of excuse if anyone questioned it.

I went to the kitchen and filled my coffee mug, taking it back to my desk. Today was Friday. I imagined some people were breathing a little easier now that no payment would be due today. Except . . . Belinda had had the book. That phone call I'd overheard wasn't about anything movie related. She was continuing Freddie's blackmail. The victim had to be someone with the bond rally tour—Angel, Kirk, Paul Davis, or even the security guard Clyde McAllister. I eliminated Angel right away, so that left the other three.

Kirk certainly had something to hide. If his secret was revealed, it would be the end of his career. I thought about his comment that Freddie had made his life a living hell. Blackmail would certainly do that. I hated to think it, but if Freddie was blackmailing Kirk, it made him the number one suspect in Freddie's murder. I heard the front door open, so I slipped the book into my top drawer.

Seconds later, Rex came into my office. He hadn't even stopped at his desk to drop off his fedora. He set a copy of a newspaper on my desk. "You need to see this. Turn to page three," he said.

Rex's tone of voice and a glance at the front page told me I wasn't going to like it. The paper was the *Hollywood Buzz*, the rag Greta Gray wrote for. I opened it to the third page. Her headline made my blood boil. I read it aloud. *"Hick Police Chief Unable to Solve Simple Murder."* I looked up at Rex.

"Believe it or not, it gets worse," he said.

I read on.

After almost a week, actor Freddie Harrison's grisly murder remains unsolved. Freddie's estranged wife, Angel, remains free. She was the very last person to see him alive, and she had more than enough reason to want him dead. Freddie had left her for the beautiful starlet, Belinda Fox, who tells me Freddie was the love of her life and they planned to marry after he divorced his current wife. It turns out that Angel is the sister of beauty shop owner Ava Dempsey, and the daughter of Ned Dempsey, who owns the diner in town. Angel's father threatened poor Freddie with a shotgun. I've been told Freddie was terrified of both his wife and father-in-law. Why hasn't Police Chief Walter Turner made an arrest? And why hasn't the town's poor excuse for a newspaper, the Progress Herald, published one word of this? Could it be because editor Irene Ingram is engaged to the chief's son? I smell the stink of a cover-up.

I slammed my fist on my desk. "Why that—that—witch!"

"You put it too mildly," Rex said. "I called her a lot worse when I read this."

"Where did you get this? They don't sell this in town anywhere."

"A friend of mine saw it yesterday. He picked up a copy for me and I drove into Pittsburgh last night to get it."

I couldn't remember the last time I was this angry. "She's not going to get away with this."

"The good thing is I'm likely the only one in Progress with a copy."

"I'm going to put a stop to it. She can't tell lies like this and not expect there to be consequences."

"And how do you plan on doing that?" Rex asked.

"Tell the chief about it for starters. Then she's going to get a piece of my mind. After that? I don't know."

"I have an idea," Rex said. "Tit for tat."

"What does that mean?" I asked.

"You know the other day when I said I had a contact in LA that could dig some things up for us?"

"I remember. But so far he hasn't."

"I'm going to give him a ring. See what he's got and ask him for dirt on Greta Gray."

I shook my head. "Find out what he knows, but I'm not stooping to her level. I'm not about to turn this paper into a gossip rag. We report the news."

"Suit yourself."

"However, I'm not above writing a scathing editorial on the damage gossip, innuendo, and plain old lies can do."

Rex grinned. "I like that idea." He pushed out of the chair. "You're definitely Pete's girl. He'd be proud of you."

I waited until he closed the door behind him before I teared up. Rex had been the hardest one to convince that I could do this job. He'd been dead set against me taking over for Pop. He had known me since I was a toddler and, until recently, he seemed to think I was still that little girl instead of a capable young woman. What Rex had just said meant more to me than anyone would ever know. I wiped the tears away, rolled a sheet of paper into my typewriter, and got to work.

* * *

I had just pulled the finished editorial from my typewriter when Peggy came in. "Rex showed me that column," she said. "I can't believe the nerve of that woman. I'd like to skin her alive."

"Get in line," I said. "I'm sure we're not the only ones, either." I handed her what I'd just written. "See what you think of this while I refill my coffee. Can I bring you one?"

"Sure. Thanks."

When I returned, Peggy was smiling. "I love it," she said. "It sure gets the point across. I'd bet anything old Greta Gray expects you to roll in the mud with her."

I set my coffee mug down so quickly, a few drops splashed onto my desk. "What did you say?"

Peggy tilted her head. "I said old Greta Gray—"

"That's it!" I yanked open my drawer and pulled out the black book. "You're a genius."

"I have no idea what you're talking about, but thanks." She pointed to the book. "Is that what I think it is? I thought Freddie's old room was occupied."

"It is." I told her what Sylvia and I had done.

"I'm glad you didn't ask me," she said. "Aren't you afraid Belinda will know what you did?"

I shook my head. "Even if she figures it out, she can't very well admit she had this and that she's blackmailing people just like Freddie was." I explained what I had figured out. "I didn't know who any of these names belonged to until you said old Greta Gray." I flipped to the page I wanted and pointed. "There. Old Gray Mare is Greta Gray. I'm sure of it."

"It makes sense. Sort of," Peggy said. "What about the others?"

"I don't know. Not yet, anyway. I'm hoping Angel will recognize some. Maybe Freddie used some of the nicknames."

Peggy sipped her coffee. "Why would Freddie blackmail Greta Gray? You'd think it would be the other way around."

"It must be bad enough that Greta kept paying instead of exposing Freddie as a blackmailer. She has a lot more clout than Freddie ever had."

"Now I want to know what it was," Peggy said. "Are you going to ask her?"

I shook my head. "No. Not yet. I don't want to expose anyone until I know which one of them killed Freddie. Rex has a friend in LA doing some checking on Greta. I'll wait and see what he turns up." I paused for a moment. "Remember when I told you Kirk said that Freddie made his life a living hell?"

Peggy nodded.

"I think Kirk might be one of the names in this book," I said.

"Why would Freddie blackmail Kirk?"

"I don't know," I lied. I couldn't tell her why. "It's just a feeling I have."

"Well, Kirk's too nice a guy to get mixed up in anything he'd be blackmailed for. I'd cross him off your list." Peggy got up. "I'd better get to work. The boss won't like me lollygagging."

I laughed as she left my office. I leaned back in my chair, thinking. I'd love to eliminate Kirk from the list, but I couldn't just yet. He still had a motive. But so did Greta Gray. The problem with that was she hadn't been in town the day Freddie was killed. She had only arrived the next day. I tried to recall where she said she'd come from. Pittsburgh. That was it. She had called it a hell hole.

Pittsburgh wasn't far. Greta could easily have driven—or had her driver bring her to Progress—to meet with Freddie, then returned to the city. I liked the idea of Greta being the killer much more than Kirk. No one was in the clear, though, and I needed to remember that. There could be no wishful thinking on my part.

When Frank, Ken, and Matt came in, we sorted out their assignments for the day. Frank was still working on the counterfeit gas stamp story. Rex would report on any war news. Ken had some local sports articles to pen, and he was planning to spend the afternoon with the demolition derby drivers preparing for the event that evening. I asked Matt to tag along and get some photographs. I had already decided I'd follow up on the murder investigation. I would start with a visit to the police department.

* * *

"Hi, Jimmy," I said as I crossed the marble floor to the police front desk.

"Morning, Irene. I haven't seen you for a while. You must be keeping busy."

I smiled. "When I stopped in the last time, Rally was at your desk. He said you were at the doctor's. How did it go?"

"It was a big fuss over nothing. He gave me some pills to take." Jimmy pointed to the door behind him. "The chief's in if you want to see him."

I thanked him, gave a quick rap on the door, and went in.

The chief was at his typewriter with papers scattered over his desk. "I can come back if you're too busy," I said.

"I've told you before, I'm never too busy for you. Besides, I need a break."

I sat in the chair opposite him. "I'm not sure how much of a break it'll be." I slid the paper with Greta Gray's column across the desk. "Rex showed this to me earlier. I thought you should see it."

Dad read it quickly. His reaction was more measured than mine—or maybe he just didn't show it. All he did was shake his head.

"Aren't you upset?" I asked.

He handed the paper to me and leaned back in his chair. "That kind of criticism comes with the job. I learned long ago not to let things like this bother me."

"But she's lying. There's no cover-up. I don't want people thinking there is."

"Everyone who knows us will see this is a bunch of baloney. No one around here reads this rag anyway." He smiled. "Anyone with sense only reads the *Herald*."

"I hope you're right," I said. "In any case, I wrote an editorial for the weekend edition."

"I'm sure it'll be a good one."

"Have you heard from the state police lab yet about the crowbar?" I asked.

"It was a dead end. The only clear fingerprints were from the boys who found it and their parents."

"I was afraid of that," I said.

"It doesn't mean the killer's going to get away with it. We're going to keep at it. I have a few leads to follow up on."

"Like what?"

"Nothing for you to be concerned about yet."

He was holding something back. I didn't like it, but then I was doing the same. I couldn't tell him about Freddie's black book until after I talked to Angel.

Dad was eyeing the papers on his desk. I took it as a sign he wanted to get back to work. I got up. "Are you going to the fair tonight?" I asked.

"I haven't missed demolition derby night for the last twenty years," he said. "I'll see you there."

I left, disappointed we weren't any closer to catching Freddie's killer. I hoped that would change after I talked to Angel.

*   *   *

It took Angel a good five minutes to answer the door when I rang the bell at Ava's house. She was still in her nightgown. "Did I wake you?" I asked.

198

"No, I just haven't felt like dressing yet." She held the door open. "Come in. I think there's still coffee if you'd like a cup."

I declined the offer of coffee and sat down on the sofa. I asked her about last night's rally, and we talked about that for a minute. I kept waiting for her to slip into a character, but she didn't. She'd opted for reality for a second time. "I have good news for you," I said.

Angel clapped her hands together. "They caught Freddie's killer? Oh, that's wonderful news!"

I shook my head. "I'm sorry to disappoint you." I pulled Freddie's book out of my bag. "I found this."

Angel jumped to her feet. "I can't believe it! I really thought he must have left it at home." She took the book from my outstretched hand and sat back down. "Where did you find it?"

I couldn't tell her that. Angel would go and confront Belinda and let it slip that I was the one who gave it to her. The last thing I wanted was for Belinda to find out I'd taken it from her room. "Does it matter?"

"Not really. I'm just curious."

"All I can say is it was still at the hotel." It wasn't a lie.

"I don't know how I missed it," she said. "The important thing is that I have it now."

"I looked through it," I said. "I hope you don't mind."

"Not at all." Angel opened it on her lap. She studied a few pages. "I don't understand why Freddie kept this a big secret. It doesn't make any sense." She looked over at me. "What do you make of this?"

I didn't want to come right out and say that I thought Freddie was a blackmailer. She'd find out eventually, but not right now. "I'm not sure," I said. "The numbers seem to be dollar amounts. Did Freddie have some kind of business on the side?"

"He said he had a lot of investments, so maybe that's what those numbers are."

"What about the names at the top of the pages?" I asked. "Do you know anything about them?"

Angel turned a few pages. "That's odd."

"What is?"

"I've heard Freddie use those names before."

Chapter
Twenty-Two

FDR Issues Order for Military Commission to Try Nazi Saboteurs
The Progress Herald, July 3, 1942

"You have?" I said.

"Yes." Angel turned a couple more pages.

"When? What did he say?"

"Freddie liked to make up names for people," Angel said. "Take this one—Pink Lady—she's a costumer at one of the studios. She wears pink all the time."

I looked at Pink Lady's page. She was paying Freddie two dollars a week. Not an exorbitant sum, but it was probably a lot to her even if she made more than the thirty cents an hour minimum wage. "What's her real name?"

"Georgette Ferrara. We call her Georgie."

"Do you know how I could reach her? I'd like to ask her a few questions." Now that Freddie was dead and Belinda didn't have the book any longer, she might be willing to talk to me.

"I can telephone the studio and see if she's working today," Angel said. "If I can get hold of her I'll have her call you at the newspaper."

"Thank you. What can you tell me about the other names?"

Angel went back a page and pointed to the top. "This one—Old Gray Mare—that's Greta Gray."

I had been right.

"I wonder why her name is in here," Angel said. "Freddie only pretended to like her to get good publicity."

I didn't know what to say to that. "Any others?"

"A couple of them seem familiar, but I don't know who they are. I heard Freddie mention the Professor once, but he never said who it was."

I had another question. "Did you and Freddie have a joint bank account, or did you have separate ones?"

"We do—we did have a joint account. I never paid much attention to it. Freddie took care of all the finances. He gave me spending money every month." She pointed to the book. "If these are his investments in a separate account, I don't know anything about it. I'll ask our banker." She sighed. "I've never even balanced a checkbook. I guess I'm going to have to learn."

She should have learned a long time ago. I was grateful that my parents had taught Lily and me about money as soon as we started collecting an allowance. I'm not a math whiz like my little sister, but I knew how to balance a checkbook before I turned twelve. I had one more question for Angel. "Did Freddie have a will?" I asked.

Angel shook her head. "Freddie thought he would live forever." Her voice caught. "He was so very wrong."

I had to agree. And he'd been wrong in more ways than one. A lot more.

* * *

Back at the *Herald*, I kept thinking about my conversation with Angel. I had hoped she'd be able to tell me more, but it wasn't her fault Freddie had kept her in the dark. It was going to be hard for her to adjust to being on her own. Ava would be able to help with that. It seemed Angel had begun to mature in the last couple of days, although it should have happened years ago. It was a good sign she wasn't trying to play a different character all the time. I hoped it would last.

When Peggy came into my office I filled her in on what the chief said and my talk with Angel.

"So you were right about Greta Gray," she said. "What are you going to do about it?"

"Have a little chat with her, but not until I hear from Georgette Ferrara. If Angel was able to get in touch with her, she should be calling soon. If she admits that Freddie had something on her and she was paying him off, it'll confirm what's in the book. If Greta thinks I know what Freddie was up to, maybe she'll admit something."

"Like what? That she killed Freddie? She wasn't even in town then."

"But she was in Pittsburgh," I said. "It's not that far away."

"Do you really think she'd get her hands dirty like that?" Peggy asked. "It seems beneath her."

"I don't think anything is beneath that woman, including murder."

"What about Kirk? You were worried he was in the book for some reason."

"Angel couldn't match any of the other names. He could still be listed. I just don't know."

Peggy grinned all of a sudden. "I wonder what Belinda thought when she couldn't find that book."

I smiled back. "That would have been something to see."

Peggy's telephone rang and she left my office. I reviewed my editorial for the weekend paper and put a few finishing touches on some articles, then took them down to Donny. He wasn't whistling, and I worried it was a bad sign. He looked up when I reached the last step.

"You're awfully quiet today," I said.

"Nothing to whistle about at the moment."

"Why is that?" I was afraid of what the answer might be.

"Betty has to work the evening shift and can't go to the fair with me."

I was relieved she hadn't broken up with him. "That's too bad."

"I was looking forward to it," he said. "Betty was disappointed too. Her foreman changed the schedule yesterday, and she won't be on daylight for another week."

"Are you still going tonight?"

"I haven't decided yet." He pointed to the papers in my hand. "You're early with those."

I passed them to him. "I have some things to do this afternoon so I thought I'd bring them down now."

"I appreciate it."

I started up the stairs, then turned. "If you do go tonight, look for Peggy and me." It was possible I'd regret saying it later, but the shocked look on his face was worth it. Betty had better never break up with him.

*   *   *

Georgette Ferrara telephoned right after lunch. "Angel Harrison asked me to call you." She spoke with a slight accent. "She made it sound important. What do you want?"

"Thanks for calling," I said. Now that I had her on the phone, I wasn't sure exactly what to ask. "I'm sure you know that Freddie Harrison is dead."

"What does that have to do with me?" Georgette asked.

"You must be relieved."

There was a short pause. "Why would I be?"

I plunged right in. The worst that could happen would be her hanging up on me. "I'm not going to beat around the bush. I think Freddie was blackmailing you."

"That's ridiculous. Why would he do that?"

"I don't care why. I just need to know if it's true." When she didn't answer, I continued. "Freddie kept a ledger of sorts. Your name and what you were paying him were on one of the pages. There were others as well."

The next pause was so long I wasn't sure if Georgette was still on the line. "Miss Ferrara? Are you still there?"

"I'm here," she said. "What do you want from me? Do you want money too?"

"No. Nothing of the sort," I assured her. "I'm only trying to come up with reasons why someone wanted him dead."

"I could give you a very long list," Georgette said. "Freddie Harrison was a horrible person. He was mean and cruel and didn't care about anyone but himself. I honestly don't know what Angel saw in him. She's kind and generous—the complete opposite of Freddie. She's the only reason I called you."

"Angel is one of the suspects in Freddie's murder. She was the last person to see him alive, and I would hate to see her charged with Freddie's murder. That's why I'm trying to get to the bottom of this. Anything you can tell me will be helpful."

"Angel would never hurt anyone," Georgette said. "Especially Freddie. What can I do to help?"

"Tell me the truth. Was Freddie blackmailing you?"

"Yes," she said. "And I'll even tell you why."

"I don't need to know why."

"It might help you to see what kind of a person he was."

"From what others have said, I have a pretty good idea."

"I want to tell you," she said. "Two years ago, Freddie found out my mother is living with me."

"Why would he blackmail you for that?" I asked.

"Because she's not here legally. I brought her up from Mexico. At first she only planned to visit, but neither one of us could bear for her to go back. Freddie threatened to have her deported. She's in very bad health. It would kill her to have to go back." She sighed. "So I paid him. I'm not proud of it, but what else could I do?"

How could Freddie have threatened such a thing—to separate a sick woman from her daughter? All for what to him amounted to a pittance. "I understand perfectly. You didn't have a choice. Frankly, I would have done the same thing." The more I heard about Freddie Harrison, the more I disliked him.

"Thank you for understanding."

"Your secret is safe with me," I said.

"I'm not sorry he's dead. I'm only sorry that whoever killed him will have to suffer for it. In my opinion they should be rewarded."

"You're not the only one who feels that way." We talked for another minute or so and I wished her the best. I was angry when I placed the receiver back in the cradle. I might have to tell it in confession, but I hoped Freddie Harrison rotted in hell.

* * *

Before I left for the day at four, I checked for any war news. Another American Liberty ship had been sunk by a U-boat, this time off the coast of Cape Cod. Fortunately, the U-boat was then sunk by a British anti-submarine trawler. The other thing of note was that the Axis had captured Sebastopol, ending a long siege. Although the Russians admitted defeat, they claimed the Germans had suffered 300,000 casualties. I told Donny to use the Associated Press articles for the weekend edition.

I stopped at Markowicz Hardware on the way home to pick up a light bulb for my desk lamp that had just burned out. Sam Markowicz was behind the counter as usual, and I was happy to see Ben Cline perched on crutches fixing a display of flyswatters. I knew Ben was planning on working at the store—at least for a while—but I hadn't known it would be this soon. Both men greeted me with a smile.

"Good afternoon, Irene," Sam said. "I have a new helper."

"I see that," I said. "How are you feeling, Ben?"

"Much better. I'm getting to be a whiz with these crutches. Pretty soon I'll be racing Sam up and down the street."

Sam laughed. "That would not be much of a race. You would most certainly win."

Ben winked at me. "I'll give you a head start."

All three of us laughed at that. It was good to see Ben like this. He'd been in a terrible state of mind after what happened. I was sure Sarah's nurturing had a lot to do with his recovery.

"What can I do for you, Irene?" Sam asked.

"I just need a light bulb for my desk lamp. Nothing too bright, though."

While Sam retrieved one for me, I asked Ben if he'd been to the fair yet.

"I went a couple of nights ago," he said. "Sam and I are going tonight for the derby."

"Sarah's not going?"

He shook his head and smiled. "She said she'd rather stay home and sew. She doesn't like the cars crashing."

"I can understand that."

"I did my part and bought a stamp book to work on getting one of those war bonds now that I'm gainfully employed again."

"So you saw one of the rallies?"

Ben grinned. "Sure did. Both those girls are something. It's hard to believe the blonde one is Ava's sister. They don't seem anything alike."

"If I see you there tonight I can introduce you," I said.

"Really? That would be great."

Sam returned with my light bulb. "What would be great?"

"Irene's going to introduce me to some movie stars," Ben said.

"I would also like to be introduced." Sam lowered his voice to a whisper. "As long as Sarah does not find out."

I paid for my purchase and walked home with a smile on my face.

*   *   *

"Only two more nights of selling cotton candy," I said to Lily as she set the table for an early dinner.

She moaned. "I can't wait until it's over. Even the smell of it makes me sick. I'll never eat it again."

"Think of the spending money you're making." I put a plate of Mom's homemade bread on the table. "You'll be able to buy all the Frank Sinatra records you want."

"That's true," Lily said. "And some new art supplies. But next year, I'm working the popcorn booth."

Mom brought a platter of baked chicken into the dining room and put it on the table. "Don't get ahead of yourself. With the war going on, there might not be a fair next year."

"I can't imagine that," I said. "Harold would never allow it."

Mom pulled out her chair and sat down. "Maybe not—"

The doorbell interrupted whatever she was going to say. I was still on my feet, so I told her I'd get it. I was surprised to see the chief standing there.

"Hello, Irene," he said. "I'm sorry to interrupt your dinner, but I need to ask your mother about something."

"Come on in." I pushed the screen door open. "Why don't you stay and have dinner with us? There's plenty."

Mom stood as we entered the dining room. "This is a surprise, Walt. Irene's right. There's plenty."

Dad looked uncomfortable. "I need to ask you a few questions first, Joan. Then we'll see about dinner."

"Certainly," Mom said.

I had a bad feeling. I'd never seen him like this. I hoped it wasn't bad news of some sort. I didn't think it could be about Pop. That news would have come by telegram. Maybe something happened to her sister? If that were the case, Donny would have called. I followed them to the living room and stood in the doorway.

Mom sat down on the sofa and Dad took the chair opposite. "What's going on?" she asked.

"I don't want you to take this the wrong way," he said.

"Take what the wrong way? You haven't asked me anything yet."

"The proceeds from the war bond sales from last night are missing," he said. "Do you have any idea what happened to them?"

Chapter
Twenty-Three

Demolition Derby Scheduled for Tonight
The Progress Herald, July 3, 1942

"What?" I said from the doorway. "Are you serious?"

The chief turned his head toward me. "Very."

Mom's mouth opened but nothing came out.

I entered the room and sat down beside her. "You can't possibly think my mother had anything to do with that."

"I didn't say she did," he said calmly. "I only asked if she had any idea what happened."

"That's the same thing," I snapped. "If she knew what happened she'd have told you when it happened."

Mom put her hand on my knee. "Why don't you go and eat dinner with your sister."

"No. Absolutely not."

She raised an eyebrow but didn't ask again. She turned to Dad. "What do you need to know?"

"What was the procedure when you finished last night?" he asked.

"Martha and I tallied up the sales just like we did every night. All the money went into a lockbox, and Martha handed it over to the security guard."

"Clyde McAllister?" I asked.

Mom nodded.

"What about after that?" the chief asked.

"Martha and I chatted with a few people while I waited for Lily to finish."

"Who did you talk to? Who else was there?"

"Ava was there waiting for her sister, so I talked to her for a bit. Let's see. Helen and Dan Petrie. A few women from church. The actors from the rally were there, of course."

"Anyone who seemed out of place?" the chief asked.

"I really didn't pay that close attention," Mom said. "There were many people milling around."

I became impatient with the back and forth. "What exactly is going on, Dad?"

He leaned back in the chair. "I don't want you to breathe a word of this. Promise me."

Mom and I both nodded.

"Somewhere between when the money was handed off to McAllister and he and Paul Davis took it to the bank, the proceeds from last night—a thousand dollars—disappeared."

"Holy moley, that's a lot of lettuce," I said. "Obviously, either McAllister or Davis took it."

"That's what I thought at first. When I questioned McAllister this afternoon, he stated he set the box down for a minute to help a woman who fell."

"Wouldn't the box have been locked?" I asked.

"It should have been," Mom said.

The chief said it wasn't. "McAllister said he set the box down before he'd had a chance to lock it. When he picked it back up, he didn't bother checking the contents and just inserted the key and turned it."

"And you believe him?" I wouldn't have.

"I didn't say that," he said.

"I should have made sure he locked the box. I should have paid more attention and kept my eyes on it," Mom said. "I feel like this is all my fault."

"It's not your fault, Mom. It wasn't your responsibility to make sure the box was locked. That was the guard's job. You had no way of knowing someone would stoop that low."

"If the guard didn't steal the money, it could have been any one of hundreds of people," Mom said.

"Possibly," Dad said. "But a stranger wouldn't have known the box was unlocked—they might have just picked up the whole thing instead of opening it and taking the money. It's likely someone who knew the procedure."

That still left too many people. Anyone could have watched how they worked and planned accordingly. The woman who fell could have been in on it. She might have been a distraction. Then there were the actors. They certainly knew the procedure, but would they risk it? Belinda might. She was familiar enough with at least one name in Freddie's book to continue his blackmail. It wasn't a stretch to think she'd steal.

"Mom, dinner is getting cold," Lily called from the dining room. "Can I eat without you?"

My mother got up. "Walt, you're staying for some chicken. We'll talk more about this later." She didn't wait for an answer.

Dad started to follow. I touched his arm. "Hold up." I waited until Mom was out of earshot. "Is this what you meant this morning when you said you had other leads?"

"Sort of. I'm thinking it's somehow connected to Harrison's murder. I just haven't figured out how."

"I might have an idea," I said. It was time to tell him about the blackmail.

"Irene and Walt, we're waiting for you," Mom called out.

"You'll have to tell me later," he said. "We'd better not keep your mother waiting."

*   *   *

The chief barely had time to eat before the telephone rang. Apparently he left word he'd be at our house, and when Jimmy couldn't raise him on the car radio, he called here to tell him there was a two-vehicle accident near the Anderson place. My revelation would have to wait.

I quickly finished the dishes while Mom and Lily headed to the fairgrounds. Peggy picked me up at six thirty to do the same. Ken had been there most of the afternoon covering the upcoming derby. The demolition derby was the highlight of the weeklong fair—even more so than the July Fourth fireworks, which Harold had decided to suspend for the duration of the war. I understood his point, but the closing of the fair tomorrow night just wouldn't be the same without them.

Peggy found a spot to park at the far end of the field used for the overflow. "There sure are a lot of cars considering gas is being rationed," she said as we got out of her father's Oldsmobile.

"Maybe they saved up," I said. "Or maybe they just don't drive much because they walk everywhere."

213

After we each paid our admission fee, Peggy went to find Ken, and I headed straight for the area where the trailers were located. The demolition derby didn't start until eight, so I had some time to snoop. The table where Mom and Martha sold the war bonds was empty at the moment, but Clyde McAllister was sitting in a wooden folding chair at his post nearby. He stood when he noticed me coming his way.

"Hi, Clyde," I said.

He nodded a hello.

"How is everything?" I asked.

"Fine."

He was back to playing statue. I couldn't blame him. He had to be on his best behavior after the theft. He wasn't in the clear despite what he'd told the chief. There was a good chance he was the thief. And for all I knew he could have killed Freddie.

"I guess you'll be glad when tomorrow is over," I said.

"Why?"

"You'll get to move on. Where are you headed next? Do you get to go home?"

"Makes no difference to me," he said. "One place is as good as another."

I tried another tactic. "Angel said she appreciates how kind you've been to her."

His stony expression softened. "It's easy to be kind to her. She's a wonderful person. She's going to be a big star someday."

"You may be right," I said.

Suddenly his countenance changed and he spun around and went into the trailer. I turned to see what had made him disappear like that. Belinda and Paul Davis were walking this way. Belinda was smiling in her cat-who-swallowed-the-canary way. Davis wore his usual bored expression.

Belinda reached for my hand and held it between both of hers. "Paul, you remember Irene, our intrepid reporter, don't you?"

Her friendliness gave me the willies. I knew she was only being cordial because she thought I'd really write the story we'd talked about.

"Sure do," he said.

"Irene's doing a feature story on me," Belinda said. "It will be out in a couple of weeks."

"How about doing one on me, too?" Davis asked. "I'm more than an emcee, and I think your readers would like it."

I smiled. "I'll think about it."

He put an arm around me. "What's to think about? Come on into the trailer and we'll talk."

I had questions to ask him, but I didn't like being manhandled. I reached up and pushed his arm away. "If you keep your mitts to yourself, we can talk."

Davis seemed surprised. I wasn't sure if it was because I agreed to talk to him or because I wouldn't let him get friendly. I'd bet he wasn't used to the latter, but I wasn't some starlet looking to advance my career.

"I'll be in the trailer," he said. "Come on in when you're ready." He turned to Belinda. "Make sure you're on time tonight. We're scheduled right after that stupid car crash thing. Nine sharp."

Belinda rolled her eyes. "You're not my boss. I'll get there when I get there."

Davis walked away, calling her a name that was definitely crude and unflattering. It didn't seem to bother her at all. I'd bet she'd been called worse.

"How was last night's rally?" I asked. "I wasn't able to make it."

"It was marvelous," she said. "I signed autographs for an hour after it was over."

"I guess that means you sold a lot of bonds."

"I suppose," she said.

"Do you know how much you brought in last night?" I asked.

"I have no idea. I'm not involved with the boring stuff. That's Paul's area," she said. "He knows the amount right to the penny. It's part of his job."

"I guess he keeps pretty good track of it then."

"The best," she said. "Paul and I don't always get along, and I would never tell him this to his face, but he makes sure everything runs smoothly, including all this." She waved her hand over the table where the bonds were sold. "Hey, if that photographer from your paper is here tonight, he should get some shots of me for your article."

I said if I saw him, I'd let him know, but I had no plan to do any such thing. Leaving Matt alone with her would be like leaving a steak for a hungry lion. After that, Belinda excused herself.

I couldn't mention the theft because I'd promised the chief I wouldn't, but Belinda hadn't even flinched when I asked about the money from the bond sales. Either she was a better actress than I gave her credit for or she knew nothing about the theft.

The door to the dressing room trailer was open, but I knocked on the frame anyway before I went in. Davis was sitting at the small table.

"Care for one of these?" He pointed to the bottle of Rolling Rock he was drinking.

"No thanks." I sat in the other chair at the table and retrieved my notebook and pencil.

"So what do you want to know?" he asked. "I'm an open book."

I asked how he became involved with the Hollywood Victory Committee, and he gave me the standard answer about helping with the war effort. After a couple of other preliminary questions I asked him how long he'd known Freddie.

"Too long," Davis said. "You probably figured out we weren't friends. Not by a long shot. Harrison didn't have many friends. He crossed too many people. It's a surprise no one offed him before now."

"What do you mean he crossed too many people?"

Davis shrugged. "Just what it sounds like."

"Did he cross you?" I asked.

"You bet he did. Looks like he won't be doing that anymore."

"Who do you think killed him?"

He shrugged again. "Could be anyone. Belinda, Angel, Kirk . . ."

"Even you?"

Davis laughed. "I'm not even going to answer that one." He looked at his watch. "That's all I have time for right now."

I thanked him for his time and went outside. Just then Clyde came out of his trailer.

"I saw you talking to Miss Fox. Don't let her fool you," he said. "She'll be nice as can be one minute and the next she'll stab you in the back. I fell for that once. She's as bad—maybe even worse than Harrison was."

I already knew her true colors. "Thanks for the warning."

"And don't get too friendly with Davis, either."

"I won't." I really wanted to ask him what happened last night. He'd given his story to the chief, but I wanted to hear it for myself. Since I couldn't come right out and ask about it, I tried something else. "In case I don't see you before you leave town, I want to thank you for doing such a good job of watching over the bond sales. My mother is one of the women volunteering here, and it's nice to know she's safe."

"I'm afraid I'm not doing a very good job," Clyde said. "Not at all."

"Why would you say that?"

He shook his head. "I can't talk about it."

"Why not?" I asked.

There was a strange look on his face. It took me a few seconds to figure out what it was. It was fear. He shook his head again, then spun quickly and went back inside his trailer.

I stared at the closed door. Clyde was frightened of something—or someone. Was he afraid of being arrested? Had he taken the money after all? Or maybe he knew who did. That made more sense to me. He must know the thief—and know them well enough to be afraid.

By this time it was getting close to eight o'clock, so I headed for the bleachers to watch the demolition derby. I kept thinking about Clyde as I walked. Had he been threatened by whoever stole the cash? Clyde was a big man and hardly seemed the type to be afraid of anyone. But he clearly was. I had another thought. Was Clyde's name in Freddie's blackmail book? Which one could he be?

I knew the identities of two people so far. Old Gray Mare was Greta Gray and the Pink Lady was Georgette Ferrara. I remembered the other names—Blue Lou, Roman Legion, The Professor, and Scarlett O'Hara. Clyde certainly didn't fit Scarlett or the Professor. That left Blue Lou and Roman Legion. With the way he stood at attention all the time, I could picture him in a Roman costume. If he was indeed in the book, he was Roman Legion. There was no doubt in my mind. Now I just had to prove it was him.

* * *

I spotted Peggy, Ken, and Matt in the front row near the chain-link fence that had been installed years ago to keep the cars from hitting any bystanders. Rust was the only thing holding the fence together. It wasn't going to stop much of anything.

"I wasn't sure you'd make it in time," Peggy said. "Where have you been?"

"Talking to the security guard."

Matt grinned. "Don't worry. I won't tell Bill you're making time with a gorilla."

"Ha, ha. You do like your job, don't you?" I teased. "I also spoke to Paul Davis and Belinda. She says hello, Matt."

"Hubba hubba. Be still my heart."

Ken elbowed him. "She's too much woman for you. You wouldn't be able to handle her."

"Maybe not," Matt said, "but I'd sure like to try."

I saw Kirk standing at the far end of the bleachers and waved to him. As he walked toward us, I noticed a lot of people nudging each other and pointing at him. Even though he wasn't well known yet, they knew he would be. Someone would be telling their child someday that they had seen Kirk Allen at the county fair.

"I loved these races when I was a kid," he said when he reached us. "I didn't want to miss this one. Who knows when I'll get back here again."

"I hope it won't be too long," I said.

"You'll probably forget all about us when you're a big star," Peggy said.

Kirk smiled. "Never in a million years."

Matt and Ken decided they wanted hot dogs before the race started. The rest of us declined. Peggy went with them and said she'd bring back drinks for us. Once we were alone, Kirk and I sat on the bench.

"I'm glad to get to talk to you alone," he said in a low voice. "Did you hear what happened last night?"

"Yes. How did you hear? I thought it was supposed to be hush-hush. The chief asked me not to tell anyone."

"I overheard Paul talking about it. He wants Clyde fired."

"That's not fair," I said. "I don't think it was Clyde's fault. From what I heard, he only turned his back for a minute to help the woman who fell. Anyone would have done the same."

Kirk was silent for a few seconds before he spoke. "The problem is it could be his fault. It's not the first time this has happened."

Chapter
Twenty-Four

FBI Rounds Up 250 Enemy Aliens in Altoona

The Progress Herald, July 3, 1942

"What do you mean it's not the first time?" I asked. "The chief didn't say anything about that."

Kirk leaned toward me. "When we were in Cleveland, three hundred dollars was missing."

Three hundred was a lot, but it wasn't anywhere near last night's take. "What happened?" I asked.

"I'm not exactly sure," he said. "While the Hollywood Victory Caravan was going cross country, plans were put into place for groups of performers to travel to smaller towns and appear at fairs and the like. As soon as the big caravan ended, we began touring. I think our third or fourth stop was a town outside Cleveland. It was for one night at a theater that held a couple thousand people." He smiled. "The turnout wasn't very good because so many people had gone into Cleveland when the Caravan passed through. I guess they figured why go see a few no-names when you can see real stars."

I patted his arm. "But someday they'll be able to say they saw you before you were famous."

Kirk laughed. "We'll see about that. Anyway, when they tallied up at the end of the night, they were short three hundred."

"What was the procedure like for that?"

"I don't know for sure, but I assume it was similar to what they do now."

"Why do you think Clyde's involved?"

"There was never an incident until Clyde was hired. That was his second night."

"What happened in Cleveland might have been a coincidence," I said. "It seems to me that the woman who fell last night could have been a distraction. Someone wanted Clyde away from the lockbox long enough to reach in and take the cash."

Peggy, Ken, and Matt returned then and our discussion ended. I didn't pay much attention to the demolition derby because my thoughts were elsewhere. Kirk left to get ready for his performance before the winner was called, and I barely noticed he'd gone. The winner was a man from a neighboring town who seemed overjoyed that he'd had a chance to smash so many cars. Ken and Matt went to interview him and take photographs, and Peggy and I walked back to the stage area, stopping long enough to buy some popcorn.

"You're awfully quiet," Peggy said.

"I'm just thinking."

"About what?"

"Do you really have to ask?"

Peggy grinned. "Murder and mayhem, no doubt."

"I might have figured out another name in Freddie's blackmail book." I told her what I thought.

"Could be," she said. "How will you know for sure? You can't just come right out and ask him."

"Says who?" It was exactly what I was considering. And as soon as I filled Dad in on Kirk's revelation about what happened in Cleveland, I wanted to ask Clyde about that too. At the very least, I'd try to be there while Dad questioned him.

"You said you talked to Belinda too," Peggy said. "Did she say anything about that book?"

I shook my head. "She'd have to admit she had it first. I'd bet she's steamed about it being gone. She was actually friendly to me again. Clyde warned me not to fall for it—that she'd stab me in the back. He let on that it had happened to him."

"No surprise there."

"Clyde also seems afraid of something—or someone. Maybe Belinda?"

"That would make sense," Peggy said. "She scares me, and I don't even know her. What about Paul Davis? Maybe Clyde's afraid Davis will have him fired."

"That's possible too. I don't know what to think, especially about who killed Freddie. When I talked to Davis he told me that Freddie had crossed a lot of people—him included."

"My money's still on Belinda," Peggy said.

I spotted my future father-in-law standing near the stage. "I'm going to say hello to Dad. I'll find you when I'm done."

"I see Ava over with your mother and Martha. I'm going to talk to them. Do you want to meet by the stage?"

I agreed and we went our separate ways.

"Here comes trouble," Dad said as I approached.

"Trouble? Me? Never," I said. "Do you have a minute to talk?"

"Of course."

"I was talking to Kirk, and he brought up the theft last night," I said.

223

"How did he know about that?"

"He overheard Paul talking about it."

"So much for keeping it under wraps," Dad said. "Go on."

I told him about the theft in Cleveland right after Clyde began working with them. "I'm still not convinced Clyde took the money. When I talked to Clyde earlier, he seemed afraid of something, or maybe someone."

"I'll need to speak with him again," he said. "I had the feeling he was holding something back."

"I think he's holding back that he's being blackmailed."

His look told me he didn't quite believe me. Before I could explain, music from tonight's guest band started up, and Paul Davis bounded onstage.

"We'll talk tomorrow," he said.

I moved to where Peggy, Ken, and Matt stood in the crowd near center stage. Davis talked about what an honor it had been to spend the week in Progress doing his part for the war effort. He invited everyone to return for their final performance the next night, when he promised there would be a special guest. "You don't want to miss it, folks," he said. "I can't tell you who it will be, but I assure you it's a once-in-a-lifetime opportunity."

Peggy nudged me. "Do you know anything about this? Did Kirk tell you anything?"

"Nope. It's the first I heard about it. I wonder who it could be."

"Well, dang," she said. "I'll just have to come back tomorrow night."

Davis told a few jokes. I'd heard all of them before. "And now I'd like to introduce the beautiful star of tomorrow, singing 'You Made Me Love You.' Let's give a warm welcome to Belinda Fox!"

Belinda glided onto the stage to applause and whistles. I'd heard her sing already and I hated to admit she wasn't half bad. When she'd finished, she gave her little speech about buying war bonds. And this was something new—she promised that tomorrow night she'd be giving out kisses to any man who bought a hundred dollars in bonds.

Angel and Kirk came out after that and did a cute rendition of "Don't Sit Under the Apple Tree." Angel's voice wasn't as good as Belinda's, but she made up for it in personality. Kirk's baritone elicited more than a few sighs from the women in the audience. They ended the song with Kirk sitting on a chair with Angel on his knee.

Pop had taught me years ago to whistle loudly by placing my thumb and forefinger in my mouth, and I put the knowledge to good use. I hoped my mother wasn't watching. She'd been appalled that Pop taught it to me. When I was twelve years old I whistled endlessly just to annoy her.

Right after the program, I found Sam Markowicz and Ben Cline and took them backstage. They were thrilled to get autographs, and even Belinda was on her best behavior. It might have been because Ben couldn't take his eyes off Angel. I was sure Belinda didn't like not being the center of attention.

The fair was open for another hour, so Peggy and Ken went to go on some of the rides. Matt left to go back to the paper to process his film, and I decided to just wander around and talk to fairgoers. I had an idea about an article I could write. I asked anyone willing to talk what having events like the fair meant to them in the midst of war. Most felt that we needed that sense of normalcy on occasion— that they wanted to forget we were at war for a little while. Others felt that having the fair was wrong—since our boys were sacrificing everything, we should be willing to do the same. I found it ironic that they were at the very fair they thought should have been canceled. One person said we were making too many sacrifices. When he started on how unfair rationing was and that he should be able to use as much gas as he wanted, I made an excuse to move on.

After that, I walked back to the bond sales area. There was no one in line and Mom and Martha sat chatting. Clyde stood in his usual spot, but tonight Rally was beside him. I waved to them. Rally waved back. Clyde didn't.

"How were sales tonight?" I asked.

"About average," Martha said.

Mom added, "We have an extra guard tonight. Walt's not taking any chances."

Martha shook her head. "That poor boy. Clyde didn't take that money."

"Why do you think that?" I asked.

"I've been married to a police officer long enough to figure that if someone stole that much money, he certainly wouldn't stick around. He'd be on his way to South America." She shook her head. "Besides that, where is the money? He'd have to hide it, and the only place would be in one of the trailers. Walt and Jimmy didn't find a thing."

I smiled. "Maybe the chief should make you an honorary officer."

Martha waved her hand in the air. "No thank you. I might have the brains for it, but not the stomach."

"It's a man's job anyway," Mom said.

She missed how hard I rolled my eyes. With all the women in factories and other places, it wouldn't be long before women were working anywhere they wanted to. Mom had grudgingly acknowledged recently that I was doing a good job taking Pop's place at the *Herald*. She was still sure, however, that I'd drop it the minute Bill and I were married to stay home and have babies. I was bound and determined to prove her wrong. There was plenty of room at the *Herald* for a nursery.

I stood back and watched the closing procedure. There were no other bystanders around tonight. Martha double checked the amount collected, then Clyde closed and immediately locked the boxes containing the cash and bonds and handed them to Paul Davis. Rally supervised the procedure, and he and Davis left for the bank in a squad car. There would be no missing money tonight.

It got me thinking, though. I needed to talk to Kirk again. I found him on the midway with Peggy and Ken. None of us were ready to call it a night, so we decided to head to the Starlight. Ken was without a car since he'd ridden with Matt earlier, so he went with Peggy in her car and I rode with Kirk in his rental. It would be the perfect time to ask some more questions.

* * *

There was a line of traffic leaving the fair. Kirk's car was parked in a restricted area behind the trailers, so we were lucky to be able to go around it. In less than a minute, we were on our way to the Starlight.

"You did great tonight," I said. "You and Angel work well together."

"I like Angel. She'll be much better off without Harrison holding her back."

"Holding her back? I thought he was helping her career."

"Only to a point," Kirk said. "If she started getting better roles and more recognition than he did, I don't think it would have gone well."

That was something I hadn't considered. Unfortunately, it gave Angel another motive.

"I doubt that Angel killed Harrison, if that's what you're thinking," Kirk said.

"So who did?"

"It wasn't me either."

"I didn't ask that," I said.

"You didn't have to. I told you I hated Harrison, and I had plenty of reasons to want him out of my life."

"He was blackmailing you, wasn't he?"

The car swerved, but Kirk recovered quickly and pulled over to the side of the road. He turned to face me. "How did you find out?"

"Freddie had a book to keep track of who he was blackmailing and the amounts."

"So my name is in there?"

"I'm not sure. It might be." I explained about the false names and that I knew the identities of two of them. "From what I've learned about Freddie, and what you've told me, I had a hunch one of the names might be yours."

Kirk closed his eyes and pinched the bridge of his nose. "What happened to the book? Do the police have it?"

I shook my head. "I gave it to Angel." I paused. "After I stole it from Belinda."

"Belinda had it?" He slapped the steering wheel. "I suppose she was going to continue Harrison's blackmail. I thought I'd be off the hook now."

"She might have started already." I told him about the telephone call I'd overheard. "I don't know who it was or if she'd deciphered the other names, but she must have known what Freddie was up to—at least in part."

"It wasn't me. I hope you believe that."

"I do."

Kirk asked about the names I'd decoded. "One was a costumer at one of the studios. I'm pretty sure the other one is Greta Gray."

"Greta Gray? I wonder what Harrison had on her," Kirk said. "I would have thought she'd have something on him and not the other way around."

"I thought the same thing. After Greta's latest column, I asked one of my reporters to see what he could find out about her from someone he knows in Los Angeles. He's still waiting to hear back."

Kirk pulled back onto the road and we continued to the Starlight.

"I'm sure the call Belinda made wasn't to Greta," I said. "I saw them both get out of Greta's limo in front of the hotel. Greta wouldn't be chummy with someone who was blackmailing her. At least I don't think she would be."

"I agree. Did you know Greta's chauffeur used to haul the tour trailers?"

"Belinda told me she got him the job," I said.

Kirk smiled. "Personally, I'd rather drive for the tour than be at the beck and call of Greta Gray."

"Me too. I'd love to know more about that phone call. If Belinda didn't call you, and she didn't call Greta or the costumer in Hollywood, who did she call?"

Kirk turned into the parking lot of the Starlight. "That's a good question." He pulled into an empty spot. "I don't even have a guess."

I trusted Kirk for the most part, but I wasn't ready to share that I thought it might be Clyde. I did have a question about the lockbox, though. "I told the chief about the theft in Cleveland. He's going to look into it and talk to Clyde again."

"I'll be happy to talk to him about it as well," Kirk said.

"I'll let him know. When Mom and Martha Feeney were finished tonight I watched Clyde close and lock the box with his key, then Paul Davis and a police officer took it to the bank. Does Mr. Davis have a key too?"

"I don't know," he said. "I always thought Clyde was the one who took the money to the bank." Kirk came around the car and opened my door. "Let's forget about all that for now. We're here to have a good time, not play detective."

I smiled. "You're right." I attempted a Scarlett O'Hara impression. "After all, tomorrow is another day."

Kirk laughed. "That was pretty good. Maybe you should be heading for Hollywood."

"Not a chance." As we walked to the door I still had Scarlett on my mind. It was one of the names in Freddie's book. I wondered who she was and if she was relieved Freddie was dead. Unlike Rhett, I did give a damn.

After an hour of dancing, I stepped outside to get some fresh air. The cigarette smoke in the dance hall was especially thick tonight, and my eyes and nose burned. I walked to the side of the building and took a few deep breaths. My nose felt better already. I started to return when I heard men's voices coming from behind the building. It sounded like an argument. I was going to ignore it and go back inside until I thought I recognized one of the voices. I moved a few steps closer.

"I'm not doing it," he said.

I definitely recognized the voice. It was Clyde McAllister.

Chapter
Twenty-Five

Allies Bomb Jap-Held Island in Dutch Celebes

The Progress Herald, July 3, 1942

What was Clyde doing here lurking behind the Starlight? More importantly, who was he arguing with? I tiptoed along the side of the building until I reached the corner and listened.

"I'm not taking the fall," he said. "You said it wouldn't happen again."

"So I lied. Sue me."

"Why can't you leave well enough alone?" Clyde asked.

I heard the back door bang and something being dumped into a metal garbage can. They were silent until the door banged again.

"You know as well as I do that we can't leave it alone. Just be smart," the other man said. "Don't do anything stupid."

"That's easy for you to say," Clyde said. "I'm going in and getting a drink."

I skedaddled to the front of the building, leaned on a post and tried to appear casual even though my heart was beating a mile a minute. Seconds later Clyde came around the corner. He stopped short when he saw me. I gave him a big smile. "Well, this is a surprise," I said. "I didn't know you were coming here tonight."

"What are you doing here?" he asked.

"I imagine the same thing you are."

"I doubt that."

"If I'd known you were coming here you could have ridden with me and Kirk. He's inside with some other friends. Would you like to join us?"

"I just want to get a drink. By myself."

I wasn't about to take no for an answer. Not until I had some idea of what was going on. I looped my arm through his and tugged him toward the door. "Not alone you're not. You're sitting with us and you can drink all you want. Kirk's buying."

The look on Peggy's face was priceless when she saw me leading Clyde to our table. Kirk just raised an eyebrow. I introduced Clyde to Peggy and Ken, then asked him what he was drinking.

"Bourbon, straight up," he said.

Ken went with Kirk to get drinks.

"It's good Irene ran into you," Peggy said.

Clyde scowled. "Is it?"

"Well, it's no fun sitting by yourself," she said. "Now you have someone to talk to."

"I'm not really in the talking mood."

It turned out to be true. Peggy and I tried our best to engage him in conversation, but all he'd give us were one word answers. When Kirk and Ken returned, Clyde downed his bourbon in one gulp. It might have been the booze, but Clyde turned into a real chatterbox ten minutes later when Ken mentioned the Pittsburgh Pirates. Apparently he was a baseball fan.

While they talked sports, Peggy and I excused ourselves to go to the ladies' room. As we passed the men's room, the door swung open, almost hitting me. The man scowled like it was my fault the door almost flattened me. We continued down the narrow hallway. Something about him was familiar. I'd seen him somewhere before, but I couldn't remember where. "Did that guy look familiar to you?"

"No, but I really wasn't paying attention," Peggy said. "How did you run into Clyde? I was shocked when you came inside with him."

I didn't tell her about the overheard conversation, only that he just happened to be outside and had been planning to get a drink by himself. We powdered our noses and freshened up our lipstick. When we returned to the table, Clyde was gone.

*　*　*

It was two in the morning by the time Kirk dropped me off. Neither he nor Ken could tell me why Clyde had left. They'd been talking about the upcoming All-Star Game, then all of a sudden Clyde got up and said he had to leave. Making him join us had been a fruitless gesture on my part anyway. I hadn't learned anything new.

Despite the late night, I only slept until seven, then Lily and I helped Mom with the usual Saturday morning housecleaning. Sylvia was working the daylight shift, so we didn't have to worry about waking her. Mom and Lily left for the fair around ten. I washed up, changed my clothes, and hoofed it to the police station. I had a lot to talk to the chief about.

The police desk was unoccupied, but the chief's door was open. Dad was seated at his desk reading what I assumed was a report. I knocked on the doorframe.

He looked up. "Come on in."

I took a seat on the other side of his desk. "Have you talked to Clyde McAllister today?"

Dad shook his head. "He wasn't in his trailer. I left a note for him to contact me as soon as possible. If I don't hear from him soon, I'll talk to him at the fairgrounds later."

"After the fair last night a few of us went to the Starlight—"

"Kind of late, wasn't it?"

I grinned. "Checking up on me, Dad?" I put emphasis on *Dad*.

"I know, I know. You're young and the night was just getting started. I vaguely remember the days of staying out late for fun instead of answering police calls."

"Rally's young. You should give all the late calls to him."

"I will, eventually," Dad said. "As soon as he learns the ropes. What were you saying before this old timer interrupted you?"

"I ran into Clyde at the Starlight last night. It was the strangest thing."

"Why is that?"

"I went outside to get some fresh air and I overheard two men arguing. I recognized Clyde's voice, so I eavesdropped. He told the other guy that he wasn't going to take the fall, that it wasn't supposed to happen again. Then the other guy told him to not do anything stupid."

"Then what?"

"Clyde told him he was going inside to get a drink. I kind of waylaid him and dragged him inside to sit with us. He wasn't in a good mood."

"No, I'd guess not."

I told him about how Clyde left suddenly with no explanation.

"Interesting." Dad leaned back in his chair. "What were you saying last night about blackmail?"

I filled him in on Freddie's black book, leaving out that I had lifted it from Belinda's room and that Angel had possession of it now.

"And Angel says she had no idea what he was doing?" Dad said. "I find that hard to believe. They were married, for heaven's sake."

"Angel spends most of her time in a fantasy world. She only sees what she wants to see. She claims that the one time she picked up that book and opened it, Freddie just about had a conniption. She only got a quick glance at names and numbers. That's it."

"Well, I can't take her word for it. I'll have to talk to her and get a look at the book for myself."

I told him that I knew for certain that a costumer in Hollywood had been one of his victims and that I was almost sure Greta Gray was too.

"Greta Gray? If he had something on her it must have been big. Who else? Belinda Fox? Paul Davis?"

"Not that I can tell." I paused. "You should know that last night Kirk admitted that Freddie had been blackmailing him as well."

"Did he say why Harrison was blackmailing him?"

"Kirk didn't say. It's none of my business." I changed the subject back to Clyde McAllister and added that I believed he was being blackmailed because of the theft.

"It's possible. Especially after what you overheard last night."

"What now?" I asked.

He stood. "I'm not waiting for McAllister to contact me. I'm going to bring him in. He has a lot to answer for." We walked to the door together.

"Because of the thefts," I said.

"Not only that." Dad held the door open and we walked outside. "From what you've told me, he had a very good reason to want Harrison dead."

"I'll go with you."

"No, you won't."

"But—"

He held up a hand. "No. That's final. I appreciate what you've done so far and passing on what you've learned to me. This is a police matter." He got into his squad car. "If McAllister is the one who killed Harrison, it could get dangerous. I don't want anything to happen to you."

Before I could protest further, he drove off, leaving me standing on the sidewalk. *Now what?* I couldn't follow him because Mom had the car. The fairgrounds were too far away to walk. Maybe I should get another look at Freddie's blackmail book to see if I could decipher anything else in case Angel handed it over to the chief. I headed to Ava's house.

*　*　*

Angel was brushing out her pincurls when she answered the door. "I hope I'm not disturbing you," I said.

"Not at all." She smiled and held up her ivory-handled hairbrush. "Don't tell Ava I'm only brushing these out now. I'm not exactly on the same schedule she is."

"I won't tell." I followed her into the living room and we sat down. "You and Kirk did a wonderful job last night."

"Thanks. It was an easy song to sing. I'd like to do better, though. When I get back to LA, I plan on taking some voice lessons. Freddie always thought it was a dumb idea."

"It's not dumb at all," I said. "Will you be singing tonight?"

Angel nodded. "The same song."

"Will the special guest that Paul mentioned be singing?" I had tried to get it out of Kirk on the way home last night, but he said he didn't know anything about it.

"I don't know," she said. "Paul's announcement was a surprise. He never mentioned it to any of us."

"That's what Kirk told me last night."

"I can't imagine who it could be," she said. "Paul could be making up the whole thing."

"Why would he do that?"

Angel shrugged. "He's done this before. I don't remember what town we were in, but he announced a special guest, then at the last minute said whoever it was couldn't make it. If it were me, I wouldn't announce anything and just make it a big surprise. Paul also likes to shake things up once in a while to keep us on our toes—especially Belinda. He goes out of his way to try and make her miserable, and vice versa. Lately it's been getting worse."

"Do you know why? You'd think he'd want to keep it all running smoothly."

"I don't know and I don't care. When they're at each other's throats it makes life easier for the rest of us."

I didn't pursue it any further. "Did you get a chance to telephone your bank to ask about the accounts?"

"No, I'll stop in next week when I'm back home. It will be easier in person."

I was disappointed, but it really didn't matter how many accounts Freddie had. "Would you mind showing me that book again?"

"Not at all." She left the room for a minute and returned with the book. "Why do you want to see it again?"

I sighed. "You might not want to know."

"Know what?"

I had to choose my words carefully. "You said that Freddie had some investments and that's what you thought these numbers might be."

Angel nodded. "Isn't that what they are?"

"No, they're not. At least I'm almost positive they're not."

"I don't understand. What are they then?"

I opened the ledger to the Pink Lady page. "You told me this was Georgette Ferrara."

"Yes, and she was going to call you."

"She did," I said. "We talked for quite a while." I pointed to the number. "She was paying Freddie two dollars every Friday."

"That doesn't make any sense," Angel said. "Why would she do that? That's a lot of money for her."

"Freddie was blackmailing her."

Angel jumped up. "That's not true. Freddie had his faults, but not cheating people. He never would have done something like that."

"But he did. Georgette verified it. She told me the whole story."

"No, I won't believe it." She paced back and forth. "He wouldn't. He just wouldn't."

"Why don't you call and ask her? She can tell you herself."

Angel stopped pacing and sank into a chair. Her face was pale, and for a moment I thought she was going to faint. Then she burst into tears. After a minute or two she pulled a handkerchief from her pocket and wiped her eyes. "Why would he do that? I don't understand."

"I don't know, Angel. Maybe he needed the money."

She shook her head. "He made plenty of money."

"Did he have a gambling problem?"

"I don't know," she said. "And I should. I was married to him for fifteen years and it turns out he was a complete stranger." She leaned forward. "And you know what else? I'm glad he's dead, because if he wasn't, I'd kill him."

She seemed to be slipping back into playing characters. I couldn't recall Bette Davis using those words in a film, but Angel sounded just like her. I picked the book up from the floor and, at Angel's prompting, I told her who else was being blackmailed. I expected her to break down again, but she didn't. As a matter of fact, she seemed stronger somehow, and I wasn't sure if that was her or if she was playing a part again. She vowed to make things right when she returned home, starting with Georgette Ferrara.

"I'm so embarrassed that Freddie was taking money from Kirk," Angel said. "Kirk must hate me."

"I doubt that. He knows it was Freddie and not you."

"I'm going to talk to him and apologize. I want to give him back everything he paid that creep," she said. "And what about poor Clyde? Are you sure he's one of them?"

"Not a hundred percent. The chief is probably talking to him now."

"About the theft the other night?" Angel asked.

I must have been the only one keeping it a secret. "You know about that?"

"Everyone does."

"The chief wanted to know more about the theft in Cleveland too."

"Poor Clyde," she said again. "If he stole that money he must have had a good reason. He's a nice man—always looking out for me."

I wasn't sure how to respond to that. "The chief will figure it all out."

"I hope so."

I didn't have anything else to ask. I stood and thanked her for her time.

Angel got up and grabbed both of my hands. "I'm the one who should be thanking you. I never would have known the truth about Freddie. I feel so stupid for being in the dark for so long."

"You're not stupid. He fooled a lot of people. And he paid for it with his life."

Chapter
Twenty-Six

Sebastopol Falls to Nazis

The Progress Herald, July 4, 1942

It was drizzling when I left Ava's house, but I made it to the *Herald* without getting too wet. I dried off in the ladies' room, made a pot of coffee, and checked the wire. An Associated Press headline caught my eye—*U.S. Air Force Celebrates 4th by Joining R.A.F. Offensive.* It made me think of Will Tabor, the new president of Tabor Industries, who was in England training pilots. I'd never met him, but Colleen Lewis, who was running the company in his absence, assured me he was a good man. I hoped he stayed safe.

I also saw that an army court would be trying the eight Nazi saboteurs who had been arrested recently. Roosevelt had appointed seven generals to hear the case, which would begin on Wednesday. I'd definitely be following the case. I wondered if Katherine had heard about the arrests, or if she was too busy singing with Sinatra to read or listen to the news. I owed her a letter. I'd write one before the weekend was over.

I poured a cup of coffee and took it back to my office. I retrieved my notes from my pocketbook and wrote my article about fairgoers' impressions on attending the fair when there was a war going on. I put the pages in my desk drawer when I finished. I'd read it over again tomorrow and have Donny put it in Monday's edition.

Rex came in when I was on my way to the kitchen to refill my coffee. "I was hoping I'd catch you in," he said.

"That's a switch."

"Just wait until I tell Pete what a smart aleck you are."

I smiled. "I'm sure he already knows."

Rex followed me to the kitchen. "My contact in Los Angeles telephoned a little while ago." He took a mug down and filled it.

"Anything useful?" I asked.

"Plenty. Wait till you hear." Once we were back in my office, he continued. "Mike really had to dig for the information. He knew there were rumors but had a hard time finding anything concrete. One of his buddies in the police department finally came through. Someone either misplaced or buried the report."

"Why would they do that?"

"I'm getting there." His chair squeaked when he leaned back. "Five years ago, a little girl was badly hurt in an automobile accident. It was a hit and run. The driver was never located. The little girl spent weeks in a hospital. Guess who paid the entire hospital bill and arranged for nurses around the clock?"

"Greta Gray."

"You're no fun. You're not supposed to answer that fast."

"So Greta was the hit and run driver?"

"The police could never prove it. They never found the vehicle, and only one witness came forward. He later recanted. You'll never believe who the witness was."

"Freddie Harrison."

Rex's jaw dropped. "How in the world did you know that?"

I could have kept him in suspense or made something up. Instead, I told him about Freddie's little blackmail business.

"No wonder someone offed the guy," Rex said. "Any one of the victims here in town could have done it."

"I know. It's not exactly easy to narrow it down. My money was on the security guard traveling with them, but now I'm not so sure." I told him about the conversation I'd overheard. I also told him about the thefts.

"So the guard's in cahoots with someone. If Harrison knew about the Cleveland theft, he could've been blackmailing the guard over it. The guard was laying low until his partner in crime lifted the cash the other night."

"That's what I figured," I said. "I just don't know if Clyde would kill over it, although he is very protective of Angel. He might have killed Freddie if he thought Angel would be hurt."

Rex pushed out of the chair. "Tell the chief what I found out. See what he thinks."

"I will. Thanks for getting the info." It was a little after noon, but I didn't want to take the time to eat lunch, so I took a nickel from my change purse and got a candy bar from the machine. I thought about everything I knew while I ate it. I had too many questions and not enough answers.

One thing I didn't get was how Belinda knew about Freddie's blackmail scheme. If he hadn't told his wife, he wouldn't have told Belinda. Was it possible she'd been a victim as well? I wasn't sure that made sense. Would she have been sleeping with him if he was extorting money from her?

And who had Clyde been talking to? I hadn't recognized the voice. If I could figure that out, I'd at least know who was behind the thefts and maybe could find Freddie's killer. I suddenly thought of something. Could the man who almost flattened me with the restroom door at the Starlight be the person Clyde had been talking to? Why had he looked so familiar? I wished I could recall where I'd seen him before.

I retrieved my pocketbook from my desk drawer and left the office. I had a lot of investigating to do and not a lot of time to do it.

* * *

Greta Gray wasn't parked on a sofa in the lobby when I entered the Excelsior, so I moved on to Plan B, which was to see Belinda. I'd been here so much lately that the elevator operator knew what floor I wanted. We chatted on the way up, and she admitted she'd be glad when "those Hollywood types"—as she phrased it—would be gone. She didn't have much longer to wait. I walked down the hall and knocked on Belinda's door.

"Just leave it in the hall," she hollered.

I knocked again and the door opened a crack.

"I said to leave it—oh. I'm sorry, I thought you were room service," she said. She swung the door open the rest of the way. "Come in."

"I hope I'm not disturbing you."

"Not at all," she said. "Frankly, I'm bored to tears. There's nothing to do in this town."

"You could go see a movie."

"I've seen it already. I can't believe you only have one theater in this town." Belinda flopped onto the bed. "Thank goodness we're leaving tomorrow. I don't think I could stand staying here another day."

"I love it here," I said.

She gave me a look like I was crazy. "You would. Everything is second rate around here. Like Greta says, it's a dump."

I'd felt bad for what I'd been planning to do, but not anymore. She was a snob. I could tolerate her making fun of me, but not my town. "I have some questions for you."

"For the article?"

"Yes," I said. "I'm trying to decide what kind of article it's going to be."

Belinda sat up. "I'll be happy to answer anything."

"Great." I opened my notebook. "How long were you and Freddie seeing each other?"

"I thought I told you already. We met on the set of a picture a year or so ago, fell in love, and were planning to be married—as soon as he dumped his wife."

That was an entirely different story than she'd told me before—she'd said Greta Gray fixed them up. I'd bet neither one was true. "So you knew everything about him."

"Of course," she said. "I knew what he liked for breakfast, what soap he used, his deepest thoughts. Everything. We had no secrets from each other."

"Perfect. Then you'll be able to tell me all about Freddie's blackmail scheme. How long did you know he was extorting money from people?" It was too bad I hadn't brought Matt with me. The shocked look on her face lasted only a second or two, but it would have been a great photo.

"I have no idea what you're talking about," Belinda said.

"You just told me you knew everything about him."

"I do. I did." She stood up. "I want you to leave. Now."

I ignored her. "Freddie had a black book he kept names and payments in."

"That book was—" She stopped suddenly.

She'd been about to admit it had been stolen. "So you did know about it."

"No. I didn't."

I closed my notebook. "How about if it's off the record?"

"I still don't know what you're talking about."

"Yes, you do. I saw the book sitting by the telephone the last time I was here. You can lie to me all you want, but you won't be able to lie to the police."

She sat back down. "The police? Why would the police want to know?"

"Maybe because blackmail and extortion are crimes."

"Freddie wasn't a criminal. Those people were breaking the law. They shouldn't have been doing that. He was only collecting what was owed to him for keeping quiet."

"And then I guess those people owed you as well?"

"I don't understand."

"Before I knocked on your door the last time I was here, I overheard you talking to someone on the telephone. You very clearly stated the payments were to continue and you expected the money before the end of the day. When I left and saw the black book on the table I realized you and Freddie had been in it together."

"No."

"Yes. The names in the book were in code. The only way you would have known who to call was if Freddie had told you who he was taking money from."

Belinda burst into tears. "You don't understand. Freddie forced me to make calls."

I wasn't falling for it. "Freddie was dead by that point. He couldn't force you to do anything."

The tears stopped. "Oh."

"If you tell me everything, I'll put in a good word with the police." I decided to put Greta's column to good use. "I'm engaged to the chief's son and he listens to me."

"Do you really have to tell the police? I have money. I'll pay you whatever you want."

I couldn't believe she had just said that. "I don't want your money. All I want is the truth. And yes, I do have to tell the police."

"You'll really put in a good word?" she asked.

"If you tell me everything."

Belinda sighed. "Where is the book now?"

"Chief Turner has it." I wasn't positive about that, but I doubted Dad would let Angel keep it.

She nodded, apparently resigned. "I don't want to go to jail. I'll tell you what you want to know."

There was a knock on the door and Belinda got up to open it. A man from room service came in with a tray of coffee and tea sandwiches and set it on a table. When he left, Belinda sat down on the chair on the other side of the table. "I didn't know I'd have company or I'd have asked for another cup."

"I'm fine. I don't need anything."

Belinda's hand shook as she poured the coffee. She added cream, then leaned back in her chair. "Where should I start?"

"How about at the beginning?"

She nodded. "I didn't actually meet Freddie a year ago. It was closer to two years ago. I was an extra on a movie he was filming. I was broke at the time, my rent money was due, and I had no money to pay it. I barely had enough for necessities. I was desperate and one day I saw an open handbag and took some money from it. It was easy and no one was the wiser. On another day, one of the stars had left some jewelry lying around. I took it. Not long afterward, Freddie said he'd been watching me. He wanted money to keep quiet. I tried to explain I didn't have any. He didn't care. I could keep doing what I was doing and pass it on to him. A month later I was on another picture and making peanuts, but it was enough to pay him a little and stop stealing."

"How did you end up lovers?" I asked. "Didn't you hate him for what he was doing?"

"I did hate him at first, especially when he said I wouldn't have to pay him anymore if I'd sleep with him."

Freddie was even worse than I'd thought. How could Angel have been so blind?

"He stayed at my place a lot, and I got to know the real Freddie. Angel made him miserable. He couldn't stand being around her. He really was going to leave her. He promised me."

I wanted to feel sorry for Belinda, but I couldn't. "What about the blackmail?"

"It wasn't blackmail," she said. "Freddie was only trying to make people pay for what they did."

"Including you."

"I had learned my lesson and Freddie forgave me."

"So you became his partner then?"

"In a way," she said. "I never knew who all the people were, or what crimes they'd committed. He said it was better if I didn't know the details. I knew Greta was paying him for something, but I didn't know what. I've been trying to find out. She went into Pittsburgh today and I offered to go with her, but she said no. I don't think she trusts me."

Imagine that. "Who else?"

"Clyde McAllister."

"Do you know why?"

"Not for sure, but I think it had to do with the theft in Cleveland."

"Is he the one you telephoned?"

"Yes."

That made it possible Clyde had been involved with the theft at the fair. Belinda had called him, and he didn't have the money. He had to steal it that night. But that didn't jibe with his conversation with that other man. It had seemed like Clyde was upset the money had been stolen. "Anyone else?" I asked.

"Others were people in the film business. One was a teacher he called The Professor. One was a police officer in LA. He was Blue Lou in the book."

It was odd she hadn't mentioned Kirk. Was it possible Freddie hadn't told her? Maybe it was too recent and Freddie hadn't made an entry yet. Or maybe he just didn't trust Belinda with that information. I only had one more question. "Were you listed in Freddie's book?"

Belinda nodded. "I was Scarlett O'Hara."

*   *   *

I left the Excelsior feeling like I needed a bath. Although I had promised Belinda I'd put in a good word for her, there was no way I could do that. She might have started out a victim, but she was just as guilty as Freddie had been. I headed straight for the police department. When I arrived, the chief was just pulling up to the curb.

"I have a lot to tell you," I said. "I just left Belinda."

"Can we make it later?" he said. "I'm heading out again in a minute."

"Of course." I didn't like the serious look on his face. "What's going on? Did you talk to Clyde McAllister?"

Dad shook his head. "And I won't get to."

"Why not? Didn't you find him?"

"I didn't, but someone else did," he said. "McAllister is dead."

Chapter
Twenty-Seven

Liberty Ship Sunk off Coast of Cape Cod; U-Boat Sunk by Brits

The Progress Herald, July 4, 1942

"What? How?" I followed him inside. "The manager of the Starlight found him behind the building," he said. "Rally took the call and identified him." He picked his eyeglasses up from his desk and headed back outside. "Forgot these this morning."

"Behind the Starlight? That's where I heard him talking to that other guy," I said. Clyde must have gone back there when he left last night. "When did it happen?"

"Don't know yet. Doc Atkins is on his way and I'm going there now."

"I want to go with you."

"Nope."

I moved in front of the driver's side door of the squad car, blocking his entrance. "I'm going."

Dad sighed. "Let me in, Irene. It's not something you want to see. He was stabbed. More than once."

I folded my arms in front of me. "If you don't take me with you, I'll just borrow a car and get there myself. Either way, I'm going. I might have been one of the last people to see him alive besides his killer."

Dad stared at me, probably trying to decide if I meant it. It didn't take him long. "Get in. If your mother finds out . . ."

"She won't. Not from me anyway." I ran to the other side of the car and hopped in. We were off in seconds.

"Tell me again about last night," he said.

I told him about the conversation I'd eavesdropped on, Clyde sitting with us for a short time, and how he left abruptly.

"Did you see where he went after that?" he asked.

"I didn't actually see him leave. When Peggy and I returned from the ladies' room, he was gone. Ken and Kirk said he just suddenly up and left."

"When McAllister was sitting with you, did he seem upset or angry? Anything out of the ordinary?"

"I don't know what ordinary would have been," I said. "I had only talked to him a couple of times and he wasn't much of a talker. He was quiet until Ken mentioned something about baseball. That's what they were talking about when Peggy and I left the table."

The chief turned into the Starlight lot, drove around the side of the building, and parked beside Rally's patrol car. Doc Atkins pulled in right behind us. "Stay here until I see what we're dealing with," he ordered.

I leaned on the hood of the car and watched from a short distance. It looked as if Clyde was wearing the same clothes as last night. What had happened to make him come back out here? I ran a scenario through my mind. When Clyde was talking with Ken and Kirk, he must have seen the guy he had argued with earlier. Maybe the man signaled to Clyde to come back outside and that's why Clyde had left so abruptly. But why did the man kill him? Did Clyde tell him he didn't want to be involved anymore? That had to be it. I thought again about the man who had almost run into me coming out of the restroom. It was too much of a coincidence that Clyde left right afterward. I still couldn't place where I'd seen him before. At one of the bond rallies, perhaps? He had to have been the man who met with Clyde. And possibly murdered him. I had to find out who he was.

The chief wouldn't let me go any closer to the murder scene until Doc had Clyde taken away. When I saw how much blood was on the ground I mentally agreed he'd made the right decision. Dad said it didn't look like Clyde had been able to put up much of a fight, that he'd likely been caught off guard. I filled Dad in on the man I'd almost run into last night and gave him whatever description I could.

On the way back into town, I told him about meeting with Belinda and that she'd admitted she had known about Freddie's scheme. "She claims she started out as one of Freddie's victims. She'd been stealing from people on the movie sets where she worked until she started sleeping with him."

Dad raised an eyebrow like I wasn't supposed to know about things like sex.

I ignored it. "Belinda knew the identities of some of the victims and decided to continue collecting from them. Clyde was supposed to pay his share before the end of yesterday."

"Did Belinda say if he paid?"

"I didn't ask," I said. "I guess I should have."

"I'll pay her a visit after I drop you off."

He left me at the *Herald*. It wasn't even four o'clock yet, and I felt like it should be much later. It had been a busy day, but I didn't have much to show for it. I knew more about the blackmail and Belinda's involvement, but that was all. Clyde's murder confused me even further. I had a strong feeling that Freddie's murder, the blackmail, the thefts, and Clyde's murder were all connected. Unfortunately, I didn't know how. Tonight was the last war bond rally, and tomorrow or the next day they'd all be leaving town. In the movies, the chief could order all of them to stay. This was real life, though, and the chance of finding the truth after they left was slim.

I needed to find the killer—or killers—before then. I definitely had my work cut out for me.

*   *   *

Since Mom and Lily would be eating dinner at the fair, I stopped at Woolworth's and got a turkey sandwich before they closed for the day. I ate half of it at the counter and the other half as I walked to the Excelsior. I still wanted to talk to Greta Gray, and I was glad to see she was sitting in her usual spot in the lobby. A bellboy lit her cigarette as I sat down in the chair closest to her.

Greta raised her head and blew out smoke. "I didn't give you permission to sit there," she said.

"I don't believe I need your permission. As a matter of fact, I'm sure of it."

"Go away. I don't want to talk to you."

"Well, I don't especially want to talk to you, either, but I'm going to."

"You are a tiresome little girl," she said.

"I'll take that as a compliment." I didn't wait for her next retort. "How long were you paying hush money to Freddie Harrison?"

Greta paused a moment too long. "I have no idea what you're talking about. Freddie Harrison was a nobody. I wouldn't give him the time of day. Why would I give him anything?"

I leaned forward. "Because you wouldn't want anyone to know about that accident you had."

Greta dropped her cigarette holder into the ashtray on the table beside her. "What do you want? How much to shut you up?"

I was surprised she didn't deny it. I told her the same thing I'd told Belinda. "I don't want money. I just want the truth."

She shrugged and picked up her cigarette again. "I was giving him money. So what? He was the only witness to the accident, and when I offered him something, he accepted. It was a small price to pay. Besides, I took care of that little girl. I paid all her medical bills and I still send money to the family."

"But why not just come clean? You probably would have only had to pay a fine. You wouldn't have gone to jail."

"It would have ruined me. I make my living telling the world others' secrets. I wasn't going to let my own get out." She removed her cigarette from the holder and ground it out in the ashtray.

"It's all going to come out anyway," I said. "Freddie kept a ledger book with names and amounts. You're not the only person he was blackmailing."

"That's such an ugly term. I wouldn't call my situation blackmail."

"What would you call it then?"

"Insurance," she said. "Have you seen this book Freddie had? Who is in it?"

"I've seen it. I can't tell you who's in it." Greta would have all their sins in black and white for everyone to see.

She fixed another cigarette in her holder and signaled to a bellboy. He was over in a split second to light it for her. She didn't bother to thank him. Instead she placed fifty cents in his hand. She turned back to me. "Who is in possession of the book?"

"I can't tell you that either."

"Can't or won't?"

I didn't answer.

"It's not Belinda. She would have told me." Greta gave me a Cheshire Cat smile. "The poor girl has been trying her best to gain my good graces. I'm indulging her, at least for now."

In my opinion they were two of a kind.

"I know who must have it," she said. "It has to be Angel, since she's his widow."

"I'm not going to tell you. How do you know it's not the police?"

Greta laughed. Once again, it reminded me of glass shards. "You are just precious. If your inept police chief had it, he'd be the one here giving me the third degree." She stood. "This has been fascinating, but I have things to do. Run along now."

I watched her slink across the lobby and get on the elevator. I doubted the chief had had time to visit Angel yet. Clyde's murder would take priority. When I saw Angel tonight I'd have to warn her that Greta was on the prowl and wanted to get her hands on Freddie's book.

I left the Excelsior and went home. Peggy and Ken were picking me up at six to go the fairgrounds. I tried to put it all out of my mind while I freshened up and changed clothes. There were still so many pieces of the puzzle missing, but I felt I was on the verge of something. I just didn't know what.

*　*　*

On the way to the fairgrounds, I filled Peggy and Ken in on my day.

"Oh, that poor man," Peggy said after she heard about Clyde. "He didn't seem like a bad sort. It sounds to me like he did what he had to do to get by."

Peggy always thought the best of people.

"And that Greta Gray. Someone should string her up by her toes," she added.

There were exceptions to Peggy's charitable thoughts.

"I suppose the chief will want to talk to us," Ken said. "I'll look for him here. It'll save him from having to track us down."

"I'm sure he'll appreciate that," I said. We split up at the entrance and I went to check on my mother at the bond sale table. She was seated with Martha in their usual spot. Martha was taking care of the only person in line at the moment, and Jimmy was standing guard in Clyde's place.

Mom got up and came over to me. "I heard about that poor security guard. It's so terrible. I'll never understand how someone can do something like that."

"I can't either," I said. "I'm glad Jimmy's here to watch over you." We chatted for a minute, then I asked if she'd seen Ava or Angel yet.

"They were both here a little while ago. They went to meet their father near the Ferris wheel."

A few more people got in line to buy bonds, so Mom went back to her duties and I headed for the dressing room trailer. I'd leave a message for Angel that I needed to speak to her in case I didn't track her down. No one was in the trailer, so I tore a page from my notebook and jotted down that I needed to see her and that it was important.

Back outside, I saw Kirk's rental in the reserved parking area alongside two limousines. One was the car Paul Davis and Belinda had been using all week. The other one must be for the special guest

Paul had mentioned. Apparently Angel had been wrong and Paul had been telling the truth this time. I wondered again who it could be—and where they were. Paul must have had them in a top secret location.

I was always sad the last day of the fair, and I was even more so this year. Because of the bond rallies, attendance had been much higher than in the past, but I had a feeling it could be because many thought it might be the last one until the war was over. The crowds were thick as I made my way past the food stands to where the rides were. Ava and Angel were no longer at the Ferris wheel, but Matt and Kirk were.

"Hiya, Irene," Matt said. "Look who I ran into."

Kirk grinned. "Would you tell him to knock it off with the pictures? He's asking every girl that passes if they want their picture taken with me."

"It's the only way they'll pose for me," Matt said. "It's a great plan. I take the picture and offer to send them an autographed copy. I get their address and telephone number. It's a winning situation."

I laughed. "Not if you want to keep your job. You'd better save some of that film for the rally."

"Drat," Matt said.

"In this poor soul's defense, only two women went for it and they were both old enough to be my mother," Kirk said.

"Have either of you seen Angel? I need to tell her something."

Neither one had. Kirk and I left Matt to his own devices.

"I saw Chief Turner not long ago, and he told me about McAllister and had a few questions. He also asked about the blackmail," Kirk said.

"I figured he would."

"When he asked why I was being blackmailed, I told him I'd rather not say. He didn't press it."

"That's good." I told him about my visit with Belinda. "She didn't mention you at all. Freddie must not have told her."

"That's a relief."

"You can tell me to mind my own business if you want, but when did Freddie start asking you for money?"

Kirk squeezed my arm. "You can ask me anything you want. He corralled me about six weeks ago outside a hotel. Said he saw me with . . . I'd rather not say who. He threatened to tell the world all about it unless I paid him. He wanted cash every Friday. I didn't think I had a choice. I couldn't very well go to the police."

I told him about the scrap of paper I'd found in the pocket of one of Freddie's jackets when I helped Angel pack his things. The dates on the paper were Fridays. We figured Freddie hadn't made an entry for Kirk in his book yet and that was one reason Belinda didn't know.

"I also talked to Greta Gray today. She'd love to get her hands on that book. That's why I want to find Angel. I need to warn her."

"There's time. The show starts in an hour so you'll see her then, if not before. I'll make sure she talks to you afterward. Speaking of the show, I'd better go and get ready."

I circled the fairgrounds and still hadn't spotted Angel anywhere. By this time, she should be on her way to the trailer, so I headed that way. As I passed the reserved parking area, the driver was getting out of the second limousine. I stopped walking, hoping to catch a glimpse of the special guest. It only took a few seconds to realize it wasn't the guest's limo at all. It belonged to the Queen of Gossip. And I now recalled where I'd seen the man who had almost run into me in the hallway at the Starlight. He was Greta Gray's driver.

Chapter Twenty-Eight

Final Day of County Fair

The Progress Herald, July 4, 1942

I only recalled seeing him in that hallway, but he could have been there all night and I hadn't noticed. He had to have been the man Clyde had been talking to. It made perfect sense, especially since the man had worked on the bond tour. I needed to hear his voice, though. It was the only way I'd know for sure. I rushed toward the lot.

He was leaning against the fender when I reached him. "Hey, aren't you Greta's driver? I didn't know she was coming here tonight." I peeked into the back seat. It was empty.

"She's not in there," he said.

It was definitely the voice from last night. "Is she at the fair?"

He laughed. "Not a chance."

"We've never officially met. My name's Irene."

"Lonnie Blake."

"Are you here for the bond rally?"

"Yeah. The rally. Gotta buy those war bonds, right?"

"Of course." I didn't think that was really why he was here. He hadn't made any effort to enter the fairgrounds, and the program started soon. He was here for some other reason. I was sure of it. Had Greta sent him to retrieve Freddie's book? Or was he here to steal the proceeds again? I couldn't ask him any of those things, just as I couldn't ask if he had been in cahoots with Clyde. I especially couldn't ask if he had killed him. I'd wanted to hear his voice and that's what I had done. I'd find the chief and let him know. "Tell Greta that I said hello. Nice talking to you." I felt his gaze on my back all the way into the fairgrounds.

There were only ten minutes until showtime, so I headed toward the stage, hoping I'd catch Angel before she went on. I didn't see the chief, but he was probably on his way. A local band was playing patriotic tunes as a crowd began gathering. Belinda exited the trailer and turned her head away when she saw me. Kirk was already backstage talking to Paul. Angel stepped out as I reached the trailer.

"Kirk said you needed to talk to me. He told me you left a note for me, but I didn't see it," she said.

I wouldn't put it past Belinda to have thrown the note away. It didn't matter. "I just wanted to warn you that Greta Gray wants to get her hands on Freddie's book. I saw her chauffeur a little bit ago, and I think he might be here to get it."

"No one is getting it except for Chief Turner. I hid it at Ava's until I have the chance to give it to him."

"Good. I learned a little more about it. I'll tell you all of it later."

Angel nodded and continued to the stage.

I added what Angel had just told me to my notes and dropped the notebook back into my handbag. I made my way around to the front and joined Peggy and Ken just as Paul Davis ran onto the stage.

"Good evening, Progress!" he said. "We have a splendid show for you tonight. But I do have some bad news. That special guest who was supposed to be here ran into some bad weather and won't be able to make it tonight."

There were groans of disappointment throughout the audience.

"I wonder who it was," Peggy said. "Why doesn't he tell us?"

"Maybe because he made up the whole thing to get more people to show up," I said.

Ken laughed. "When did you become so cynical?"

I shrugged. "I learned it from Pop. Never take anything at face value. My mother would say it's unbecoming."

"So would mine," Peggy said.

"Besides, Angel told me he's done this before." I saw the chief standing near the corner of the stage as Paul introduced Belinda. I had no desire to watch her sing, so I told my friends I was going to talk to him.

"Too bad about the guest," Dad said.

"I don't think there ever was one." I told him about seeing Greta's driver here and that he had been at the Starlight the previous night. "Before the show, I talked to him long enough to hear his voice. He told me his name is Lonnie Blake."

"You're sure that's the voice you heard?"

"Definitely. And he used to drive for the bond tour hauling the trailers. Belinda got him the job with Greta." I then told him about my encounter with Greta earlier. "Blake might be here to try and get Freddie's book from Angel. She said it's hidden at Ava's until she gives it to you. It's possible he's also going to attempt another theft."

"Thanks. You've been a big help. I'll take it from here."

"Gladly."

262

"I'll go tell Jimmy and Rally to keep an eye out. Let me know later if I miss anything."

"Sure thing." I went back to my friends to watch the rest of the show. Kirk and Angel put on another impressive performance. I hated to admit that Belinda did too, and she was the perfect foil for Paul's jokes. Each made impassioned cases for buying war bonds.

Kirk was the final speaker. He pulled up a wooden stool, took the microphone off the stand and half-sat on the stool. He hadn't done that before. "Thanks for coming out tonight," he said. "This week has been especially important for me. Many of you don't know it, but I'm a hometown boy. I grew up here and graduated from Progress High School."

Murmurs and confused looks went through the crowd.

Kirk smiled. "I know you're all thinking *we don't know any Kirk Allen.* Some of you might remember Eugene Allen, though."

There were a few nods and gasps of recognition from those who had known him.

"I have a story to tell about why it's critically important to buy these bonds. My good friend in high school wanted to be a pilot as badly as I wanted to be an actor. I was a chubby kid with bad skin, convinced I'd never go anywhere. I never imagined I'd be on this stage and getting ready to star in a major motion picture. But my friend knew it. He truly believed I could be an actor and he encouraged me to never stop dreaming. When he had doubts that he'd ever be a pilot and fly a plane, I encouraged him to do whatever it took. After high school, I went to Hollywood and he joined the service. Neither one of us imagined that in a few short years we'd be at war. I'll regret till my dying day that we never got to see the other fulfill their dream. Folks, the friend I'm talking about was Richie Finnerty. As most of you know, he was killed during the Battle of Midway. He should have been able to live a long, successful life flying the planes he loved. Instead, he was cut down by the Japanese. It's not fair. And there will be more boys cut down in the prime of their lives unless we sacrifice and buy these bonds. The more you buy, the better equipped our fighting men will be and the sooner they'll get to come home. If that's not enough of a reason for you, buy one for Richie. He didn't get to come home."

There was complete silence for a moment, followed by thunderous applause. There were few dry eyes, including mine. I was blubbering like a baby. So was Peggy. Angel ran across the stage and hugged Kirk so hard he almost fell over. Even Belinda dabbed at her eyes with a handkerchief.

Afterward, people clamored for autographs, especially Kirk's. Belinda was none too pleased about it. When her line dwindled to nothing, she stalked back to the trailer mumbling to herself. Peggy and Ken wanted to take a last spin on some of the rides, so I told them to go ahead. I waited with Angel, who didn't seem to mind playing second fiddle to Kirk. I thought back to when I'd met her. I hadn't realized it when Ava brought her to the *Herald*, but she'd been playing a character that day. I had thought she was a spoiled brat. Nothing could be further from the truth.

I looked over to where Mom and Martha were. The lines were longer than I'd seen all week. Ava was pulling up a chair beside Mom to assist, and a minute later Ellen Petrie did the same thing. Both Jimmy and Rally stood guard. If Lonnie Blake was planning to steal the cash tonight, he was out of luck.

While I stood with Angel, I thought about the conversation between Clyde and Blake, trying to remember exactly what was said. Clyde told him it shouldn't have happened again and they should have left well enough alone. Blake's answer was something like, *you know we can't leave it alone.* Then he told Clyde not to do anything stupid. I wondered what Blake meant by saying they couldn't leave it alone.

It occurred to me that it was likely they weren't the only ones involved. Someone else was pulling the strings. Greta? But why would she? She surely didn't need the money, but then neither had Freddie. Greta was a lot of things, but I had a hard time believing she'd steal what for her amounted to petty cash. Blackmail was more her style—that's why she wanted Freddie's book. If it wasn't Greta, then who?

Belinda was another option. She'd been helping Freddie with his scheme, and she'd attempted to continue it without him. She'd been angry that he'd broken off their relationship, which would put her back to making her own way and scraping by. And unlike Greta, she'd been on the fairgrounds. She knew Blake well enough to recommend him to Greta. Belinda knew I was a reporter. If Blake had been keeping tabs on Clyde at the Starlight and he had seen Clyde with me, would he have contacted Belinda? I didn't like Belinda, but would she have resorted to murder? Especially Freddie's murder. She claimed to love him, but did she?

There was one more person I had to consider. Just then Angel broke my concentration.

"I've been thinking," she said.

"About what?"

"That book of Freddie's has been nothing but trouble. Maybe we should go and get it now and give it to Chief Turner. Then I won't have to worry about it anymore."

"That's a good idea," I said. When we handed it over, I could tell Dad my theory that Blake and Clyde weren't the only ones involved.

"Let me get keys from Ava and we'll be on our way."

"No need," I said. "I keep an extra key for my father's car in my pocketbook."

Angel and I were quiet as we walked, giving me a chance to think about the last suspect on my list. It made perfect sense. All the pieces were there—I just hadn't seen them before. As we reached the reserved parking, I was so lost in thought I hadn't heard anyone come up behind me until I felt a hand grab my elbow. Something hard dug into my back. I glanced at Angel beside me. Lonnie Blake had an arm around her waist, holding her tight. Without looking, I knew who had a grip on my elbow. I squirmed to get away.

"I wouldn't do that if I were you."

I recognized the voice immediately. I'd been right about who had been pulling the strings. I only wished I'd figured it out sooner. The voice belonged to Paul Davis.

Chapter
Twenty-Nine

Arrests Made in Murder of Actor Freddie Harrison
The Progress Herald, July 5, 1942

"What the deuce is going on, Paul?" I tried to sound calm, like having a gun shoved into my spine was an everyday occurrence. My insides were quaking, though. "Is this some kind of a joke?"

"It's no joke. Keep walking."

"I demand to know the meaning of this," Angel said. She sounded like Katharine Hepburn.

"Shut up," Lonnie Blake said.

They led us to Greta's limousine. Blake forced Angel into the front seat as Paul opened the back door and gave me a shove. I had to think fast. I dropped my purse on the ground as I got into the car. Everyone knew I always carried it, and the chief knew about Greta's limo being parked here. I had told the chief that Freddie's book was stashed at Ava's and I'd written it in my notebook. He'd put two and two together and go to Ava's. At least I hoped so. If that didn't work, we were in big trouble. I'd have to come up with another way to save our skins. I had no doubt in my mind that after they got what they wanted we'd be done for.

Blake pulled out of the parking lot while Davis kept his gun stuck to my ribcage. "Where's the book?" Davis asked.

"What book? I don't know what you're talking about." Maybe playing stupid would work.

"You know what book. The one Freddie had that he was black-mailing half of Hollywood with."

"You're a laugh riot, Paul," Angel said, sounding like Gracie Allen. "Freddie didn't have no book. He could barely read."

"Not that kind of book," Blake growled.

"Keep your eyes on the road," Davis said. "I'll do the talking. So where is it?"

"Honestly, I have no idea what you're talking about," I said.

Davis pressed the gun into my side. "You'd better figure it out real soon, sweetheart."

"Tell me more about this book," I said. "What's it look like?"

"Knock it off," Davis said. "I heard enough from Belinda to know one of you has it."

"We'd better tell them," Angel said. "I don't want anything to do with it anymore. I just want to get rid of it."

I needed to buy a little more time. I had to stall long enough for the chief to realize what had happened. "I don't think that's a good idea, Angel. Don't you want to know why they want it so badly?"

"I'd listen to Angel if I were you," Davis said.

"Why?" I asked. "As soon as you get what you want, you'll have no use for us."

"I don't have any use for you now," Paul said.

"Sure you do," I said. "Chief Turner already knows you're behind this whole thing. He was planning to arrest you as soon as the fair comes to a close."

Blake turned his head to look at Davis, and the limousine swerved.

"Watch the road," Davis said.

Blake faced front again. "You said we were home free. Nobody knew it was us."

"She's bluffing," Davis said.

"No, she's not," Angel told him. "I was there. Chief Turner knows everything."

"That's a load of bull," Davis said. "Enough talking. Where's the damn book?"

I let out an exaggerated sigh. "Oh, all right. It's at her sister's beauty parlor."

"It's n—" Angel stopped in mid-word. She must have realized what I was doing.

We'd have a better chance of getting out of this alive if I led them to Ava's shop instead of her house. Some of the chemicals Ava used might come in handy. "Now that you know where it is, why don't you stop and let us off. We won't tell anyone," I said.

Lonnie Blake laughed. "You must think we're really stupid."

"We'd never think that, would we, Irene?" Angel now sounded like a southern belle. "Why, y'all are smart as the dickens to figure this all out."

"Knock off the act, Angel," Davis said. "I'm sick and tired of it. Neither one of you is going anywhere. Where's the beauty shop?"

I gave Blake directions, taking the long way around town. Thankfully, he didn't seem to notice. While we drove, I asked Davis why he wanted Freddie's book so badly.

"You don't need to know that," he said.

"Maybe not, but I'd like to at least try to understand why you killed two people over it."

"Fair enough. That book is a gold mine. Harrison didn't even know it."

"Why do you say that?" I asked.

"One of the names in there was a U.S. congressman. I saw him handing money to Harrison one day."

I tried to remember some of the other names. The Elephant. That had to be it. It was the one that had been paying exorbitant amounts. "Freddie didn't know he was a congressman?"

"Oh, he knew," Davis said. "What he didn't know was that the schmuck was planning to run for president."

In other words, he could have collected even more from the man. "How did you know Freddie was extorting money from all these people?"

"Because I was one of them until I threatened to expose what he was doing. My indiscretion was minor compared to some of the others. I slept with a married woman. Big deal. I didn't care anymore if it got out. So Harrison started paying me to keep quiet. Until he found out about that congressman, that is."

"So you killed him."

"I had no choice," Davis said. "We argued. He told me he was done paying me anything. I wasn't about to let him get away with that. I wasn't going to let him cash in on that congressman all by himself. He reached for that crowbar, but I beat him to it. If I hadn't killed him he would have killed me."

Angel was quietly crying through this. "He wouldn't have. Freddie wasn't a killer."

Before I had a chance to ask him about Clyde and the thefts, we reached the main street. Blake parked the limousine in front of

Ava's shop. It was dark now and everything was closed. The vehicle stuck out like a sore thumb. Surely someone would notice lights on in Ava's shop when they shouldn't be. At least I hoped so if the chief didn't arrive in time.

The men got us out of the car, and the gun was still glued to my side as we walked to the beauty shop door.

Blake turned the knob. "It's locked. Give me the key." He stuck out his hand to Angel.

"I don't have a key," she said.

"What do you mean you don't have a key?" Blake said.

"It's my sister's shop, not mine. Why would I have one?"

"We'll just break the glass then," he said.

I'd been ready to tell him Ava hid a key on top of the door-jamb, but a broken window would certainly call attention to any-one going by. I kept my clam shut.

Blake got a tire iron from the trunk and smashed the window in the door, then reached in and turned the lock. They pushed us inside and closed the door.

"Where's the book?" Davis asked.

Angel hesitated. "I'm . . . I'm not sure."

"You're not sure?" he said. "Didn't you say it was here?"

"I did say that," Angel said. "And I did bring it here. I'm just not sure where it is."

"You stupid broad," Blake said. "How could you not know?"

"Well, I gave it to my sister for safekeeping," Angel said. "She didn't tell me where she put it."

Davis was ready to blow a gasket. He shoved me against the wall of shampoos and solutions, then grabbed Angel by the arm and pushed her over beside me. "Don't move. Neither one of you." He turned to Blake. "We'll tear the place apart if we have to."

271

"You can't do that!" Angel said. "My sister will kill me."

"That's gonna be the least of your worries," Davis said.

"Wait. Let me think. It might be in the back room," Angel said. "Or maybe in the cash register drawer. That would be a safe place, right?"

While Angel spoke, I reached behind me and grabbed a glass bottle. I couldn't tell what it was, but it was our only chance. Behind my back, I twisted the lid open.

Davis told Blake to look around in the back room. "I'll check the register."

Blake disappeared through the doorway. When Davis leaned over the register to open it, I removed the lid on the bottle and tossed the contents into his face. A strong ammonia odor filled the room. He screamed and dropped his gun.

"My eyes! You bitch! What did you do?"

I snatched the gun up from the floor as Blake charged out of the back room. I aimed it at him. "Stop right there," I said.

I heard a siren and Davis's shrieks turned to moans of pain as a car screeched to a halt outside. Seconds later Dad and Kirk ran into the shop.

Kirk looked surprised, then he smiled. "We came to rescue you."

I was too shaken up to return the smile. "A little late, don't you think?"

*   *   *

Dad took both men into custody. Davis had to be taken to Providence Hospital to have his eyes flushed. I probably should have felt bad about that, but I didn't. Kirk and I helped Angel clean up the mess and cover the broken window.

"How did you end up riding with the chief?" I asked Kirk.

"I saw them push you into the car," he said. "I found Chief Turner and told him what happened. We found your purse on the ground and the chief remembered that Angel left Harrison's book at her sister's. We drove past Ava's house first. The car wasn't there, so we came here. How did you figure out it was Paul?"

"Process of elimination," I said. "For a while I thought it was Belinda or Greta Gray. But I didn't think either one of them could commit cold-blooded murder."

"I always thought Paul was a nice person," Angel said. "I thought Freddie was too. I'm finally realizing there are a lot of bad people in this world."

I wanted to ask what took her so long, but she'd been through enough.

By the time we finished cleaning up, the fair had closed for the night—for the year, in fact. I telephoned home and told my mother I'd be at Ava's house for a while and not to wait up. I didn't tell her why. I thought Ava would be upset over her broken shop window, but she wasn't. She was only concerned that her little sister had had such a close call. She hadn't been quite as worried about me. I was fine with that.

Dad arrived at Ava's around midnight. We were all anxious to hear the rest of the story—or at least as much as he had learned so far. He sipped the coffee Ava gave him and leaned back in his chair.

Angel picked up Freddie's book from the coffee table and handed it to him. "I never want to see this again. It's brought too much misery to too many people."

"I'll be handing this over to the FBI, especially since there's a congressman involved," Dad said. "Both men will be facing murder charges in addition to numerous federal charges for extortion and the theft of the bond money." He looked at Angel. "Federal agents will want to talk to you about your husband."

"That's not fair," Ava said. "Angel had nothing to do with any of this."

"They're not going to take my word for it that Angel was unaware of his activities, Ava," he said.

"It's still not right," Ava said.

Angel touched her sister on the arm. "It will be all right. I'm prepared to do whatever I have to."

"What did you learn about the thefts?" I asked.

"I'm still sorting out some of that," Dad said. "I gather that McAllister, Davis, and Blake were in cahoots—at least to a point. The second theft wasn't planned, but when McAllister helped the woman who fell, Davis took the opportunity to lift the cash."

"Why would Davis take a chance like that?" I asked. "Someone could easily have seen him."

"Greed," Ava said,

"Not entirely." Dad put his mug down on the end table. "Davis owed money to some, let's say, not so savory types."

"Why wouldn't he just wait until he was on the way to the bank?" Kirk asked.

"Because then everyone would have known he was the one who took it," I said. "Mr. Reardon would make sure it was all accounted for before locking it up."

"What else did Paul say?" Angel asked.

"McAllister wasn't happy about Davis taking the money since he knew he'd be blamed. McAllister decided to turn himself in and implicate the other two. When he left Irene at the Starlight, he met Blake outside and told him. And . . . well, you know what happened."

"Poor Clyde," Angel said.

Ava rolled her eyes. "Poor Clyde nothing," she said. "He was a criminal."

"I don't think he was. Not deep down anyway," Angel said. "In the end, he wanted to do the right thing."

Kirk spoke up. "What about Belinda? How involved was she?"

I didn't wait for Dad to answer. "She was helping Freddie with the blackmail and would have continued it if I hadn't lifted—oh, crapola."

Dad raised an eyebrow. "If you hadn't what?"

I put my hands out in front of me. "Go ahead, put on the handcuffs. I stole the book from Belinda's hotel room."

Dad laughed. "I probably don't want to know how you got into her room."

"Nope," I said. "You don't."

Dad wasn't sure yet what Belinda would be charged with. It could depend on her cooperation with the feds and the authorities in Los Angeles. I was glad she wouldn't get off scot-free and I hoped she learned a lesson from all this. I didn't count on it, though.

Greta Gray wasn't involved at all, other than being the victim of blackmail because of her hit and run, which she'd likely never be punished for. I disliked the woman and hated her tactics, but I gave her credit for never driving a car again after the accident and relying on a driver. I only hoped she had better discernment and wouldn't take Belinda's advice when she chose a new chauffeur.

I finally got home and fell into bed at three in the morning. I was glad it was all over.

*   *   *

Mom, Lily, and I gathered at the train station on Sunday afternoon to say goodbye to Kirk. The FBI had questioned Belinda that morning and were permitting her to fly back to Los Angeles. The local authorities would meet her at the airport. Greta Gray had checked out of the Excelsior last night and flown to New York. It would be interesting to see what she wrote about what happened, and if she'd retract what she'd written in her last column.

Angel had decided to stay with Ava for another week since the remainder of the tour had been canceled, but she, Ava, and their father had come to the station. The train was headed west to Chicago, where Kirk planned to stay for a couple of days to visit a friend before catching a plane to Los Angeles. He was scheduled to start filming on his new picture a week later. I expected great things from him. I truly believed he was destined to be a big star.

While we waited for the train, Ned Dempsey pulled me aside. "I hear you're the one to thank for saving my little girl."

"That's not exactly true," I said. "Angel and I made a good team."

"Well, thank you anyway," he said. "Lunch is on the house the next time you stop into the diner."

I told him that wasn't necessary, but he wouldn't take no for an answer. I went back to where Mom and Lily waited with Kirk. Lily had her sketchbook with her and had been drawing for the last ten minutes. She wouldn't let anyone see it until she carefully tore it from the pad.

"All done." She handed the drawing to Kirk.

I might have been biased because she was my sister, but it looked exactly like him in every detail.

"Lily, I'm so touched," he said. "I'll treasure this. As soon as I get home I'm going to have it framed and hang it on my wall."

She beamed. "Maybe I can visit and see it someday."

"I hope you do." Kirk gave her a hug.

Someone was coming our way, and I was surprised to see it was Richie's sister. I took a few steps toward her. "Hello, Louise," I said.

"Hi, Irene. I'd like to see Eugene for a minute if he doesn't mind."

I hoped she wasn't going to make a scene. "That's up to him."

Kirk came over to us. "It's good to see you again, Louise," he said.

"I owe you an apology," she said.

"That's not necessary. I understand how you feel."

Kirk was a lot more gracious that I would have been in the same situation.

"I was at the fair last night and I heard your speech." Louise had tears in her eyes. "I knew that Richie liked airplanes as a kid, but I had no idea he wanted to be a pilot that badly. I thought his enlistment was because of . . . well, never mind that. I just wanted to tell you I'm sorry and I'm glad Richie had a friend like you."

"Thank you for saying that," Kirk said. "Will you give your mother a hug for me?"

Louise nodded and they embraced. She went on her way as the train pulled into the station.

All of us gathered around Kirk to say goodbye except for Angel. I wondered where she had gone. After a minute she joined us with a big grin on her face.

"Everyone follow me, please," she said. "There's someone I want you to meet."

"What's going on, Angel?" I asked.

"You'll see. I've been planning this since I arrived in town. Paul Davis might not have had a special guest, but I do." She linked her arm through Ava's. "This is especially for you, sis," Angel said.

We followed Angel and Ava down the platform to a first-class passenger car. Angel led us inside. I couldn't do anything but stare. Ava was speechless for perhaps the first time in her life. She looked like she was going to faint at the tall, black-haired man with a rakish grin who was standing there.

Angel giggled, very pleased with herself. "Everyone, I'd like you to meet my good friend, Mr. Clark Gable."

Acknowledgments

I can't believe this book is out already! It seems like yesterday when I got the call from my agent that Crooked Lane wanted to publish the Homefront News Series. It's a joy to write this series, and frankly it's been wonderful to go back in time to 1942 and let myself forget that the real world was in the midst of a global pandemic.

There are a few people I want to thank. First is my agent, Melissa Jeglinski. I am so happy and feel so fortunate that we ended up together. She's been a true champion of my writing, and she's a whiz with titles! Next I want to thank my editor, Faith Black Ross. All the good things I've heard about her are absolutely true. She knows exactly what each book needs to make it the best it can be. I'm so fortunate to have her editing my books.

Finally, thanks to everyone else at Crooked Lane who has made this such a wonderful experience, especially Melissa Rechter, Madeline Rathle, Dulce Botello, and cover artist Trish Cramblet.